Annie Burrows has been writing Regency romances for Mills & Boon since 2007. Her books have charmed readers worldwide, having been translated into nineteen different languages, and some have gone on to win the coveted Reviewers' Choice award from *CataRomance*. For more information, or to contact the author, please visit annie-burrows.co.uk, or you can find her on Facebook at facebook.com/AnnieBurrowsUK.

Also by Annie Burrows

Reforming the Viscount
Portrait of a Scandal
Lord Havelock's List
The Captain's Christmas Bride
In Bed with the Duke
Once Upon a Regency Christmas
The Debutante's Daring Proposal

Brides for Bachelors miniseries

The Major Meets His Match
The Marquess Tames His Bride

Discover more at millsandboon.co.uk.

THE MARQUESS TAMES HIS BRIDE

Annie Burrows

MILLS & BOON

First published in Great Britain 2018
by Mills & Boon, an imprint of HarperCollins*Publishers*
1 London Bridge Street, London, SE1 9GF

Large Print edition 2018

© 2018 Annie Burrows

ISBN: 978-0-263-07477-2

MIX
Paper from
responsible sources
FSC® C007454

This book is produced from independently certified
FSC™ paper to ensure responsible forest management. For
more information visit www.harpercollins.co.uk/green.

Printed and bound in Great Britain
by CPI Group (UK) Ltd, Croydon, CR0 4YY

To Louise Marley—
because she says it's about time!

Thanks for persistently tweeting,
sending me congratulation cards
every publication day, and generally
cheering from the sidelines.

Chapter One

'Well, well...what have we here?'

Clare's heart sank. It was just typical of Lord Rawcliffe to take it into his head to travel through Bedfordshire on the very same day as her. Trust him to stroll in through the back door of the inn where she was changing stages, looking so expensive and elegant, at the very moment she was on her way out to visit the necessary, wearing a coat she'd dyed very inexpertly in the scullery. How did he do it? How was it that whenever she was at her lowest, or caught in some humiliating predicament, he always managed to be there to witness it?

And laugh at her.

'No, don't tell me,' he drawled, taking off his gloves with provokingly deliberate slowness. 'A missionary visit to the raff and scaff of Biggleswade.'

And this was the way he always spoke to her. Every time their paths crossed, he would mock her beliefs and she would retaliate by denouncing his morals and informing him that just because he had a worldly title higher than most, and was rolling in filthy lucre, it did not give him the right to assume he was better than everyone else.

But today, she had no time for his games. Nor was she in the mood.

'Don't be ridiculous' was therefore all she said, lifting her chin and attempting to dodge past him.

She might have known he wouldn't permit her to do so. Instead of stepping aside politely, the way any other man would have done, he raised his arm, creating a barrier across the narrow passage, under which she'd have to duck to get past him.

In years past she might have attempted it. But she wasn't a child any longer. And she'd learned the folly of trying to dodge him when he didn't wish to be dodged.

'Will you excuse me?' she said in her most frigidly polite, grown-up voice.

'Not until you tell me what you are doing here,' he said, curving his thin lips into a mocking smile. 'Preaching sobriety to the parishioners of Watling

Minor lost its appeal, has it? Need to spread your gospel farther afield?'

She winced. Why did he always have to make her sound as though she was some sort of religious maniac?

'Surely you, of all people, must know why I have so much sympathy for the message preached by the Methodists,' she retorted, reacting the way she invariably did when he addressed her in that sarcastic tone. 'Not,' she added hastily, when his smile hardened, presaging an escalation in hostilities, 'that I am here to preach at *any*body for *any* reason.'

'Joan,' he said, shaking his head. 'You cannot help yourself. Your whole life is one long sermon. You even manage to preach hell and damnation by the very way you look down that sanctimonious little nose of yours at the entire human race.'

She knew she shouldn't have mentioned his mother's fatal weakness for alcohol. Not even indirectly. It was the equivalent of poking him in the eye.

But when it came to the Marquess of Rawcliffe, she just couldn't help herself. He was so infuriating that no matter how sternly she lectured herself about keeping her tongue between her teeth, he only had to half-lower those lazy lids of his over his ice-cold eyes and utter some puerile taunt, and reason flew out of the window.

'You should know,' she heard herself saying. 'Since you look down your own, arrogant, *big* nose at the whole world and everything in it.' Blast it. That wasn't what she'd meant to say. And now she was even *thinking* in profanities. 'And how many times do I have to tell you not to call me Joan?'

'As many times as you like and I shall still do so, since it is what your father should have called you.'

'No, he shouldn't.'

'Yes, he should. Since he named all your brothers after popes, then he should have done the same for you. But then consistency,' he said with a curl to his upper lip, 'has never been his strongest suit, has it?'

'There was no such person as Pope Joan, as you very well know,' she snapped, falling into the same argument they'd had countless times over the years. 'She was a myth. And would you please just leave my father out of it for once?' Did he have no compassion? At all?

'Absolutely not,' he said, his eyes hardening to chips of ice. 'For one thing, I cannot believe even he would approve of you frequenting places of this sort. If he were any longer in a fit state to know where you were or what you were about.'

The beast! How could he rub her nose in it like this? Oh! She'd always known he was the hardest-hearted person she'd ever met, but this? This was too much.

All the frustrations and hurts of recent weeks played through her mind in rapid succession and crystallised in the mocking smile on the hand-some face of the last man she wished to witness her degradation.

There was nothing she could do about her broth-ers. Nothing she could do about her father, or her future. But right now, there was one thing she could do.

She could knock that sneering, cruel, infuriating smile off the Marquess of Rawcliffe's face.

Before she had time to weigh up the conse-quences, her fingers had curled into a fist. And all her grief, and anger, and confusion, and sense of betrayal hurled along her arm and exploded into movement.

She'd meant to punch him on the jaw. But just as she was letting fly, he moved and somehow her fist caught him right on the nose.

It was like hitting a brick wall.

If she hadn't seen his head snap back, she wouldn't have known she'd had any effect upon him at all.

Until a thin stream of blood began to trickle from his left nostril.

For a moment they just stood there, staring at each other in stunned silence. As if neither of them could credit what she'd just done.

'A fight, a fight!'

The excited voice came from somewhere behind her, reminding her that they were in a corridor of a public inn. And that other people travelling on the stage, or in their own vehicles, had a perfect right to be walking along this same corridor.

'It's a woman,' came a second voice.

'And stap me if it ain't Lord Rawcliffe,' said the first.

Lord Rawcliffe delved into a pocket and produced a handkerchief, which he balled up and pressed to his nose. But she could still see his eyes, boring into her with an expression that boded very ill. He was plotting his revenge. For he was not the sort of man to let anybody, but especially not a female, get away with striking him.

Her stomach plunged. The way it had when she'd almost fallen out of Farmer Westthorpe's oak tree…and would have done if a strap of her pinafore hadn't snagged on the branch she'd just been sitting on. And left her dangling, three feet from the ground, her dress rucked up round her neck. If Lord Rawcliffe—or rather Robert Walmer, as he'd been in those days—hadn't found her, she might still be dangling there to this day. Only of course he *had* found her. And freed her.

Though not before he'd had a jolly good laugh at her expense.

He wasn't laughing now. But she was as unable to move as she'd been that day. Unable to do anything but stare up at him helplessly, her stomach writhing with regret and humiliation and resentment.

She could hear the sound of tankards slamming down onto tables, chairs scraping across a stone floor and booted feet stampeding in their direction.

But she couldn't drag her horrified eyes from Lord Rawcliffe's face. Or at least his cold, vengeful grey eyes, which was all she could see from over the top of his handkerchief.

'What do ye think he'll do?'

Something terrible, she was sure.

'Have her taken in charge? Should someone send for the constable?'

'My lord,' said someone right behind her, just as a meaty hand descended on her shoulder. 'I do most humbly apologise. Such a thing has never happened in my establishment before. But the public stage, you know. Brings all sorts of people through the place.' She finally managed to tear her gaze from Lord Rawcliffe, only to see the landlord, who'd not long since been standing behind a counter directing operations, scowling down at her as though she was some sort of criminal.

'Remove your hand,' said Lord Rawcliffe at his most freezing as he lowered his handkerchief, 'from my fiancée's shoulder.'

'Fiancée?' The word whooshed through the assembled throng like an autumn gale through a forest. But not one of the bystanders sounded more stunned by Lord Rawcliffe's use of the word than she felt herself.

Fiancée?

'No,' she began, 'I'm not—'

'I know you are angry with me, sweetheart,' he said, clenching his teeth in the most terrifying smile she'd ever seen. 'But this is not the place to break off our betrothal.'

'Betrothal? What do you—?'

But before she could say another word, he swooped.

Got one arm round her waist and one hand to the back of her bonnet to hold her in place.

And smashed his mouth down hard on her lips.

'Whuh!' It was all that she managed to say when, as abruptly as he'd started the kiss, he left off. Her mouth felt branded. Her legs were shaking. Her heart was pounding as though she was being chased by Farmer Westthorpe's bull. Which would have been her fate if she'd fallen into the field, rather than become stuck on one of the lower branches.

'The rumours,' he said in a silky voice, 'about my affair with…well, you know who…are exactly that. Merely rumours.'

'Affair?' What business did he have discussing his affairs with her?

'It is over. Never started. Hang it, sweetheart,' he growled. 'How could I ever marry anyone but you? Landlord,' he said, giving her waist an uncomfortably hard squeeze, which she took as a warning not to say another word, 'my fiancée and I would like some privacy in which to continue our…discussion.'

And naturally, since he was the almighty Marquess of Rawcliffe, the landlord bowed deeply, and said that of course he had a private room, which he would be delighted to place entirely at their disposal. And then he waved his arm to indicate they should follow him.

Back into the interior of the building she'd just been about to vacate.

Chapter Two

Lord Rawcliffe kept his arm round her waist, effectively clamping her to his side.

'Not another word,' he growled into her ear as he turned her to follow the landlord. 'Not until there is no fear of us being overheard.'

She almost protested that she hadn't been going to say anything. She had no wish to have their quarrel witnessed by the other passengers from her coach, or those two drunken bucks who'd staggered out of the tap at the exact moment she'd punched the Marquess on the nose, or even the landlord.

'This will do,' said Lord Rawcliffe to the very landlord she'd been thinking about, as they entered a small room containing a table with several plain chairs standing round it and a couple of upholstered ones drawn up before a grate in which a fire blazed even though it was a full week into June.

'You will be wanting refreshments, my lord?'

'Yes. A pot of tea for my fiancée,' he said, giving her another warning squeeze. 'Ale for me. And some bread and cheese, too. Oh,' he said, dabbing at his bleeding nose, 'and a bowl of ice, or, at least, very cold water and some clean cloths.'

'Of course, my lord,' said the landlord, shooting her a look loaded with censure as he bowed himself out of the door.

'And one other thing,' said Lord Rawcliffe, letting go of her in order to give the landlord his full attention. Clare didn't bother to listen to what the one other thing might be. She was too busy getting to the far side of the room and putting the table between them for good measure.

'Look,' she said, as soon as the landlord had gone. 'I know I shouldn't have hit you and I—' she drew a deep breath '—I apologise.' She looked longingly at the door. Rawcliffe might have all the time in the world, but she had a stage to catch. 'And thank you for the offer of tea, but I don't have time to—'

He was nearer the door than she was, and, following the direction of her gaze, he promptly stepped in front of it, leaned his back against it and folded his arms across his chest.

'What,' she said, 'do you think you are doing?'

'Clearly, I am preventing you from leaving.'

'Yes, I can see that, I'm not an idiot. But why?'

'Because I am not going to permit you to walk into a scandal.'

'I am not going to walk into a scandal.'

'You think you can strike a marquess, in a public inn, and get away with it?'

'I don't see why not. You might be notorious, but nobody knows who *I* am.'

His mouth twisted into a sneer. 'You flew here on angel's wings, did you?'

'Of course not. I came on the stage.'

'Precisely. A stagecoach, crammed, if I know anything about it, with plenty of other passengers.'

'Yes, but none of them took much notice of me...'

'That was before you indulged in a bout of fisticuffs with a peer of the realm. Now they will all want to know who you are. And it won't take them long to find out.'

She thought of her trunk, sitting out in the yard awaiting her connecting coach. The label, bearing her name, tied to the handle. And then, with a sinking heart, the ostler who'd wrested it from the luggage rack and the withering look he'd given her after she'd dropped her tip into his hand. A tip so meagre he'd clearly regarded it in the nature of an insult.

She swallowed.

'It…it cannot really matter though, can it? At least, it wouldn't have,' she added resentfully, 'if you had not claimed I was your fiancée.'

'You think people would have been less interested in a random woman assaulting me in a public inn? Do you have any idea of the story they would have concocted had I not given them a far better one? You would have been a cast-off mistress, at the very least. Or possibly the mother of a brood of my illegitimate offspring. Or perhaps even a secret wife.'

'Well, I don't see how any of that would have been any worse than for them now to believe you have a fiancée nobody knew anything about.'

'You cannot just say thank you, can you? For rescuing you from the consequences of your own folly?'

She lowered her gaze. Studied her scuffed boots for a moment or two, weighing his words. She supposed she did ought to thank him. After all, she'd hit him and he hadn't done anything in retaliation.

On the contrary, he'd covered for her behaviour by making up a story about her being an insanely jealous fiancée, so that everyone would believe she was perfectly entitled to waylay him in a corridor and bloody his nose.

'Very well.' She sighed. 'Thank you for attempting to rescue me from myself. And now—'

He let out a bark of laughter. 'Good God! An apology and an acknowledgement that I have actually managed to do something decent, in your opinion, in the space of five minutes. From you, that is nothing short of a miracle. If you continue at this rate you will become a model wife. Within about fifty years,' he finished on a sneer.

'You and I both know I am never going to be your wife—'

'But I have just announced our betrothal.'

'Yes, well, I know you didn't mean anything by that.' Just as he hadn't meant anything by it the last time he'd spoken to her of marriage. She gave an involuntary shiver as that particular episode came to remembrance, since it was not exactly her finest hour. She'd been emerging from the duck pond, covered in slime and with ribbons of weed tangled in her hair. And with the sack full of drowned puppies clutched to her chest. She'd been distraught, because she'd taken far too long to find them. Only later did she discover that the reason the sack into which they'd been tied had sunk deep into the mud was because it was weighted down with rocks. She'd been horrified by the cruelty of the wretch who'd thrown those poor innocent little creatures into the pond and there he'd been, bowed over with laughter, holding himself up by propping his hands on his knees at the sight of her. And then to make matters worse, she'd lost her footing as she'd been clambering out and fallen back into the water. To set the seal on her humiliation, her sense of failure, he'd extended his hand and laughingly said something to the effect of having to marry her if this was what she sank to the moment he took his eyes off her.

And her heart had fluttered. Even though she should have known better, should have known that a man as handsome, and wealthy, and elevated in rank as him could never seriously consider marrying a diminutive, red-haired, penniless vicar's daughter, some pathetic, lovesick part of her had dared to hope. For a moment or two. Which had been the height of absurdity. Because, deep down, she couldn't imagine any man losing his heart to her, let alone the one man in the county who could have any woman he wanted for the clicking of his fingers—and very probably had.

Which had, thankfully, prevented her from making any sort of reply apart from a haughty toss of her head—which had made him laugh all over again since in doing so it had dislodged a clump of weed—and stalking off with her nose in the air. Leaving her with at least one tiny shred of pride still intact. Because of course it turned out he had merely been teasing her. For if he'd been in earnest, he would have come calling on Father to make a formal offer. Or at least ask if he could start to pay his addresses, until such time as she was old enough to consider marriage.

But he hadn't.

Because he hadn't meant a word of it.

Any more than he meant what he'd just said about her becoming a model wife, even if he had put in the bit about it taking fifty years. Men like him didn't marry girls like her.

It was ridiculous.

'Did you indeed?' He pushed himself off the door, and sort of loomed over her. 'Then why did I say it? Why tell the world you are my fiancée?'

'I don't know!' She backed away. There was something so overwhelming about him. So dangerous. And now that he'd kissed her, she knew what that danger was. A danger to her self-respect which would shrivel away to nothing should she permit the attraction she felt for him to govern her actions. And right now, self-respect was all she had left.

But, oh, how tempting it was to latch on to his carelessly spoken words and make him stick to them, for once. It would serve him right...

But, no. Though the temptation surged swift and strong, she must thrust it aside. She couldn't marry a man simply to get revenge on him for all the hurts he'd inadvertently caused her over the years. What sort of marriage would that be? Not the kind she read about in the bible...not that she'd ever actually seen anyone in real life attain the state of being an image of Christ and his church. But if she ever did marry, she would at least hope the man would regard the estate as holy and make an effort to be *faithful*, if not actually be ready to lay down his life for her.

Oh, but she might as well wish for a castle and a chest full of jewels and an army of servants to see to her slightest whim while she was at it.

'Why do you ever say anything? And anyway,

it's not as if it was to anyone who matters, is it? They didn't look to me like anybody you knew.'

'One of those bucks is a member of one of my clubs. The news of my betrothal to a short, red-haired shrew will be all over town within hours.'

'I am not a shrew!' He just brought out the worst in her. Deliberately.

'Only a shrew would have punched me in a public inn, when all I'd done was tease you, the way I have always teased you.'

'*Not* the way you have always teased me,' she seethed. 'What you said was unforgivable!'

A frown flickered across his brow. 'I said nothing that I have not said before.'

'Only now, to say such things about Father, when he is gone, that, that, that…' She shuddered to a halt as her emotions almost got the better of her.

'Gone? What do you mean, gone?'

'Don't pretend you don't know!'

'I am not pretending,' he said, taking her by both shoulders and looking into her eyes as though searching for the truth. 'Where has he gone?'

She swatted his hands from the patchily dyed shoulders of her coat and took a step back, before she gave in to the temptation to lean into him and sob her heart out.

'I was not surprised that you did not attend his funeral. I know you are far too busy and important to bother with—'

'Funeral? He died? When? Good God, Clare,' he said, advancing and taking hold of her shoulders once again. 'You cannot think that I knew? Would have spoken of him in that way if I...' His fingers tightened almost painfully on her before he abruptly released her with a bitter laugh. 'You did, in fact, believe that I knew. And, knowing, that I would be cruel enough to taunt you...' He whirled away from her, strode across to the rather grubby window and stood gazing out.

Now that he wasn't trying to prevent her from leaving, Clare found herself strangely reluctant to walk through the unguarded door. There was something about the set of his back that, in any other man, would have looked...almost defeated. Weary.

'If you really did not know...'

His back stiffened.

'Then I am sorry for thinking that you would deliberately taunt me with...with...well...' She faltered. He'd never been cruel. Not *deliberately* cruel. Oh, he might have hurt her time after time, but he'd never been aware, not really, how much power he had to hurt her. He just thought she was funny. A joke. Because, although she tried her hardest to live up to the precepts set down in the gospels, her temper kept on overruling her better judgement. Time after time she fell into scrapes. And somehow he always heard about them and mocked her for them when next he crossed her path.

Unless he actually happened to be present when she was in one, when the chances were he was at the root of it, like today.

'I suppose...' she began, on a flood of remorse. But was prevented from making another apology by the return to the room of the landlord and a waiter. Between them they'd brought all the items Lord Rawcliffe had requested. Not that he acknowledged them. He just stood there, with his back to the room, in stony silence while the men set everything on the table.

While she stood by the door, shifting from one foot to the other.

Why were they taking so long to set out a few dishes? Why couldn't they take the hint that both she and Lord Rawcliffe wanted them to go away?

Because, even though it was highly improper to remain in the room with only Lord Rawcliffe for company, she had too much pride to make her apology to him in front of witnesses.

And too highly developed a conscience to leave without making it.

Chapter Three

'You had better remove your gloves,' he said, once the landlord and the waiter had bowed their way backward out of the room.

'My gloves? Why? I am not staying. My coach is due in any moment and I—'

With an expression of impatience he strode across the room and seized her wrist. 'You need to get some ice on your hand,' he said, wrenching the buttons undone and tugging at her fingers.

Oh, good heavens. He was removing an item of her clothing. True, it was only a glove and he was doing it as though she were a naughty child, but still it was making her insides go all gooey.

Until something he said jolted her out of that pathetic state.

'Ice?' The bowl of ice he'd ordered, while he was standing there staunching the blood flowing from his nose, was for her hand? She'd assumed it was for his nose.

'Yes, ice,' he repeated, drawing her over to the table. 'It is the best thing for injuries sustained when boxing,' he said, thrusting her on to a chair. 'I know how painful it must be.' He took some chunks of ice and wrapped them in one of the cloths the waiter had brought. 'It is just fortunate that your hand connected with my nose, rather than my jaw, at which,' he said as he placed the cloth over her knuckles and held it there, 'I believe you were aiming.'

'Are you saying you deliberately moved your face so that it was your nose I struck, rather than your jaw?'

He shrugged one shoulder. 'You don't seriously think you could have landed a blow unless I permitted it, do you?'

'Well, now you come to mention it, I was a bit surprised you didn't try to block me.'

He gave her one of those withering looks that made people say he was insufferably arrogant.

'There are a lot of little bones in the hand,' he said, looking at hers as he dabbed at it with the napkin full of ice. 'And not one of them, as you should know, as strong as the jawbone.'

'What do you mean, *as I should know*?' Did he think she went round punching people on a regular basis? And had he really, deliberately, put his nose in the way of her fist, rather than letting her injure herself on him?

'Judges 15, of course,' he replied scathingly. 'How do you think Samuel managed to slay all those Philistines with the jawbone of an ass, if it wasn't harder than all their skulls?'

Oh, that was more like him. To quote scripture at her in order to make her feel stupid. And yet... he was taking care of her. Tending so gently to her hand, which did hurt rather a lot. When never, as far back as she could recall, had anyone ever tended to any of her hurts.

She had always been the one tending to others. She'd started learning to care for her brothers, and her father, well before Mama had died and left the task of running the bustling vicarage entirely in her ten-year-old hands.

'There,' he said, giving her hand one last gentle pat. 'Does that feel better?'

She nodded. Because she couldn't have spoken even if she'd been able to think of the right words to describe how she felt. The ice did indeed feel soothing. But the fact that he'd sent for it, that he'd made it into a compress, that he was applying it… *that* was what was bringing a lump to her throat.

Oh, this was why Lord Rawcliffe was so dangerous. Why she'd always stayed well away from him. Because he made her want things she had no right to want. Feel things she had no right to feel.

Eventually she pulled herself together sufficiently to lift her chin and look straight into his face, and even give him a tremulous smile.

'Thank you for tending to my hand. And accepting my apology. And…and even for dodging so that I got your nose rather than your jaw.' She got to her feet. 'But I really must be going now. My coach is due in any minute and—'

His face hardened.

'I have *not* accepted your apology.'

'What? But—'

'Sit down,' he said sternly. 'You are not going anywhere until you have given me a full explanation. Besides, have you forgotten?' He gave her a cold smile. 'You are my fiancée. Do you really think I am going to permit you to go jauntering off all over the countryside, on your own?'

'Don't be ridiculous. I am not your fiancée. And I don't need your permission to do anything or go anywhere!'

'That's better,' he said, leaning back in his chair, an infuriatingly satisfied smile playing about the lips that had so recently kissed her. 'You were beginning to droop. Now you are on fighting form again, we can have a proper discussion.'

'I don't want to have a discussion with you,' she said, barely managing to prevent herself from stamping her foot. 'Besides, oh, listen, can't you hear it?' It was the sound of a guard blowing on his horn to announce the arrival of the stage. The stage she needed to get on. 'I have a seat booked on that coach.'

'Nevertheless,' he said, striding over to the door and blocking her exit once again, 'you will not be getting on it.'

'Don't be absurd. Of course I am going to get on it.'

'You are mistaken. And if you don't acquiesce to your fate, quietly, then I am going to have to take desperate measures.'

'Oh, yes? And just what sort of measures,' she said, marching up to him and planting her hands on her hips, 'do you intend to take?'

He smiled. That wicked, knowing smile of his. Took her face in both hands. And kissed her.

'Mmph,' she protested, raising her hands to his

chest to ward him off. He paid no attention. He just wrapped his arms round her and kept right on kissing her.

'Mbrrrhgh!' She wriggled in his hold. To no avail. His arms were like bars of iron. Besides, she wasn't only fighting him. She was also having to fight the stupid, crazy urge to push herself up against him, to open her mouth and kiss him back.

And just as she was starting to forget exactly why she ought to be fighting him at all, he gentled the kiss. Gentled his hold. Changed the nature of his kiss from hard and masterful, to coaxing and... oh, his clever mouth. It knew just how to translate her fury into a sort of wild, pulsing ache. She ached all over. She began to tremble with what he was making her feel. Grew weaker by the second.

As if he knew her legs were on the verge of giving way, he scooped her up into his arms and carried her over to one of the upholstered chairs by the fire. Sat down without breaking his hold, so that she landed on his lap.

And instead of struggling to break free, she subsided on to his chest, burying her face in his neck. Because she could see absolutely no point in struggling to escape from the one place she'd always wanted to be: in his arms, the focus of his whole attention.

'Now,' he growled into the crown of her bonnet, 'you will tell me why you are in this godforsaken spot, trying to get on a coach, when you should be snug and safe at home in the vicarage.'

'The vicarage is not my home anymore, as you very well know,' she said, jerking upright under the impact of a dose of that bleak truth. 'Now that Father has died.'

'The vicarage *is* your home,' he said. 'Even,' he laid one finger to her lips when she took a breath to protest, 'even when the vicar is no longer living. There was no need for you to leave, the moment you buried him.'

'But the curate—'

'The curate should have damn well contacted me before evicting you and presuming to move in, which is what I have to assume he did?'

'Well, yes, but he did contact you. At least, I mean, he tried to. And when you didn't respond, he—' Well, everyone in Watling Minor believed that Lord Rawcliffe knew everything. Which meant that if he hadn't responded in the negative, then he simply didn't care what arrangements had been made for the late vicar's daughter.

'Assumed I would be happy to have you evicted?' His eyes narrowed. 'I shall have to have words with the Reverend Cobbet.'

'No, no, it wasn't like that.' She laid one hand on his chest. 'It wasn't him. I just… There didn't seem any point in me hanging on there. Not when Clement had arranged everything for me so…so… kindly.'

'Clement? Kind?'

'Yes, well, it *was* kind of him to go to so much trouble on my behalf.' He'd told her so. 'He didn't have to make *any* arrangements.' As Lord Rawcliffe raised one cynical eyebrow, Clare hastened to add, 'I mean, I would have thought if anyone had the duty to provide for me it would have been Constantine.'

He made a scoffing noise, expressing his opinion of her oldest brother. Since it pretty much coincided with her own, after the way he'd behaved lately, she made no objection.

'And what form did this kindness of Clement's take, dare I ask?'

'He found me work. A good, honest job. One I am well qualified to take up.'

'You are going to be housekeeper for another

family of ungrateful, lazy, hypocritical, sanctimonious prigs, are you?'

'Don't speak of my brothers like that.'

He closed his mouth. Gave her a look.

Which somehow had the effect of reminding her that she was still sitting on his lap, with her arms about his neck, though she couldn't recall the moment she'd put them there. And that he was running his big hands up and down her back, as though to soothe her. And that, although she had just, out of habit, leapt to defend her brothers, right at this moment she couldn't help agreeing with him. For she'd spent years keeping house for them. Then nursing their father, while they'd all left and got on with their own lives. But when she'd needed them, all they'd had to offer her were excuses. Constantine's wife was due to give birth to their third child at any moment, he'd written, and couldn't be expected to house an indigent sister. It was asking too much.

Cornelius had no room for her, either. Though, since he lived in bachelor quarters in the bishop's palace she hadn't really hoped for anything from him apart from sympathy. But even that had been in short supply. Instead of acknowledging how hard it was going to be for her to leave the vicarage, the only home she'd ever had, he had, instead, congratulated Clement on his foresight in arranging for her removal so swiftly, so that the curate, a man who had a wife and a baby on the way, could move out of the cramped cottage where he'd been living before. He'd even gone so far as to shake Reverend Cobbet by the hand and say how pleased he was for him to finally be moving into a house where he and his family would be comfortable.

It had felt as though he'd stabbed her in the back.

At which point in her bitter ruminations she heard the sound of wheels rattling across the cobbles.

'Oh, the coach, the coach!' Finally she did what she should have done in the first place—she made an attempt to get off his lap. But he tightened his hold, keeping her firmly in place.

'Too late,' he said smugly. 'It has gone without you.'

'But my luggage! Everything I own is in my trunk…'

'Which has been conveyed to my chaise.'

'What? How can you know that?'

'Because I told the landlord to have it done when I ordered the tea and ice. Did you not hear?' He widened his eyes as though in innocence, when he must know very well she had heard no such thing. That he must have mumbled it while she'd been busy getting the table in between them. Which had worked really well, hadn't it? Since she'd somehow ended up not just in his arms, but also on his lap just the same.

'Well, you shouldn't have.'

'Of course I should,' he said with a touch of impatience. 'If I hadn't had the foresight to do so, you would have just lost everything you own.'

'Instead of which, I have fallen into the hands of a...a... Why, you are so high-handed, ordering people about and...and forcing people into fake betrothals that you... Why, you are little better than a kidnapper!'

Chapter Four

Rawcliffe drew in a deep breath and started counting to ten.

Just as he got to two, he realised he wasn't angry enough to need to resort to his usual method of dealing with Clare. He was still far too pleased with the ease with which he'd finally got her on to his lap, and into his arms, to care very much about what she had to say about it.

He smiled down into her furious little face.

'Far from kidnapping you,' he pointed out, 'I have rescued you from the consequences of your own folly. However,' he interjected swiftly when she drew a breath to object, 'I concede you must have been at the end of your tether, to hit me when all I did was tease you the way I have always done.'

And it hadn't hurt that much. Not as much as discovering she thought him capable of such casual cruelty that she'd ended up being evicted from her home before her father was even cold in his grave. When she'd said he'd gone, he'd just assumed she meant that he'd managed to get on to a coach when she wasn't watching and that she was searching for him. Reverend Cottam's behaviour had been getting increasingly erratic of late after all. And his sarcasm had been mainly aimed at her brothers, who'd left her with a burden she should no longer have to shoulder all on her own. He'd never dreamed the irascible old preacher could actually have died.

'But you cannot deny,' he continued when she drew her ginger brows together into a thwarted little frown, 'that had I not announced you were my fiancée, you would have been ruined.'

'I don't see that it would have been as bad as that,' she said, defiant to the last.

'Johnny Bruton, the man who is a member of my club, is a dedicated gossip. He would have left no stone unturned in his quest to discover your name and station in life.'

She shifted on his lap, giving him a delicious experience of her softly rounded bottom.

'That was why I instructed the landlord to have your belongings placed in my own chaise. So that he would not be able to read your luggage label with, no doubt, its destination thereon. Not for any nefarious notion of abduction.'

'Well, if you've prevented him from discovering my name, there is no need to carry on with this deception, is there?'

Need? No, it wasn't a question of need. But it was so deliciously satisfying to have the proud, pious little madam so completely at his mercy for once. True, she was still spitting insults at him, but they lacked the conviction they might have had if she wasn't sitting on his lap. If she hadn't put her arms round his neck instead of slapping his face when he'd kissed her.

Not only that, but she'd actually apologised to him. And thanked him, though the words had very nearly choked her as she'd forced them through her teeth.

Oh, no, he wasn't finished with Clare just yet. There were just too many intriguing possibilities left to explore.

'That depends,' he said, as though considering her point of view.

'On what?'

Hmmm. She'd stopped scowling. It was worth noting that pretending to be taking her opinion into account made her sheathe her claws. He would have to bear that in mind.

'On where you were planning to go. I presume, to the home of your new employer?'

'Yes, I told you, Clement arranged for me to begin work as a companion to an elderly lady.'

'No, you didn't tell me that.'

'Oh. Well, he did. You see, he is involved in all sorts of charitable work. And one of his causes is to find honest work for…er…fallen women.'

Something like an alarm went off inside him. Because he'd just spent the better part of a month searching for a girl who might have criminal connections. A girl who'd disappeared after the elderly, vulnerable woman she'd been working for had been robbed. And Clement's name had come up then, as well.

'He finds work for fallen women, does he?' He only just prevented himself from asking if he also found work for professional thieves. Just because he was on the trail of a group of criminals who'd been systematically robbing elderly ladies, it did not necessarily mean that Clare's brother was behind it. It could be just a coincidence that one of the people he'd questioned had mentioned Clement Cottam's name.

'What sort of work? And, more to the point, how does this affect you?' Because he couldn't see Clement being fool enough to ask Clare to rob an elderly lady she was supposed to be looking after, even if he was involved in the crimes Rawcliffe was currently investigating. She was too conscientious. 'Are you not insulted?'

'No, no, he… It is just that he has a sort of network, I suppose, of elderly ladies with charitable dispositions, who are willing to give that sort of woman a chance to reform. At least, that is how he explained it to me when I couldn't credit how swiftly he'd managed to find me a post.'

'That does sound hard to credit,' he agreed. So, Clement had a network of elderly ladies who would agree to take in servants with a shady past, on his recommendation, did he? Even though that could be a coincidence as well, two coincidences regarding a man he already suspected of being up to no good, coming in such rapid succession, were hard to ignore.

'You had better explain how it came about.'

'Well, I wrote to him, naturally, to inform him of Father's passing.'

'Naturally.' And somebody must have written to him, as well. What a time for him to be trying to stay beyond the reach of anyone who might have been able to reveal his identity.

'And within two days he was back, helping to arrange the funeral. And, say what you like about him, I cannot deny that I was very grateful for his help. He is very, very good at organising things. Keeps a cool head, you know, when I…'

He reached up and tapped the end of her nose with the tip of his forefinger. 'You feel things too deeply. You don't need to explain it to me.'

She jerked her head back, out of his reach. And he let her do so.

For now.

'No, and you don't need to bring up the curse of my red hair, either,' she said mutinously.

'It would, patently, be absurd to do so, when Clement has hair of almost exactly the same shade as yours.' His features were similar, too, so that nobody looking at the pair of them together could doubt they were siblings. Yet Clare's sharp little features and pale gold eyes made her look like some kind of sprite, or a woodland nymph, whereas Clement's face just reminded him of a fox. A fox that was contemplating a raid on the nearest hen coop.

'But do, pray, continue to explain how the saintly Clement provided you with employment.'

'Oh, well, as I said, he has this network of elderly ladies willing to employ girls on his recommendation. So he just sent a letter to one of them recommending me as her companion. And she accepted me by return of post. So, you see, before the funeral was over, I had work and somewhere to live, whereas before that I...'

She didn't need to say more. She'd had nothing. Believed she had no options. As she bit down on her lower lip, which had started to tremble, a strange feeling came over him. A feeling compounded of admiration for her bravery in the face of such adversity, coupled with a very strong urge to protect her from ever having to go through anything like it again.

Who would have thought he'd ever consider that the crusading Clare needed anyone to protect her from anything? But then who would have thought she could ever look so vulnerable as she did, sitting there trying not to give way to tears? Having just spoken of what must have been a horribly lonely experience in such a matter-of-fact way?

It made him want to hold her tighter. Tell her

she was not alone anymore. That he would look after her...

'And I am sure,' she said, removing her arms from about his neck, reminding him that he was the last person she'd willingly accept help from, 'she will still take me, if only you will arrange for me to get on the next coach.'

'I am sure she will not,' he said, tightening his own hold round her waist in instinctive reaction to her attempt to escape him. She was going nowhere until he was ready to let her go. Until he'd wrung every last drop of satisfaction from this encounter. She hadn't anything like begun to repay him for the insults she'd heaped on him over the years. If he couldn't make her eat her words, precisely, then he could at least rub her nose in the fact that she was where she was because she'd fallen so very far short of the exacting standards she'd always been waving under his nose. 'Nobody wants to employ the kind of girl who gets into fist fights in public inns.'

'I didn't!' She glanced guiltily at his nose. 'That is, she isn't likely to find out about it.'

'Oh, but she is. Things like this get out. People like Johnny Bruton make sure of it.'

'But she lives so far away from London...'

'If she is part of a network of elderly women, who have little better to do with their time than write letters, somebody is bound to write and inform her of your part in this fracas.'

Clare's mouth turned down at the corners as the truth of his observation struck home. Oh, but revenge could be sweet.

'Even if she does not know anything about it to start with,' he persisted, 'the fear of discovery will hang over your head from the moment you inveigle your way into her household.'

'I would not be inveigling my way anywhere!'

'Oh, but you would. No doubt Clement promised her, and her family, the companionship of a gently reared, caring, competent young lady. Once they hear about this little escapade, they will think you have deliberately deceived them. That your *brother* deliberately deceived them.'

'No, no. You are making it sound far worse than it was!'

'And how do you think the likes of Johnny Bruton will make it sound? And how much do you think the tale will be embellished every time it is repeated? Why, the gossips will probably have the pair of us repairing to one of the bedrooms in this establishment and making up our quarrel in the most uninhibited fashion.' Which would, now he came to mention it, be the way he'd rather like this interlude to progress. The taste of her lips had been every bit as sweet as he'd once dreamed it would. And, though she'd fought her response, there was no hiding the fact that she had responded to him. If this were any other woman, they'd be negotiating terms by now.

But Clare, being Clare, was looking wildly round the perfectly respectable coffee room, then wrinkling her nose in disgust.

'You are probably right,' she said gloomily. 'Particularly given your reputation.'

And even though he'd been thinking along the very same lines, to hear her estimation of his character come out of her lips in such a disdainful manner was like a slap to the face.

He tried not to tense. He was not a rake or a libertine, but Clare had never managed to comprehend that a young man, with tolerable looks and plenty of money, was bound to make the most of the opportunities that came his way. In her opinion, men and women should never yield to the temptations of the flesh, outside the marriage bed.

'Exactly,' he purred, injecting every ounce of lasciviousness into his voice that he could muster.

Living right down to her low expectations of him, the way he always did.

'Nobody will ever believe that I could take a young woman into a private room, particularly not one to whom I have declared myself to be betrothed, and allow her to walk away with her virtue unsullied.'

'Oh, dear.' She buried her face in her hands and bowed over as though trying to curl up into a ball.

And hang it if another surge of protectiveness didn't choose that very moment to sweep away his urge to needle her. Causing him to start rubbing his hands up and down the curve of her back.

'Never mind,' he said, wondering why humbling Clare wasn't making him feel like the victor. 'I am sure there are worse fates than marrying a marquess.'

She made a strangled little squeal as if of half-swallowed outrage. Bringing any inclination to show mercy grinding to a juddering halt.

Last time she'd acted as though his proposal was an insult, he'd had to walk away, licking his wounds. He'd been smarting under the insulting manner of that rejection ever since. So that every time their paths had crossed, he'd felt he had to make a point of demonstrating that he was over it. Over her. That he didn't give a rap what she thought of him. In fact, on occasion, he'd gone so far out of his way to show her how unimportant she was that he'd even disgusted himself.

Yet she could still wound him by shuddering in genuine horror at the prospect of marrying him.

And suddenly, he couldn't think of any sweeter form of revenge than actually doing it.

Marrying her.

Because, for the rest of their lives, if ever she felt inclined to look down her nose at him, or complain about his lax morals, or...*anything*...he'd be able to point out that it was entirely her own fault she was shackled to such a reprobate.

His lips quirked. He couldn't help it. She could be his, now. For as long as they both would live, if he dug in his heels. And she would have nobody to blame but herself.

Because she'd lost her temper and swung that punch a split second before he'd made his own move. Since, he'd reasoned, she couldn't think any less of him than she clearly did, since he hadn't thought he had anything to lose, he'd decided he might as well kiss her. It would, he'd thought, have taken the wind out of her sails. Taken her down a peg or two.

Thank God for her temper. Because now *she* was the instigator of the scene which had fatally compromised her and he was the magnanimous one, stepping in to save the day. Rather than playing the role of villain for the rest of their lives, the villain who'd ruined her reputation by kissing her in the corridor of a public inn, he would always be able to claim the moral high ground.

He could hardly wait.

Chapter Five

'You don't really mean that, do you?' She lifted a tragic face to his.

He hadn't. Not to begin with. Announcing she was his fiancée had simply been the only thing he could think of, on the spur of the moment, that would both extricate her from her immediate difficulty and thoroughly annoy her at one and the same time. But now that he'd considered carrying through on his threat, the advantages were becoming clearer by the second.

Especially since he'd kissed her.

Because he'd been longing to get her into his bed for years. Even after she'd rejected him, she'd continued to fascinate him. He'd watched, with mounting frustration, as she'd blossomed from captivating girl to alluring woman. Always dancing just beyond his reach.

But now she was sitting on his lap. And once he got that ring on her finger, she'd have no excuse for refusing him. Not considering the vows she was going to make, in church. Vows which she, with her heightened religious conscience, would consider binding.

'Don't I?'

She peered at him as though trying to understand him. *Really* understand him, rather than jumping to conclusions based on the lies and half-truths fed to her by the likes of Clement.

'Well, I rather thought,' she said, 'that you only said it because it was the one thing that would guarantee getting me out of hot water. And while I appreciate the, um, brilliance of your quick thinking—'

'Trying to turn me up sweet?'

'No,' she said with exasperation. 'I was *trying* to give credit where it is due. But since I know you cannot really wish to marry me—'

'Can't I? And just why would that be?'

'You are going to make me spell it out?' She narrowed her eyes. 'Very well, then. Since you seem determined to amuse yourself at my expense today, then I will freely admit that you ought to marry someone who is all the things I am not. Someone beautiful, for a start.'

And Clare was not beautiful, not in the conventional sense.

'Someone with all the social graces.'

She certainly didn't have any of those.

'Someone with a title and money, and, oh, all the things I haven't got. But because of my temper, my awful temper, you have told people you are going to marry me.' Her eyes swam with regret and penitence. 'But I'm sure, if we put our heads together, we can come up with another plan, an even better plan, to stop you from having to go through with it. We could perhaps tell everyone that we discovered we do not suit, for example, or—'

'Put our heads together?' Everything in him rose up in revolt. If he thought she could wriggle out of this, she had another think coming. There was only one way he wanted their heads close together. 'Do you mean, like this?' he said, before closing the gap between their mouths and stopping her foolish objections with a kiss.

She made a wholly feminine sound of surrender and fell into his kiss as though she was starving for the taste of his lips. With a sort of desperation that made him suspect she intended it as a farewell. As though she was giving in to the temptation to sample what she considered forbidden fruit just one last time.

At length, she pulled away and turned her face into his neck. She was panting. Her cheeks were flushed.

But when she eventually sat up, her face wore an expression of resolve.

'That was not what I had in mind,' she said, unnecessarily. Though it was pretty much all that was in his mind and had been from the moment he'd pulled her onto his lap.

'Poor Clare,' he murmured, without a shred of sympathy. 'So determined to escape my evil clutches...'

She went rigid, as though his words reminded her she'd been making precious little attempt to escape him from the moment he'd taken her in his arms. And bit down on her lower lip, the lip he'd been enjoying kissing so much not a moment before. And with which she'd kissed him back.

Her expression of chagrin made him want to laugh.

She nearly always made him want to laugh.

It was a large part of why he'd proposed to her that first time. He'd just endured one of those days that were such a factor of life in Kelsham

Park. His mother barricaded in her room. His father out shooting. The staff tiptoeing around as though scared of rousing a sleeping beast. Life had seemed so bleak. And then there she'd been, so full of life, and zeal, and all the things that were lacking in his. And she'd made him laugh. When he'd thought there was nothing of joy to be found anywhere in his life.

And he'd wanted to capture it. Capture her. So that he could...warm himself at the flame that was her spirit.

The proposal had burst from his lips before he'd thought it through. But then, as now, the moment he'd spoken he'd wanted it to become real. Wanted her by his side. In his life. Keeping the chill of Kelsham Park at bay.

He cleared away the lump that came to his throat, so that his voice would not betray the swell of emotion which had just taken him unawares.

'So determined to escape me. Yet you are the only woman to whom I have ever made an honourable proposal.'

'What?' She looked completely flummoxed by that.

'Yes. All the others,' he put in swiftly, before the conversation could turn to that first proposal and all the hurt that had ensued, 'were quite happy to receive *dis*honourable ones.'

Her puzzled frown turned to a veritable scowl. And she made her first real attempt to get off his lap.

Since he'd already decided they'd been starting to venture rather too close to territory he would rather not revisit, he let her go. All the way to the table where she seized the teapot with what looked like relief.

But the expression faded as she set the pot down after pouring herself a cup of tea, as if she'd realised that, although she'd scored one point in escaping his lap, there was still a major battle to fight. And the look she darted him as he got to his feet and followed her to the table was one of outright desperation.

'I, um, should thank you, then, for doing me the honour of…though actually, you didn't propose, did you? You just informed the world that I was your fiancée.'

'Nevertheless,' he said, pouring himself a glass of ale, 'you will become my wife.'

'I—'

'And you will make the best of it. In public, at

least,' he added grimly. Even his own parents had managed that. 'In private—'

'There isn't going to be any *in private.*'

'You mean, you wish me to make love to you in public?'

'Don't be…oh! You provoking man! You know very well what I mean. That there isn't going to be *any* making love, *any*where, since we are *not* getting married. You know we are not.'

'But, Clare, what will become of you if I don't make an honest woman of you?'

She flung up her chin. 'I will be fine. I will… well… I will work something out.'

He couldn't help admiring her stance, even though he still felt rather insulted by her determination to survive without his help. She was so brave. So determined to stand on her own two feet. No matter what life flung at her.

'There is no need to work anything out. This solution will do as well as any other either of us could come up with. And it saves us the bother of racking our brains for an alternative.'

'But—'

'Really, Clare, this is getting tiresome. I am offering you a position amongst the highest in the land. Wealth you have never been able to imagine.'

'I don't care about your money, or your position,' she retorted. 'Worldly vanity, that is all you have to offer me—'

'Have you never considered how much good you could do, as a marchioness? You will be mixing with the people responsible for making the law. You will be able to preach your beliefs to their faces, whenever they eat at our table. You will be able to use your wealth to make a difference to the lives of very many of the poorest and most deserving, should you care to do so.'

She froze. Like a hound scenting prey. 'You would let me spend your money however I wish?'

'I will give you a generous allowance,' he corrected her, 'which you may spend however you wish.'

Her eyes went round and she stared right through him, as though she was imagining all the ways she could spend that allowance. For a moment or two. Before she lowered them to the table and bit down on her lower lip, as though chastising herself for indulging in some extremely mercenary daydreams.

Time to put some steel in her spine again.

'However,' he said sternly, 'I shall expect you to look the part whenever you appear at my side in public. I most certainly do not wish to see you out and about wearing garments that make you look like a bedraggled crow.'

Which served to put the mutinous look back on her face.

'How dare you! I am in mourning for my father—'

'Which is no excuse for looking shabby.'

Her eyes flashed. She took a deep breath. He cut in, swiftly.

'I can see I shall have to engage one of those abigails who do nothing but take care of clothes. A top-notch one,' he said, running a deliberately disparaging look over her complete outfit.

'You don't need to—'

'I always expected whomever I married to cost me a pretty penny,' he cut in again, deliberately misconstruing whatever objection she'd been about to make. 'Though unlike most husbands, instead of dreading the bills flooding in from the modistes, I may have to curb your enthusiasm for supporting beggars and cripples.'

'Now, look here…' she began, indignantly. And then petered out. Lowered her head again. Fiddled with her teacup.

'Damn me for being right?'

She nodded. 'It's terrible of me, isn't it? But, the

thought of being able to do some good, *real* good, for once. It is so terribly tempting…'

Clare Cottam must be the only woman alive who would regard the opportunity to do good in the world as a *temptation*. It was all he could do to keep a straight face.

'Then let it be a consolation to you. For the terrible fate,' he said drily, 'of having to marry me in order to be able to do so.'

'Look, I never said it would be a terrible fate to marry you. You mustn't think that. It's just…it doesn't seem fair you have to marry the likes of me just because I…'

'Struck me?'

She hunched her shoulders. Lifted her teacup and took a large gulp, as though hoping it could wash away a nasty taste.

'It is true,' he said, provocatively, 'that you are obliging me to enter a state I would not willingly have walked into for some considerable time—'

'I am not! I am trying to think of a way out for you. While all you are doing is—'

He cut through her latest objection. 'But I would have had to marry somebody, some day. Because I must produce an heir.'

For a moment it looked as though Clare's tea was in danger of going down the wrong way.

'Yes,' he drawled. 'That is one very real function you could fulfil just as well as a titled, wealthy, beautiful woman.' He reached across the table and stroked the back of her wrist, where it lay beside the plate of bread and butter.

'Oh!' She snatched her hand away.

'Yes, Clare, you could be the mother of my child.' And what a mother she would be. He couldn't see her taking to drink when she didn't get her own way. Nor taking lovers, nor only visiting the nursery when she wanted to complain about his behaviour and telling her child that he was the spawn of his father and that the sight of his face made her sick to her stomach.

'Oh,' she said again in a rather softer voice, her eyes taking on a faraway look as though she, too, was imaging a child they could create together.

And then her face turned an even deeper shade of red and she began squirming so much he decided it was time to give her thoughts another direction.

'Possibly, I *should* have looked for a woman with all the qualities you listed. And a very tedious business,' he said, with a grimace of genuine distaste, 'it would have been making my choice from all the many candidates for the privilege.'

She gasped. 'How can you be so arrogant?'

He raised one eyebrow at her. 'You yourself have already pointed out that I could have had my pick of society's finest specimens of feminine perfection. I was only agreeing with you.'

'You—how typical of you to turn my own words against me like that.'

'Indeed,' he said affably. 'And you should have expected it, knowing me as well as you do. I have no shame, have I?' He'd added that last when she opened her mouth as if to say it. 'But never mind. There is no point in us quarrelling over this. Just accept that I am relieved that you have saved me a great deal of bother.'

'You...you...'

'Yes, and now I come to think of it,' he said, leaning back in his chair and looking her up and down speculatively, 'I may as well tell you that I don't mind having to marry you as much as you seem to think.' Not at all, to be truthful. But whenever had being truthful got him anywhere with Clare?

'Rubbish,' she said. 'I know full well that I am not fit to become your marchioness.'

'Why not? You are the daughter of a gentleman. Besides, I have known you all my life.'

'Exactly! You know we are not at all suited.'

That was only *her* opinion. 'On the contrary. With you there will be no surprises. You could never fool me into thinking you would be a compliant wife by being all sweet and syrupy whenever we meet, then turning into a shrew the minute I got the ring on your finger. Which could happen with any woman I got to know during a London Season. No,' he said, smiling at her in a challenging way as her little mouth pursed up in the way it always did when she was attempting to hold back a scathing retort. 'I already know that you are a shrew. That the last thing anyone could accuse you of being is compliant.'

Her hand tightened on the handle of her teacup.

'Are you planning on throwing that at my head?'

She deliberately unclenched her fingers and tucked her hands into her lap.

'Good, then, if we are finished here, may I suggest we get on our way?'

'Our...our way?' Once again, she looked slightly lost and bewildered. 'Where to?'

'London, of course. It is where I was going when I stopped here for a change of horses. I have pressing business there.' He had to report back to his friends on the progress he'd made so far with investigating the disappearance of some jewellery from not only Lady Harriet Inskip's aunt, but also from the family of his chaplain, Thomas Kellet.

'Oh, but…' She twisted her hands in her lap. 'I thought you were trying to avoid scandal. If you take me to London and parade me about the streets…'

'I have no intention of doing anything so fatheaded,' he said, 'since I know full well that nobody could parade you anywhere you did not wish to go.'

She shot him a narrow-eyed look, one with which he was all too familiar when attempting to pay her a compliment. As though she suspected him of concealing an insult behind his comment, one that she hadn't immediately perceived, but would discover on further reflection.

'I shall, instead, take you directly to the house of a respectable female, where you will stay while I arrange our wedding.'

She frowned. 'A respectable female?'

'Yes. A lady who has recently become…a friend.'

'I see,' she said, glowering at him. And bristling all over.

If he didn't know better, he'd think she was jealous. The irony was, that Lady Harriet, the lady to whom he was referring, would probably have applauded if she'd seen Clare punch him on the nose, since she'd often shown signs she'd like to do something very similar.

They would, when Clare had climbed down off her high horse and realised Lady Harriet was indeed respectable, get on like a house on fire.

Chapter Six

Clare couldn't believe she was getting into Lord Rawcliffe's luxurious chaise to travel to London, when not half an hour since she'd been planning to get on to the public stage and head in the opposite direction.

She couldn't believe she'd let him sweet-talk her into going along with his ridiculous proposition, either.

He couldn't possibly really want to marry her.

In spite of the outrageous claims he'd made about saving him the bother of choosing one from among the hordes of females who practically swooned whenever he walked into the room.

They were too far apart. Socially, to begin with. And morally, which was more important. He was a rake and a libertine, and a…well, no, she could not accuse him of being a drunkard.

Nor, if she was being completely honest, did he deserve the label of rake. He had never littered the countryside with his by-blows, nor taken any woman against her will.

No, because he didn't need to. Women had been throwing themselves at him since he'd first started sprouting whiskers on his arrogant chin and he hadn't thought twice about enjoying what they had to offer. He only had to smile at them, in that certain sort of melting way he had, and they'd...well, melted.

All except her. On the contrary, she'd lifted her chin and told him exactly what she thought of his promiscuity whenever he'd smiled at her in that lascivious way. Had kept all the melting she'd done hidden, deep down. Concealed it behind a smoke-screen of invective. Told him he should be ashamed of attempting to corrupt a vicar's daughter. Informed him she would never become yet another victim of his dubious charms. And when all else failed, simply hidden if she'd seen him coming.

Not that she'd had to resort to such measures all that often. Thankfully. She cringed as her mind flew back, for about the third or fourth time that day, to the time she'd almost fallen out of the tree into the field where Farmer Westthorpe kept his bull. She'd climbed the dratted tree in the first place because she'd seen him coming down the lane. Shinned up it fast, so that she wouldn't have to bid him good day, or face the sniggers of Betsy Woodly, who was clinging on to his arm. And the innkeeper's daughter *would* have sniggered, because there could only be one reason why she was strolling along the lane on Lord Rawcliffe's arm. Which was that they were looking for a convenient place to...*urgh.*

Unfortunately, it was directly after they'd passed the tree whose leafy branches were doing such an admirable job of concealing her that Betsy had pulled him behind a hedge and flung her arms round his neck. Clare had squeezed her eyes shut so she wouldn't have to witness the unspeakable things they proceeded to do to each other. Which was why she'd lost her footing and almost tumbled to her doom.

Of course Lord Rawcliffe had found it hilarious. Had taunted her with getting her just deserts for spying on him. And she'd been too mortified to offer a coherent explanation as to what, precisely, she had been doing up that particular tree at that precise moment. So that every time their paths crossed, for several months after that, he'd smile at her in a knowing way and offer to satisfy her curiosity.

She'd always managed to escape with her dignity intact. Until today, when he had proved that he was every bit as devastating as she'd always feared. His skilful kisses had not only melted her, it was as if they'd lit a fire in her blood and scrambled her brains. How else to account for the fact she'd ceased trying to find a way out of their predicament and agreed to marry him, instead? Yes, now she looked back over the past hour or so, it seemed to her that every time she'd almost come up with a rational alternative, he'd kissed her again and reduced her to a quivering heap of jelly on his lap.

On his lap!

She shifted on the seat.

'Trying to keep your face averted from my corrupting presence is clearly giving you a crick in your neck,' he said provokingly. 'Why don't you just turn your head and stare out of the other window? Pretend you cannot see me.'

She didn't need to see him to be aware that he was sitting right next to her. Even though he didn't allow a single part of his body to touch any part of hers. He was so…*there*. So vital and male, and sure of himself. Dominating the whole carriage just by the act of sitting in it.

How did he do that? Dominate whatever place he happened to be, just by breathing in and out?

'Have you ever been to London? I am not aware that you have done so, but you might have sneaked up to town in secret, on some mission you wished to conceal from me.'

She gritted her teeth. How could he accuse her of being sneaky, when she could not tell a lie to save her life? Everything she thought was always written on her face, or so he kept telling her.

Although—she darted a sideways glance at him under her lids—he'd never discerned the one secret she would die rather than have him discover. Which was the way she felt about him, in spite of herself. The way her heart pounded and her insides melted when he turned that lazy smile of his in her direction. The way her insides knotted with feelings she couldn't name or even fully understand whenever she'd heard about his latest conquest.

'You mean you don't know?' she said with mock astonishment. 'I thought you were infallible.'

His face hardened. 'No. As we have both discovered today, I do not know everything that occurs even within my own sphere of influence. Clare, you still cannot think that I would have stayed away had I known of your father's death?'

'Yes, I can think that,' she retorted. There had been no love lost between the two men she cared about the most and she could easily believe he would prefer not to attend the funeral. 'But,' she put in hastily when his lips thinned and his eyes hardened to chips of ice, 'I do acquit you of deliberately hurting me earlier. I do believe, now, that you just fell into the way you always have of teasing me.'

'How magnanimous of you,' he drawled, looking far from pleased.

They fell into an uneasy silence for some considerable time. Such a long time that she began to wonder if he was ever going to speak to her again. How could he think a marriage would work between two people who couldn't even conduct a civil conversation?

Perhaps, she reflected darkly, he didn't consider conversation important. His own mother and father never seemed to speak to each other. Whenever they were out in public, it was as if there was a wall of frost separating them. She almost shivered at the memory. Surely he wouldn't be as cold a husband as his father had been to his mother?

Although…they'd still managed to produce him, hadn't they?

A strange feeling twisted her insides at the thought of conceiving his child. Under such circumstances. Though a pang of yearning swiftly swept it aside. That had been what had silenced her very last objection, the prospect of becoming a mother. To his child. She'd have had to be an idiot to carry on insisting she'd rather spend the rest of her life tending to an unfamiliar and probably cantankerous old lady.

She'd actually seen it. The child. Seen herself rocking it in her arms, holding it to her breast. Imagined what it would feel like to belong to someone. And have someone belong to her in a way she'd never truly known.

'We are now crossing the section of the Heath,' he suddenly said, jolting her out of her daydream which now featured not just one baby but three little boys of varying ages, 'where once a serving girl, armed only with a hammer, fought off a highwayman with such vigour she left him dying in the road.'

'Why on earth,' she said, half-turning in her seat to gape at him, 'would you think I would be interested in hearing that?'

He gave a half-shrug. 'I thought you would find her behaviour admirable.'

'What, clubbing a man to death? With a hammer?' She caught a glint in his eye. 'Do you take me for a complete idiot?'

'I do not take you for any kind of idiot.'

'Then kindly cease making up such outrageous tales. As if a maidservant would have been wandering around with a hammer in her hand, indeed. Let alone have the strength to fell a fully grown man with it.'

His lips twitched. 'I beg your pardon. No more tales of grisly crimes.'

He fell silent for only a few moments, before pointing out a ditch into which he claimed an eloping couple had met their grisly end when the gig in which they'd been fleeing to Gretna had overturned.

'I thought you were not going to regale me with tales of grisly crimes.'

'It was not a crime. It was an accident,' he pointed out pedantically.

'Well, I don't want to hear about grisly accidents, either.'

'No? What, then, shall we discuss?'

He was asking her? She swallowed. Then noted what looked like a mischievous glint in his eye.

He was trying, in his own inimitable fashion, to break through the wall of silence that she'd thrown up between them by being so ungracious. It made her want to reach out and take hold of his hand.

Rather than do anything so spineless, she said, instead, 'You could…point out the landmarks as we pass them. Explain what they are.'

'I could,' he said. And proceeded to do so. So that the ensuing miles passed in a far more pleasant manner. Especially once they reached streets thronged with traffic and bounded on either side by tall buildings. She was actually sorry when, at length, the chaise drew up outside a white house with at least three storeys that she could make out, in the corner of a very grand square.

'Is this your house?'

'No. This is not Grosvenor, but St James's Square. This is the home of that friend I was telling you about. The one who will be looking after you until we can be married.'

'If you can make her,' Clare mumbled as one of the postilions came to open the door.

He shot her one of his impenetrable looks. 'She will be an ally for you, in society, if she takes to

you, so I hope you will make an effort to be agreeable to her.'

Which set her back up all over again. How dared
he assume she would be anything but agreeable to
a woman who was going to be her hostess?

She avoided taking his hand as they alighted and
even managed to evade the hand he would have
put to the small of her back as he ushered her into
the portico that sheltered the front door.

A smart butler admitted them and took Lord
Rawcliffe's coat and hat as a matter of course.

'Lady Harriet is in the drawing room, my lord,
Miss...'

'Miss Clare Cottam,' said Lord Rawcliffe in answer to the butler's unspoken question.

For some reason, the butler's demeanour squashed
any lingering suspicion that Lord Rawcliffe might
be bringing her to the home of his mistress. Which
made her slightly less annoyed with him. Which,
she decided the moment they entered the most opu-
lent drawing room she'd ever seen, was probably a
mistake. Because it was only her anger which was
shoring her up. Without it, she felt rather insecure
and out of her depth. And had to fight the temptation to grab his hand and cling to it. Or the sleeve
of his coat.

'Oh, Zeus, thank heavens,' said a young woman getting to her feet and coming over to them, rather than staying in her chair by the fire. She had non-descript hair and a rather square face. Not a bit like the kind of woman she could see Lord Rawcliffe taking for a mistress. At all.

'I am so glad to see you. Is this Jenny?'

Jenny? She looked up at Lord Rawcliffe's impassive profile. Why on earth would this woman think he was going to bring someone called Jenny into her front parlour?

'Ah, no, I am afraid not. Allow me to intro—'

'Then it was a wild goose chase? Just as you predicted?' Lady Harriet wrung her hands. 'Oh, this is dreadful. Dreadful. You see—'

'This is neither the time nor the place,' began Lord Rawcliffe, only to be interrupted almost at once.

'It most certainly is the time,' said Lady Harriet indignantly. 'Past time, you see, Archie—'

'We will not discuss that matter now, if you please,' he said sternly, jerking his head slightly in Clare's direction.

'You mean…you don't wish this person to know?'

'Astute of you,' he said sarcastically.

'Oh, well, then, perhaps we can leave her here and go into the kitchen to—'

'We are not leaving her here alone while we go off to discuss anything,' he bit out. 'And will you stop referring to her as *this person*. Clare is my fiancée!'

'Your fiancée?' Lady Harriet stared at her with all the shock Clare had felt last time he'd announced their betrothal. 'Good heavens. But she looks...'

'Be careful, very careful, what you say next,' he growled.

'I was only going to say she looks quite sensible. Whatever came over her to agree to marry you?'

'She has been recently bereaved. She was distraught. She had nowhere else to go—'

'Excuse me,' said Clare, goaded beyond patience by being talked about as though she wasn't there. 'But I had a very good place to go. And I was not distraught until you decided to taunt me with my misfortunes.'

'I thought we had already agreed that was an oversight.'

'Yes, we had. Which is why I cannot permit you to go about telling people it was anything other

than it was. I think we've had quite enough econ-
omies with the truth for one day.'

Lady Harriet turned to gape at her. 'If what he
said wasn't true, then how come you are going to
marry him?'

'She hit me,' said Lord Rawcliffe, 'if you must
know. In front of several witnesses who would
have torn her reputation to shreds had I not made
them believe it was a…lovers' tiff. She would not
have been able to gain respectable employment,
if word got out, which it was bound to do. Which
left us with no alternative.'

'You hit him,' said Lady Harriet, ignoring all
the rest.

'Well, yes, but—' Clare meant to explain that
he could have blocked her, easily, if he'd been in
the mood to do so. She didn't want this lady, in
whose home she was going to have to stay until
she could come up with a better plan, to think she
was violent.

But Lady Harriet was smiling. 'I know, you
don't have to explain how it was. I have very often
wanted to hit him myself.'

'I am so glad,' Lord Rawcliffe interjected sarcastically, 'that you are hitting it off…'

'Nice pun,' said Lady Harriet.

'Since,' he continued as though she'd said nothing, 'I am going to have to leave her in your care while I go and procure a marriage licence.'

'Oh! Yes, of course. Only, well, you won't mind, will you,' said Lady Harriet turning to Clare, 'that this household is a little, um, disorganised at present? You see, I am getting married in a day or so myself and you wouldn't believe the amount of work and upheaval it creates.'

Clare turned to Lord Rawcliffe. 'It clearly isn't going to be convenient for me to stay here. Can't you take me to a hotel, or something?'

'My wife does not stay in hotels,' he said implacably.

'I am not your wife. Yet.'

He waved his hand as though dismissing her remark as irrelevant. 'I can see no difficulty about your staying here. You are a most capable woman. I am sure that you will be able to help Lady Harriet with whatever tasks *she*,' he said with a distinct sneer, 'is finding so onerous.'

Oh. Had he just intimated that he thought she was better, in some respects, than Lady Harriet? He'd called her capable. Had suggested that Lady Harriet wasn't coping as well as she ought.

And Lady Harriet was wearing the exact expression on her face that Clare was sure *she'd* worn on many occasions, when crossing swords with his lordship.

'I am not finding arranging my own wedding onerous in the slightest,' she said through gritted teeth. 'I was just explaining that I might not have time to...to entertain in the manner to which she might be accustomed.'

'Please,' said Clare, stepping forward and laying a hand on Lady Harriet's arm. 'Do not let him annoy you. I am perfectly happy to give you any help I may, since you are being so kind as to have me stay with you at what anyone with a modicum of sensitivity—' she shot Lord Rawcliffe a look loaded with reproach '—would know is a very difficult time to entertain strangers.'

'Besides, Clare isn't used to being entertained in any manner whatever,' he said coldly. 'She is far more used to being a drudge. Put her to work and she will immediately feel at home.'

She whirled on him. 'What a beastly thing to say!'

He shrugged. 'The truth? I thought you had been exhorting me to tell the truth. And not to be economical with it.'

'Yes, but that is quite different from wielding it like a weapon!'

'I think I'd better ring for some tea,' said Lady Harriet, darting across the room to a bell pull and yanking on it with a slight air of desperation.

'You have somebody to bring it now, do you? When last I came here,' he said to Clare, as though they had not just been on the verge of yet another quarrel, 'I had to come in by the back door because she had neither butler nor footmen to answer the front.'

'Clearly, I have rectified my lack of staff,' said Lady Harriet, 'since Stobbins let you in and announced you. Oh,' she said, clasping her hands together in agitation. 'What kind of hostess am I? Please, Miss... I forget your name, but it is Clare something, isn't it?'

'Cottam,' supplied Lord Rawcliffe.

'Please, won't you sit down? You must be exhausted if you've travelled up to town today.'

'And it was such a long way,' said Lord Rawcliffe sarcastically.

'I am sure it felt like it, if she was shut up in a coach with you the entire time,' shot back Lady Harriet.

'Fortunately,' said Lord Rawcliffe, turning to

subject her to one of his lazy-lidded, stomach-melting smiles, 'Clare is not you. Clare and I have known each other practically all our lives, you see. And we…understand each other.'

He took her hand. Kissed it.

And her heart soared.

Because he'd declared he preferred her to another woman. True, he'd only implied he thought she was more capable that Lady Harriet and that he was glad she'd been the one in the coach with him, but for the first time, he'd made it sound as though she wasn't a total disaster.

And he wasn't laughing at her. Or mocking her. Or provoking her into an argument.

Suddenly she had to sit down. Because her knees were buckling. Oh, dear, whatever was she going to do? She was used to sparring with him. But if he started paying her compliments and kissing her whenever he felt like it, however was she going to resist him?

Because she had to.

Or he would, one day, casually break her heart without even noticing.

Chapter Seven

'Well, this is all very romantic, I'm sure,' said Lady Harriet tartly, eyeing the way Clare had just practically swooned on to the nearest chair just because Lord Rawcliffe had kissed her hand. 'But I need to tell you what happened to Archie. Because I cannot believe even you could indulge in some sort of elopement, or abduction, or whatever this is—' she waved her hand indiscriminately between them both '—if you knew.'

'Knew what?' Lord Rawcliffe dropped her hand and turned his head to fix Lady Harriet with one of his chillier looks. 'What has happened to Archie?'

'He…oh, dear, there is no easy way to break it to you. I'm so sorry, Zeus,' she said, going over to him and laying one hand on his arm. 'He's… he's dead.'

Zeus? Why was she addressing him by that

name? Last time she'd thought it was some fashionable sort of oath she'd uttered.

He flinched and drew back a step, effectively shaking Lady Harriet's hand from his arm.

'Dead?' He was looking at Lady Harriet as though she'd been personally responsible for it. If he'd looked at her that way, Clare thought she would be begging his forgiveness, even if she was completely innocent. Of anything.

'How? When?'

'He…he drowned.'

Lord Rawcliffe went white.

'I'm so sorry.' Lady Harriet clasped her hands together at her waist. 'It was only a day or so after you went to—' she darted a glance in Clare's direction '—to Thetford Forest.'

'He's been dead all this time.' Lord Rawcliffe stood as though rooted to the spot. 'While I have been pursuing a woman who doesn't exist…' His hand curled into a fist.

'We tried to reach you, but nobody could find you…'

He flinched. 'The one time I abandon my responsibilities and travel incognito, everything goes to hell in a handcart.'

Clare had never seen him look so utterly devastated. Her heart went out to him.

'I'm sure there was nothing you could have done,' Clare began.

His head whipped in her direction, his pain so intense she could almost feel it like a physical blow.

'That is your considered opinion,' he snarled, 'is it?'

'Well,' she said, determined not to quail just because he was lashing out at her. It was what people did when they were grieving. She'd had enough experience visiting the recently bereaved to know that it was best to just absorb their hurt, rather than react as though they were angry with her, personally. 'There was certainly nothing you could have done to prevent Father dying. When it is time for someone to…to go…'

'Archie was not an old man. He was young. And talented, dammit. He had a brilliant future ahead of him. And I should not have let him out of my sight. He wasn't equipped to deal with the likes of—' He broke off, his jaw working.

'Death always comes as a shock, no matter what age the person was. And those left behind often feel guilty, but…'

'But nothing! I *am* guilty. I might as well have—'

He stopped short again, this time with a shudder of what looked like self-loathing.

Lady Harriet stepped forward. 'Jack and Atlas reacted in pretty much the same way when they heard, Zeus. They both feel responsible, too. But, the thing is, none of us could have foreseen—' She was the one to stop mid-sentence this time, with the addition of a guilty glance in Clare's direction that made her feel as though *she* was the one who ought to go to the kitchen and give them the privacy to speak to each other freely.

'Would you like me to leave you alone? I can see you are both terribly upset and—'

'No!' Lord Rawcliffe seized her hand as she made for the door. 'No. It is…' He looked down at her hand with a touch of bewilderment. Then he let it go. As he did so, she could see him pulling himself together. 'I am the one who should go,' he said in a voice that was far more like the Lord Rawcliffe she knew. Cool. Slightly disdainful.

'Do you happen to know,' he said, turning to Lady Harriet, 'where I might find Ulysses and Atlas?'

The transformation was astonishing. He sounded as though he was merely asking the time of day. If she hadn't seen how upset he really was, she would never have guessed it from his demeanour now.

Lady Harriet glanced at the clock on the mantelshelf. 'Probably at Jack's town house. Atlas has moved in there with him for now.'

He gave one brief nod. 'More discreet. Using the excuse that he is acting as groomsman?'

Clare was becoming increasingly bewildered by the rapid-fire questions and answers, but decided that to interrupt and demand an explanation, when both of them were so upset, would be highly insensitive.

'Yes,' said Lady Harriet.

'Then that is where I shall go. Clare,' he said, turning to her, though it didn't look as though he was really seeing her. 'Clare, I will bid you goodnight. I have much to attend to, as you can probably gather.' Even so, he had collected himself enough to remember his manners. 'I shall call tomorrow.'

'Very well. And, oh—' she took his hand and pressed it '—I am so sorry for your loss. And that I expressed my condolences so clumsily.' No wonder he was always accusing her of being sanctimonious and preachy. Instead of just offering him the sympathy he'd so clearly needed, she'd, well, *preached* at him.

He blinked. 'Another apology? My goodness,' he said in the sarcastic tone with which he usually addressed her. 'At this rate you will make a decent wife in merely a decade or so.'

He lifted her hand to his lips. Bestowed a brief kiss upon it, then set it firmly aside. Effectively dismissing her.

'We shall be married the day after tomorrow.'

'Oh,' said Lady Harriet. 'But that is the day I am to marry Jack. He will want you to be there.'

'And I shall be,' he said over his shoulder as he made for the door. 'We will make it a double wedding.'

'Oh, how lovely,' cried Lady Harriet.

The look he gave her could have curdled milk. 'Efficient, rather. Since you will have already booked the church, the minister and ordered the wedding breakfast. And the guests at both events would have been more or less the same. It will save me, and my own bride, no end of bother.'

'Oh,' cried Lady Harriet again as he left the room, closing the door behind him. Only this time she didn't look at all pleased. 'What a beast! Oh, I do beg your pardon,' she said, looking contrite. 'I know you are going to marry him, but—'

'No need to apologise,' said Clare. 'That was a beastly thing for him to say.' And just typical of him.

'Yes, but,' said Lady Harriet, coming over to the chair where she sat, 'it will be rather lovely having a double wedding. What with Jack and Zeus being so close.'

'Zeus?'

'I mean to say Lord Rawcliffe, of course. Only I have got used to calling him that because that is how Jack always refers to him. It started when they were at school together. Since he acted as though he was above most mere mortals.'

'Oh, I see.' And she did. Especially after this little scene. She could just see him looking down his nose at the other boys, setting them all at a distance, to disguise his hurt and bewilderment at his banishment. His father had put the word out that he'd sent him to school to learn how ordinary people thought and behaved, so that he would be a better judge of men when he came into the title. Though local gossip had it that he'd really done it to get him away from his mother's influence. Anyway, whichever it had been, he would have hated all the speculation about his sudden banishment. Was that when he'd started erecting defences behind which to hide? Because that was what he did, she perceived. He'd just done it before her very eyes. Pulled a cold, aloof demeanour round him like some kind of armour.

She didn't know why she hadn't understood it sooner. Because he hadn't been icy or aloof before he'd gone away to school. He'd even played with her brothers, occasionally. The vicar's sons and the young viscount, who was one day going to be a marquess, had fought King John's men with toy bows and arrows through the woods, swum together in the lake in Kelsham Park, flicked paper pellets across the aisle at each other in church and traded jokes in basic Latin and Greek.

While she had watched them wistfully, wishing they'd let her join in. Until her mother had died and she no longer had the leisure to trail after them. After that, she'd pretended she didn't care that she was stuck indoors, running the house while they carried on exactly as they'd always done. Acted as though she was too high-minded to even wish to descend to their level.

No wonder Lord Rawcliffe had started to tease

her about her puritanical attitude. She taken on the airs of an early Christian martyr.

While he…he'd hidden his own hurts and resentments behind a shield of icy sarcasm.

'Perhaps I should explain,' said Lady Harriet, 'that Jack, the man I am going to marry, has the nickname of Ulysses, though his title is Lord Becconsall. But of course I always call him Jack.'

'Of course,' said Clare, trying to smile. Though she couldn't imagine Lord Rawcliffe ever letting her close enough to permit her to call him Robert. The boy he'd once been hadn't minded her doing so, but the man? Good grief, she wouldn't be a bit surprised if he didn't insist she address him by his title.

Which was what many people of his class did, she believed.

Oh, well, if he did insist she call him Rawcliffe, it was at least marginally better than Zeus, which, to her way of thinking, bordered on the blasphemous.

'And Atlas,' Lady Harriet was saying, 'that is Jack's groomsman, he is really Captain Bretherton, who was also at school with them and quite their hero, on account of him being so tall and so defensive of the smaller boys who were prone to being bullied. And Archie...' She trailed off. 'Oh, dear, I don't know how much I'm allowed to tell you about all that.' She twisted her hands together. 'And you must be beside yourself with curiosity.'

Funnily enough, Clare wasn't all that curious. She felt as if she had enough on her plate with everything that had happened the last few days.

'I would not want you to feel you were breaking any sort of promise you have made.'

Lady Harriet sat down on the nearest sofa to where she'd been standing. Frowned. Shook her head. 'I haven't made any sort of promise, actually, have I? He just sort of shook his head to show he didn't want to tell you about what he's been up to of late...'

'Which wasn't surprising, since it sounds as if he was in pursuit of some female. I suppose that is his idea of being tactful.'

'Oh, no, it wasn't anything like that! It was...' She wrung her hands.

'Perhaps, instead, you could tell me a little about the man who died? I admit, I am curious about him, since I have never seen Lord Rawcliffe so utterly...' Yes, she wouldn't mind learning something about the person whose death had upset Lord Rawcliffe so much that he'd let his true feelings show, even if it had only been for a moment or two. Especially since she'd done such a poor job of offering him comfort.

'Yes,' said Lady Harriet with what looked like relief. 'There is no reason I may not tell you about poor Archie. He was another friend from Jack's schooldays. And later he worked for your Lord Rawcliffe as his chaplain...'

'Chaplain? No, he couldn't have. I mean, the chaplain at Kelsham Park was Mr Kellet.'

'Yes, that's him. Archie was the nickname they gave him. On account of his being so clever. After Archimedes, the Greek chap who did a lot of inventing. And mathematics.'

'Thomas Kellet? He is dead?' She could hardly believe it. 'And drowned? But...last I heard, he was coming to London to attend some lectures and consulting some scientific chaps who were working in the same area as him.'

'You knew him?'

'Of course I knew him. He was Lord Rawcliffe's tame scientist. I mean,' she added hastily, 'that is the way everyone in Watling Minor referred to him.'

'Oh. I see. Zeus said you had known each other for a long time. You live near Kelsham Park?'

'Yes. My father was the vicar of Watling Minor. That is the nearest parish. I used to see Mr Kellet occasionally. He didn't leave the grounds of the manor very often. Oh, dear. No wonder Lord Rawcliffe was so upset.'

'Yes, and it was all my fault,' said Lady Harriet, pulling a handkerchief out of a concealed pocket in her dress and blowing her nose.

Clare went to sit next to her and patted her hand. 'I don't see how it can possibly be your fault.'

'But it was,' wailed Lady Harriet. 'If only I… I could tell you…' She bit down on her lower lip, looking absolutely torn.

'But you cannot break your word, I understand. Besides, it sounded to me as though Lord Rawcliffe feels responsible. So I don't see how it can be your fault, as well.'

'Because I was the one who sent Lord Rawcliffe to…to Norfolk. If he hadn't gone there, Archie would never have gone to Dorset to confront his great-godmother and he wouldn't have drowned.'

'You *sent* Lord Rawcliffe to Norfolk?' She shook her head. 'Surely not. Knowing Lord Rawcliffe as I do, I could not see anyone being able to persuade him to do anything he didn't wish to do.'

As soon as the words had left her lips, it was as

if she was hearing somebody else reminding her of that fact. Lord Rawcliffe never did anything he did not wish to do.

Did that mean he *wanted* to marry her?

No…no, that couldn't be possible.

Although…he'd said all that about not wanting to go through the bother of choosing a suitable bride. And him knowing her so well that he wouldn't be getting any unpleasant surprises, after he'd put the ring on her finger.

So…did that mean…?

Lady Harriet blew her nose very loudly and in a most unladylike fashion, jerking Clare out of her rather nebulous train of thought.

'I suppose I know that really. And Archie was like a dog with two tails at the prospect of searching his great-godmother's house for any signs of the missing jewels. He was so determined to prove that Lady Buntingford…' She slammed her mouth shut. 'I shouldn't have said that…'

Clare reached out her hand and touched Lady Harriet's.

'You are very upset. I can see that this has been a terrible thing to happen and right before your wedding, too.'

'Yes, I'm positively distracted. And with having

so much to do, too, since Mama is rather...' She waved her hand in an agitated fashion.

'Well, perhaps it is a good thing I am here, then.' Hadn't her father been fond of saying that God moved in mysterious ways? Perhaps this was why her day had gone the way it had. He'd known Lady Harriet needed a friend, right now. And that she needed...well, to be useful. 'As Lord Rawcliffe said, I am used to hard work. And I will feel much more comfortable about being foisted upon you if I can make myself useful.'

And as Lord Rawcliffe had said, she was a very capable, practical sort of person.

Growing up in the vicarage, without a mother and with three brothers and a father to keep house for, she'd had to be.

Chapter Eight

'I should never have let him go down to Dorset,' said Lord Rawcliffe, taking the glass of brandy Lord Becconsall held out to him.

'You couldn't have stopped him.'

'Yes, I could. I am his employer. Was his employer,' he corrected himself. 'I could have forbidden him...'

Jack took him by the upper arms and gave him a little shake. 'Damn it, Zeus, don't you think we all feel guilty? I could have gone down to Dorset in his stead. Or to Thetford, while you went to Dorset. But the truth was we all saw how blue-devilled Archie had been lately and thought it would do him good to prove himself.'

'It was his family that had been robbed, don't forget,' put in Atlas, from the chair in which he was slouched, clearly having got on the outside of a fair quantity of brandy already. 'It was his right to be the one to investigate.'

'I was responsible for him, though…'

'It wasn't your fault,' said Ulysses firmly. 'It was the fault of whoever is behind the jewel thefts. Because you can depend upon it that is why Archie was killed. Because he was getting close to the truth.'

'You are right,' said Rawcliffe. 'I know you are right. The trouble is, the moment he told us his great-godmother lived in Lesser Peeving, I smelled a rat.' He downed his drink, which had the effect of flinging Lord Becconsall's hand from his arm, as well as giving him the hit of alcohol he sorely needed after the day he'd had.

'What do you mean?' Atlas raised his head and peered at him, blearily, across the room. 'You *knew* there was something fishy going on down there?'

'Not for certain.' Lord Rawcliffe stared into the bottom of his empty glass. 'Though I do know of someone with a…shady past, who was sent there to…' He shook his head in frustration.

'Who?'

That was the worst part of it. 'One Reverend Cottam.' Clare's brother. Clement. The one who'd given her a reference for a post with an elderly lady with suspicious swiftness. The one who'd been so good at organising that she'd been glad when he'd arrived to supervise their father's funeral.

'A *vicar*? A vicar with a shady past?'

Rawcliffe nodded and held out his glass for a refill. The tale wasn't going to be an easy one to tell. 'He lost his post in a parish in Exeter after the bank began to complain about the amount of counterfeit coins being handed in to them from the collection plate. The young Clement Cottam was the one responsible for counting the money and taking it to the bank.'

Ulysses whistled. 'So, how did he end up in Lesser Peeving?'

'Partially as punishment. The parish is poor, in-habited mostly by fishermen and quarrymen. Posi-tively infested by smugglers, too. Not the kind of place where he'd have the opportunity to enrich himself by stealing from the collection plate. And also…' He got a bitter taste in his mouth, which he washed away with another gulp of purifying brandy. 'Well, you do not think the church is will-ing to advertise the fact that one of its clerics is a thief, do you?'

'They wanted to hush it up?'

'That's about the size of it. Also, as I think I

mentioned to you before I left for Norfolk, his father held the living in the parish close to Kelsham Park. He probably used what influence he had to get clemency for… Clement.' He glanced into his empty glass, wondering if draining it so swiftly had been responsible for him speaking so clumsily.

'Which reminds me,' said Ulysses. 'Did you discover anything about the girl from Norfolk, while you were *in* Norfolk?'

'It wasn't her,' he said, setting down his glass and walking away from it before he was tempted to ask for another refill. 'That is, there *was* a girl called Jenny Wren, who came from that hamlet.'

'Bogholt,' supplied Ulysses.

'Yes. And a more aptly named place I have yet to discover,' he said with a sneer as he recalled the extreme simplicity of the place and all its inhabitants. 'However, by casting out lures, which mostly involved inventing a brother with a dubious talent for compromising innocent young females and insinuating that I had heard of a child who must be provided for by my family, I did track down a girl of that name. Who bore no resemblance whatever to the description given of the person who worked as a maid for both Lady Tarbrook and Mrs Kellet. However,' he continued, when both Ulysses and

Atlas groaned in disappointment, 'it turned out that she had spent some time in a charitable home where they hoped to reform unmarried mothers. Find them respectable work. And it was run by a group of ladies filled with evangelical zeal, who had a most understanding young cleric come in to hear their confessions and offer absolution on a regular basis.'

'Not...'

'Yes. One Reverend Cottam. The trouble is...' the words stuck in his throat '...I have just, this very day, become betrothed to his sister.'

'Good God! How did that come about?' That was Atlas.

Ulysses, however, gave him a knowing look. 'You already have a plan, don't you? Damn it, but as usual you are one step ahead of us.'

Rawcliffe toyed, for a fraction of a second, with admitting that it had been a total coincidence that he'd stopped for a change of horses at the very same inn where Clare had been waiting for her connecting coach. But it would take too long to explain the history between them which had re-sulted in her bloodying his nose. 'I came across Clare in an inn, just as she was about to take the stage to employment which her brother had organised for her. And…effectively compromised her,' was all he was willing to say. Especially since he still couldn't quite believe he'd practically forced her to marry him, in spite of all her objections.

'My God,' said Ulysses, giving him a hard stare, 'that's cold, even for you. Using the family connection as the perfect excuse for going down to Lesser Peeving and carrying on the investigation Archie started.'

Rawcliffe thought about protesting that he'd never considered that aspect of things, but then, to be honest, Ulysses had a point. Clare's relationship to Clement *was* a factor he could exploit in regard to their investigation.

'We are dealing with a man who has murdered,' he pondered out loud, 'or perhaps has caused to have murdered one of my oldest, closest friends. Do you think there is anything I should not do to see him brought to justice?'

'You cannot know, for certain, that this Cottam person is responsible,' Atlas pointed out. 'Don't forget Lady Buntingford's part in it all. She was the one who provided the references that got those girls into the houses where they stole the jewels.'

'Now that I know Clement Cottam has connections to a group of women with dubious morals, and a network of elderly ladies intent on helping reform such women, and has, moreover, taken up residence in an area renowned for harbouring smugglers who would know exactly how to get stolen jewels into the hands of buyers, I think it is fairly certain that he is the one who has been organising the whole enterprise. All I need to do is find some proof. Some concrete proof that will expose one of the most godless, devious, sanctimonious hypocrites it has ever been my misfortune to know.'

'And to that end, you'd even go to the length of marrying his sister,' said Ulysses, shaking his head.

That wasn't why he was marrying Clare. The thought had never entered his head until Ulysses had planted it there.

Not that he was going to admit any such thing. Not even to these men.

'I would have had to marry and beget heirs at some stage,' he said with a shrug, using the same excuse he'd given Clare. 'As well her as another.'

Atlas gave him a reproachful look. Ulysses appeared more sympathetic. 'It isn't going to be easy, marrying a woman whose brother you will be dragging off to prison. Possibly even the gallows.'

He got a vision of large golden eyes looking at him as though he'd betrayed her. And bade farewell to his dream of being able to occupy the moral high ground throughout their marriage. Instead of featuring as her benefactor, she'd regard him as a monster.

'Then I had better get her with child quickly,' he said with a sinking feeling. 'Before she discovers what I am about. And to that end, I had better inform you that I have told her we will be marrying the day after tomorrow.'

'What? The same day as Harriet and me?'

'The same ceremony. I have already put the matter to Lady Harriet and she has seen the wisdom of having a double wedding.'

'Harriet has? When did you see her?'

'Well, where do you think Clare is staying? She has no family in London. And I had no intention of leaving her in a hotel, where she might have been able to…contact her brother and seek to escape me.'

'You think she could be in league with her brother?'

'No!' His whole being revolted at the notion she could have anything to do with anything the slightest bit shady. 'She is so puritanical that were this the sixteen hundreds she would probably have become a prophetess in one of those outlandish sects that sprang up all over the place. No, the trouble with Clare is that she can believe no ill of any of her family. Even when evidence is thrust right under her nose.'

He'd tried to explain, a number of times, why he could no longer consider any of her brothers his friends. But she wouldn't countenance a word of criticism against any of them. Not from his lips, anyway.

'If she were to get wind of my suspicions about Clement, she would be so incensed that she would probably tell him. And alert him to the fact that we are on to him.'

'Archie probably did just that,' said Ulysses thoughtfully. 'He would have trusted a fellow cleric, wouldn't he?'

'Yes. Also, he knew Clement, slightly, from when he first took up his post at Kelsham Park. Knew, and respected, his father, too.'

'Then the chances are that Clement already knows we're on to him. If you go down there, you aren't going to be able to poke around and find out enough to bring him to justice. Especially not with his sister in tow.'

'Actually, I rather think that Clare might be a very effective weapon to use against him. He is fond of her, in his own way.'

'You think you can use her as a sort of...hostage?'

'I might be able to make him believe I would do so. At the very least, I think he would think twice before making an attempt on my life while she is with me. Since it would be extremely difficult to do away with me without her suspecting who is behind it.'

'You do realise, then, that going down to Lesser Peeving will be dangerous?'

'Dealing with Clement Cottam was never without its dangers,' he said, recalling the many instances of the vicar's son's malice and cunning he'd witnessed as a boy and young man. 'The difference between me and Archie, though, is that I am up to his weight. And I know what I am walking into. Whereas Archie did not.'

'So, you seriously mean to take your bride to Lesser Peeving, the moment you've signed the marriage lines?'

'No. Not straight away. I am as keen to avenge Archie as either of you,' he said, raising one hand to prevent either of them from interrupting. 'But as Ulysses has already pointed out, once I bring Clement to justice, it is going to take my bride some time to forgive me. If she ever does. So I need a little time, before then, to…see to the matter of an heir.'

Both men looked into their glasses, rather than at him. Which was probably as well. He wasn't sure he could have looked them square in the face. Not after outlining what sounded, even to his own ears, like a most dastardly way of treating any woman. Let alone a woman who deserved so much better.

'Then we are in agreement,' he said with determination. 'I will marry Clare, and bed her before I take our investigation any further.'

Both men nodded, although Atlas was now looking at him as though he was some kind of monster.

He let it go. Because Atlas couldn't possibly think any worse of him than he did of himself, right at that moment.

Chapter Nine

The church was packed with a lot of people Clare had never seen before and all of them there to witness Lady Harriet's marriage to Lord Becconsall. It didn't look as if any of them had any idea Lord Rawcliffe was getting married in the same ceremony, to judge from the curious stares people were giving her as she walked up the aisle on the arm of Lady Harriet's father.

And oh, how glad she was now that he'd been thoughtful enough to make the suggestion.

'Don't seem right,' he'd said as they'd all been gathering in the hall before setting off for St George's, 'for you to have to walk down the aisle on your own behind me and Harriet. Bad enough you've just lost your own father, without having your nose rubbed in it. And I have two arms,' he'd finished gruffly. 'You don't mind sharing, do you, Harriet?'

Lady Harriet didn't. But then she was so full of love for her groom, so happy to be marrying him, that Clare didn't think anything would have dimmed her joy. Besides, Lady Harriet had a very generous disposition. It was entirely thanks to her that Clare was wearing the most beautiful gown she'd ever *seen*, let alone owned.

'I have more clothes than I know what to do with,' Lady Harriet had said airily when they'd started discussing the tricky question of what she ought to wear for her wedding, since she was in mourning. And to prove it, she'd flung open the lid of a trunk absolutely crammed with clothes. 'And it will be much quicker to have something of mine altered to fit you than attempting to get a dress-maker to create something in the scant time his High and Mightiness has agreed you may have,' she'd finished acidly, 'before he screws his ring on to your finger.'

Which was true, since Clare was much shorter than Lady Harriet. It had been fairly straightfor-ward to remove a couple of rows of flounces from the hem and put a few darts into the bodice of the one she'd chosen, and substitute a black sash for the green one. Black gloves and a black ribbon to tie up her posy would suffice, Lady Harriet had assured her, to satisfy conventions.

So that now Clare was walking up the aisle on the arm of Lady Harriet's father, a belted earl no less, wearing a gown of shimmering white satin, embroidered here and there with a tasteful motif of ivy leaves, under a delicate overdress of black lace.

But instead of feeling like a glowing bride, the way people were craning their necks to stare and then whispering about her behind their prayer books made her very conscious it was a borrowed dress she was wearing and someone else's father upon whose arm she was leaning. And that she was heading toward a groom who was marrying her for all the wrong reasons.

She kept her head held high, but she could feel her cheeks heating and knew they must be bright red. For nobody could be saying anything worse about her than what she was feeling about herself. She'd spent the last day or so keeping the kindly Lady Harriet at arm's length by talking of nothing but clothes. Of speaking to her future husband of nothing but trivialities.

Because she couldn't help fearing that if she mentioned any of her fears, everyone might see she was correct and would call off the wedding. And then she'd be facing a lifetime of servitude to an elderly and probably cantankerous old lady instead of marrying the man who'd featured in far too many of her girlish dreams and having his child. And she knew it was selfish, but the prospect of having her own baby was just too precious to risk. In spite of knowing she was not fit to take Rawcliffe's title, she'd stopped arguing when he'd pointed out that she could give him the heir he needed. And had avoided any sort of conversation that might prompt him to think of a way out of the proposal he'd fabricated on the spur of the moment.

So that now, here she was, standing beside him at the altar as he drawled vows he couldn't possibly mean. *Forsaking all other* indeed? She would wager not a single person in the entire congregation believed he had any intention of doing any such thing. Particularly not her.

Which made her want to fling her own responses back at him like a challenge. Because she would, of course, stick to vows made in church. They were sacred.

But just as she was opening her mouth to speak she made the mistake of glancing at the other couple who were gazing at each other in a sort of smug mutual adoration. And her heart contracted painfully. Because Lord Rawcliffe was only marrying her on sufferance. And instead of sounding defiant and brave, her voice quavered with all the fears and doubts that she was struggling to control.

As though he knew exactly how she felt, and sympathised with her, Lord Rawcliffe kept hold of her hand after he'd slid the ring on to her finger. Which meant they stood hand in hand while the vicar intoned the blessing. The warmth and strength of his hand clasping hers was strangely comforting, so that she made no attempt to shake it free until the moment the vicar ought to have been joining their right hands together to symbolise their union before God.

But Lord Rawcliffe would not let go. Instead he gave the vicar a very haughty look, as though declaring he'd already taken her to wife, thank you very much, and nothing the vicar could say or do would make any difference.

And once again, Clare was ready to sink through the floor.

After an awkward pause, the vicar turned to the other couple, who allowed him to join their hands in the prescribed manner, while she stood there fuming. What gave Lord Rawcliffe the right to think he didn't need to observe the traditions that had been laid down by the church and adhered to for hundreds of years?

By the time they all turned to process down the aisle, as two married couples, she had worked herself up into such a state of righteous indignation that she scarcely noticed the rude stares and the wave of shocked, thrilled whispers foaming in their wake.

Until they were almost at the door. At which point she was glad he'd tucked her hand into his arm so possessively because it spared her the necessity of having to cling to him for support.

Because she couldn't really blame anyone for being shocked at this mésalliance. If she'd been a guest at Lady Harriet's wedding, she might have been speculating as to why on earth Lord Rawcliffe was getting married at all, let alone to a complete unknown. And in a double wedding to boot. The whole thing reeked of scandal.

As they stepped out into the colonnaded portico, she heaved a sigh of relief. Just before Lord Rawcliffe leaned down and put his mouth close to her ear. 'Well done,' he murmured.

'What? What for?' She blinked up at him in a

mixture of confusion and reaction to coming into such a bright light after the gloom of the interior.

'For bearing up so splendidly through the ordeal,' he said in a tone she could only interpret as withering.

'You mean the very opposite, I suppose. You think I should have skipped down the aisle, looking as radiant as Lady Harriet. And said my vows as though I believed I was the luckiest woman on earth.'

'I should not like being married to a woman who thought it permissible to skip in church,' he replied caustically, 'no matter what the ceremony she was attending.'

Oh. Well, it ought not to matter, but she was still rather glad she'd managed to do *something* of which he approved.

And then she recalled how comforting it had been when he'd held her hand when she hadn't been able to disguise how nervous she'd felt. Even though the vicar had disapproved. And she wondered if perhaps he wasn't taunting her. If perhaps he might truly be attempting to support her through what he termed *the ordeal*.

She darted him a look, but could see nothing on his face but a sort of weary contempt for the crowds gathering on the steps and the air of gaiety surrounding the other newly married couple.

'We shall have to attend the festivities organised by Lady Harriet's family,' he said. 'I hope you can continue to behave as bravely as you have just done in church.'

She frowned. Did he mean that as a compliment or a criticism? Well, whatever it was, marriage to a man like Lord Rawcliffe was going to be hard enough without fretting herself to flinders trying to work out what he meant by every casually uttered caustic comment.

She'd do better to give as good as she got.

'I can endure it,' she therefore declared, 'if you can.'

He turned to look at her. And gave her the benefit of one of his most penetrating stares. And then suddenly, the corner of his mouth kicked up in an ironic smile.

'I shall find it easier to endure than you, I suspect.'

'Yes, since all these people are your friends.'

Whereas she'd only known most of them for a couple of days. She did recall seeing Lord Becconsall visit Kelsham Park once or twice, during the long vacation from school, and later, when he'd been on furlough from his military service. Not that she'd ever spoken to him, or known that he answered to the name of Ulysses. But she'd paid close attention to everything Lord Rawcliffe did every time he returned from school. And suffered agonies of mortification when people had gossiped about his conquests, with a kind of salacious glee, whether he made them in the villages surrounding Kelsham Park, or London, or anywhere else.

'Some of them, yes,' he replied cryptically. 'But most of them are mere acquaintances.' Just then his carriage drew up at the foot of the steps and he urged her in its direction. Not that she needed much prompting. She was jolly glad to climb inside and shut out all the people who were looking at her as though she was some kind of fairground sideshow.

He said nothing during the short ride back to Lady Harriet's house, where the wedding breakfast was being held. She'd been told that just the bridal parties and close family would be invited. But as they alighted, it felt as if an awful lot of people were converging on the enormous mansion. It was one good thing about having such a massive house, she supposed. You could sit thirty to dinner and not feel cramped.

You could, however, feel small and lonely and out of your depth, she reflected. Especially as both Lord Becconsall and Captain Bretherton, who were her new husband's closest friends, kept giving her most peculiar looks. Halfway between pity and suspicion.

If she'd had any confidence in him, she'd have asked Lord Rawcliffe what he'd told them about her. But she didn't think she'd be able to look them in the face if she knew for a fact that he'd described the way she'd hit him, and the steps he'd taken to salvage her reputation. If he *had* told them, it would definitely account for their air of disapproval.

And the pity? Well, anyone who knew him well would expect him to make any woman a devil of a husband. Why, even she had almost said *hah!* when he'd come to the part of the vows about staying faithful.

Practically any other woman would be able to bear that better than her. The kind of woman who'd been brought up to expect a fashionable sort of marriage might have expected nothing else. But Clare wasn't fashionable, or brought up to expect to contract a fashionable marriage. So she could foresee him hurting her on a regular basis. And not only by being unfaithful. It was the fact he didn't love her, would never love her…and probably wouldn't even be able to consider her as a companion, let alone a partner in life. He had too much pride to consider *anyone* his equal.

Not that she believed a wife should think herself *equal* to her husband. A husband represented Christ and the woman the church. Which was why she'd promised to obey him.

But couldn't he just glance at her, from time to time, even if he couldn't think of anything to say to her? He didn't even meet her eyes when he handed her into her chair before sitting down at table beside her. It wasn't that she expected him to act like Lord Becconsall, who was fawning all over his bride in the most revolting manner. But did he really have to make her feel about as attractive as somebody's maiden aunt?

She reached for her wineglass, which a footman had obligingly filled. And reminded herself it wasn't Lord Rawcliffe's fault her feelings were all over the place like this. He was being remarkably affable, all things considered. He *had* held her hand and he *had* spoken a word or two of encouragement. She'd got to stop comparing his behaviour with that of Lord Becconsall. Stop hankering for the impossible. Stop being so ridiculously sensitive.

Besides, a man who took his bride's hand for himself, rather than allowing the vicar to join them, was declaring that the marriage would be entirely of his own design. He'd conduct himself the way he wished, no matter what was written in the prayer book.

And she was just going to have to accept it.

She got through the meal by keeping her eyes fixed firmly on her plate, or her lap, and since nobody attempted to converse with her, she didn't need to come up with any kind of response. But, oh, how glad she was when Lord Becconsall eventually got to his feet and made a short speech. It made everyone else laugh, with its allusions to how he'd fallen at Lady Harriet's feet, but only served to make her feel a bit apprehensive. For what could Lord Rawcliffe say about his own bride when it came to his turn to make a toast? Not that she could believe he would really relate how she'd shouted at him like a shrew, then punched him on the nose. Or that he'd had to marry her, or she would have ended up without a shred of reputation and without a job or a home, as well. Because he'd done all that to *prevent* gossip. He might share some things with his closest friends, but he would never broadcast his private business to all and sundry.

Nevertheless, when Lord Rawcliffe got to his feet, she gripped her hands together in her lap, bracing herself for whatever might come next.

'I thank you all for coming,' he said, just as if it was his own house they were sitting down to dine in. 'And for all your good wishes for my future happiness.' Though to her knowledge, nobody had actually given him any. 'But now my wife and I must bid you farewell. As you probably know, she has recently been bereaved and feels that it would not be appropriate to stay for the dancing.'

She laid her napkin carefully on the table next to her plate, hoping that her fingers did not resemble those of a woman who could cheerfully wring her husband's neck. How dare he use her father's death as an excuse to leave a gathering he had not wished to attend in the first place? Let alone make everyone believe it was *her* wish? Not that she did want to stay and dance, because she couldn't, anyway, what with her father having so recently died…

Oh…*swear words and profanities!* He might at least have asked her what she was thinking before informing everyone else what it was.

'But before we go, I invite you to raise your glasses to absent friends.'

"Absent friends," went the sombre echo around the table. The contrast between his toast and the cheerful one Lord Becconsall had made could not have been more stark. Which hurt and angered her in about equal measure.

'Come.' He held out an imperious hand to hers, which he clearly expected her to take like a meek little biddable...*serf.*

It was the last straw. She might have just promised to obey him, but that didn't give him the right to speak for her as though she had no mind of her own. And it was all very well telling herself she must expect a man like him to go into marriage on his own terms and make it what he wanted, but if she didn't make a stand at some point, he'd trample all over her, the way he appeared to trample all over everyone else.

'I must just bid Lady Harriet farewell,' she said. 'She has been so very kind to me over the last couple of days.'

His mouth thinned. And he gripped her elbow as she walked to the chair upon which Lady Harriet was sitting, as though he didn't trust her to get there and back to him on her own.

Lady Harriet got to her feet as they approached and flung her arms about Clare's shoulders in a fierce, brief hug.

'Good luck,' she whispered, under cover of the hug, then darted a glance in Lord Rawcliffe's direction and one back to her, full of sympathy. Suddenly, Clare had had enough. No matter what she thought of him, Lord Rawcliffe was her husband now and part of her duty as a wife was to support him. She'd always despised those women who did nothing but complain about every single little flaw their husband possessed. It was so disloyal.

So she lifted her chin. Patted her husband's hand where it lay on her arm.

'Thank you for your good wishes, Lady Harriet. And for your generosity to me.'

And then, with her head held high, she walked out of the room on her husband's arm, determined not to look back.

Chapter Ten

His heart was beating so fast it was making his hands shake. She'd clung to his arm. Recoiled from the way Lady Harriet had practically invited her to bemoan her lot and walked out with her nose in the air as though she felt offended.

The way a wife *ought* to behave.

He wasn't sure what it meant, but whatever it was, he was not a man to look a gift horse in the mouth. He kept her hand clamped to his arm until the very last moment, handing her into his carriage himself rather than allowing his footman the pleasure.

By the time he climbed in she was sitting bolt upright, her hands folded primly on her lap.

'Are you comfortable?'

'Yes, thank you,' she replied, looking anything but.

Still, he acknowledged her statement with a

nod before thumping on the roof with his silver-topped cane.

Her eyes widened as the coach lurched forward. As though she couldn't believe that he'd consulted her before giving the driver the office to depart. As if he was incapable of thinking of anyone but himself and his own comfort.

Which was much more like her. For this was the woman who had never believed him capable of doing *anything* good. Even today, even after all he'd done for her, her little mouth had pursed up with scepticism as he'd repeated his marriage vows. And when he'd tried to offer her some comfort by holding her hand, when he'd seen how nervous she was, to demonstrate that at least he could fulfil the cherishing part, all he'd got was a dirty look for defying the vicar.

He'd been sorely tempted to show her exactly how a man behaved who didn't give a rap for his marriage vows, on the way to their wedding breakfast. He'd had to grit his teeth and recite whole chunks of Ovid under his breath to prevent her from arriving with bruised lips and rumpled clothing, rather than with her dignity intact.

He'd been the very model of propriety. And what was his reward?

There wasn't one.

'Don't look so surprised,' he drawled, leaning back in his seat as though her total lack of faith in him didn't matter in the slightest. 'It is only good manners to ensure that any passenger in my coach is ready before signalling to the driver to depart. I wouldn't want anyone flung from their seat and landing on the floor with broken knees.'

'Not even me?'

She had that look on her face. The one that showed she was spoiling for a fight.

'Especially not you,' he flung back at her. 'Since I have so recently vowed to cherish you.'

'Yes, well…'

There! He knew it. She thought him the kind of man who would make vows, in public, he had no intention of keeping.

'But then, you surprised me, too,' he continued. 'When you resisted the temptation to join Lady Harriet in bemoaning your fate.'

'I have never approved of wives,' she retorted, 'who behave as if their husband was a cross they had to bear.'

It felt like a slap. He should have known it would be something to do with her principles, or her pride, that had made her refuse to stoop to Lady

Harriet's level, rather than any tender feelings she might be developing towards him.

'Not even the ones,' he bit out, determined to force her to see how absurd she was being, 'whose husbands come home intoxicated and beat them?'

'Oh, well, yes, those ones may have some excuse for complaining, but ironically those are the ones who rarely do. In my experience, that is. In the parish of Watling Minor, anyway. I cannot speak for wives of violent men in general.'

'What a little pedant you are,' he drawled in the most mocking tone he could muster.

Up went her chin. 'Would you prefer it, then, if I was to make sweeping generalisations about topics I am in complete ignorance of? Or take every opportunity that presents itself to let everyone know our marriage is not a happy one?'

Not a happy marriage? How could she tell? It had been less than two hours since he'd put his ring on her finger. She had no notion whether they were going to make each other happy or not.

As usual, she'd judged him and found him wanting without giving him any chance to put his side of the case.

'It would certainly make you seem more like a

normal woman,' he said out of bitterness, 'and less like a plaster saint.'

'Oh!' After throwing him one look of searing reproach, she turned her back on him and spent the rest of the short journey to Grosvenor Square staring out of the window.

And so they arrived at his town house in a state of silently eloquent resentment. Though she placed her hand upon his arm as he led her into the house, she managed to do it without even glancing at him. And she stalked up the front steps and into his house with her nose in the air.

Looking, ironically, every inch a marchioness.

Ponsonby, the man who'd served as butler both here and at Kelsham Park for as long as he could remember, raised one eyebrow at the dignified little creature standing at his side. Hardly surprising. The man had known her as the threadbare firebrand of a vicar's daughter and couldn't have expected her to alter so much simply because she was now draped in satin and lace. But after only that brief and barely perceptible start, the butler inclined his bald head deferentially. 'Welcome to your new home, my lady,' he said. 'May I present Mrs Chivers, your housekeeper? She will make known to you the members of staff who serve you here in London.'

It was just as well Chivers was ready to do so, since Ponsonby had staged this introduction, *en masse*, of every person who lived and worked here, because he was pretty certain he'd never clapped eyes on about half of them. They probably inhabited the nether regions of the house and never crept up to his level during his waking hours.

Mrs Chivers confirmed that conjecture when she told his new bride that the skinny little girl who bobbed a clumsy curtsy with eyes round with awe was the one who went round lighting all the fires first thing in the mornings.

'I shall conduct you to your rooms,' said Mrs Chivers once she'd accounted for the very last person in line, a rather idiotish-looking boy described as the boots, though he was sure Cadogan, his valet, would never permit someone like that to lay so much as one greasy finger on his gleaming Hessians. 'I hope they meet with your approval,' she finished, folding her hands at her waist.

'I am sure they will do very well,' said Clare, 'since I know you did not have much time to prepare them.'

She couldn't have said anything more likely to

impress them all. Mrs Chivers was appeased by the acknowledgement that she would have done better had she had more warning, whilst put on notice that Clare had such exacting standards that she would find something that needed improving.

Clare would be good with the staff, who had been without a proper mistress for far too long. Since well before his mother had died. In fact, all the previous Lady Rawcliffe had achieved when she'd been in charge of things was to create chaos. Clare, on the contrary, would find out all about them and know, within days, which of them were good workers and which needed a swift kick up the backside. And she'd administer it, too—metaphorically, of course. She'd run her own father's house on a shoestring, from what he could gather, and had still managed to make charitable donations to the really needy in the parish.

He watched the sway of her own backside as she began to mount the stairs, following Mrs Chivers to her bedroom. Where he had half a mind to go himself, right now, so that he could sink his hands, if not his teeth, into those tempting little mounds of flesh. After all, it was his right now. At long last, there was not a single excuse she could make for keeping him at bay.

Except…if he appeared too keen, she might assume…

No, she wouldn't be able to assume anything. She was too innocent. But she *would* be shocked if he went straight upstairs and pounced on her. She'd accuse him of being an animal, driven by base lusts. A rake. A fiend.

So he'd better leave her for a while to settle into her new room before making what she'd probably consider his beastly demands upon her.

With a grimace of distaste at the prospect of such a response, he took himself off to his study.

His hands shook as he unstoppered the heavy decanter and lifted it. Damn it! He slammed the crystal decanter back down on the table, picturing the way Clare's nose would wrinkle if she smelled brandy on his breath. Held his trembling hands before him, imagining the scorn in her eyes if she assumed he was nervous. Not that he didn't have a right to be nervous. So much rested on the outcome of his performance this night. He *had* to break down Clare's dislike and distrust of him enough to get her to relax, so that she could enjoy her initiation into married life.

Though it wasn't nerves. It was anticipation that was making him tremble. The thought of finally having her in his bed was enough to make him drop to his knees and give thanks to the God he wasn't at all sure he believed in anymore.

Though, ironically, that was a gesture she might approve of—her husband dropping to his knees beside their bridal bed and offering up thanks to the deity who'd brought them there. A wry smile touched his mouth at the image—her sitting in her bed, piously approving while he knelt on the rug, ranting like a dissenter.

Ah, Clare, poor Clare. He shook his head. Chained for ever to a confirmed sinner, when all she wanted was to rise above every temptation the world had to offer.

Well, tonight, he was the one who was going to rise to the challenge. And she was going to sin.

And enjoy every damned second of it.

He had the skill. He had the experience.

And tonight he was going to unleash it all on her.

With a mirthless smile, he left his study, crossed the hall and mounted the stairs two at a time.

Chapter Eleven

There was a short, imperious rap on the door before Lord Rawcliffe strode in, claiming the room.

'You…that is, I…that is, I hadn't expected you to come to me so soon,' she stammered.

She'd thought he would at least have given her time to get out of her wedding dress and into her nightgown. She was hoping she'd even have time to down the glass of wine she'd just sent for.

But, no. There he was, standing in the doorway, looking all harsh and determined and handsome and wicked.

Temptation in the flesh. And what flesh. He was so tall and muscular, and the way his lids drooped ever so slightly as he ran his smoky eyes over her with a look that made her insides melt…

She swallowed.

She'd always thought that marriage was a sacrament. That joining with a husband ought to be a holy occasion.

But the man she'd married was the walking embodiment of sin.

Her stomach flipped.

'I am not ready.' Her heart started pounding. Parts of her that never ought to be mentioned were throbbing. Because of him.

He strolled across the room, going straight to the bed, across the foot of which lay the nightgown Lady Harriet had insisted she wear tonight. He picked it up and let the fine lawn sift through his long, supple fingers. Then held it to the light, which shone right through it.

He shook his head as though in disbelief. 'I take it Lady Harriet procured this scandalous piece of frippery?'

She flinched at his implication she was not the kind of woman who could get away with wearing anything so sensuous.

'Yes, well,' she said, flinging up her chin, 'she thought she was being kind. She went right through my clothes and threw up her hands in horror when she saw the patches on my nightgown. Said it was not what a bride should wear for her husband on their wedding night. And that I shouldn't allow your servants to see it, or they might think I wasn't worthy of you. And there just wasn't time to do any shopping for the kind of thing that would have suited me and make it look as if I was the kind of woman you *should* have married, and…' She faltered to a standstill as he tossed the flimsy bit of nothing aside and stalked towards her.

She swallowed. Again.

'And I, um…' She didn't get to finish what she'd been going to say about not wanting to let him down and how she would do her best to be a good wife to him, even though he wouldn't have chosen her in a million years, for he took her in his arms and kissed her. Full on the mouth. As though he couldn't stand listening to another single word of the nonsense she was babbling.

Or…no…better to pretend he was showing the eagerness of an impatient bridegroom. Yes, yes, that was better. For her self-esteem. It also gave her the courage to yield to the temptation to slide her arms up his muscular body and round to the back of his broad shoulders. After all she was his wife now and so this was no longer a sin. On the contrary, it was positively her *duty* to appreciate her husband's caresses and return them. With fervour.

'You are shaking,' he observed huskily after a few deliciously fevered moments of doing what she'd always wanted to do. At which point she made a startling discovery.

'So are you!'

'It is merely lust,' he said dismissively. 'In *my* case, that is. Though I dare say you are trembling with nerves.'

'Umm...' She felt her cheeks heat with shame. At the fact that she was, apparently, as responsive to his kisses as any of the other women he'd bedded. And also at her reluctance to admit it. Because to let him think she was trembling with *nerves* was a sort of a lie. And surely no marriage founded on lies, or half-truths, could possibly prosper. Could it?

'Which is why I decided not to wait,' he said, stroking one finger along her jaw line. 'I could see you working yourself up to such a pitch that making you mine tonight would have become impossible.'

'Oh.' That was actually rather thoughtful of him. He could be considerate, in his own fashion. No, no, considerate by *anyone*'s standards. Only think of the way he'd sent for ice after she'd punched him, knowing her knuckles would be sore.

And…he was trembling, too. With lust, he'd said. For her. When he was such a connoisseur of women.

'Oh,' she said again. Or rather, sighed. For his admission he was so filled with lust he was shaking with it made her feel desirable for the first time in her life.

Womanly.

'Turn around,' he growled.

'Wh-what?'

Instead of repeating his order, he spun her round in his arms and his intent became clear as he began to tug open the fastenings at the back of the gown Lady Harriet had given her for her wedding. She'd wondered how she was going to manage it, tonight, without the help of a maid. All her own gowns fastened at the front, or under the arms since she'd never had a personal maid to help her dress and undress.

Though it looked as though she wasn't going to need one now. Her husband was amazingly efficient. He had her gown and stays undone before she could say Jack Robinson. Had slid them down her arms, and kicked them away, and spun her back to him and was kissing her again as though he needed to have his lips upon hers without wasting one second.

Which was fine by her. After all, she'd longed, for years, to know what it would feel like to have him kiss her. And, oh, it was everything she'd dreamed. Exciting, and pleasurable and...golly! He was picking her up and carrying her over to the bed.

He set her down with deliberation on top of the counterpane, before straightening up and removing his neckcloth. Jacket. Waistcoat. Shirt.

She lay still, licking her lips and breathing rather fast. My, but he had a beautiful body. Lean and muscular. With just a smattering of hair in the centre of his chest. Which formed an arrow, pointing down to where his hands were impatiently tugging at the fall of his breeches. Oh, dear. That was just a bit much.

She squeezed her eyes shut before she caught sight of anything too...masculine.

She heard him chuckle. Heard the noise of fabric rustling, the thud of a garment landing on the floor. Felt the bed depress as he climbed on to it.

She might not be ready to look at him, naked, but she didn't want him to think she was too prudish to make love with her own husband. So she reached for him blindly. And he let her catch him before drawing her close to his firm, naked body and kissing her.

'Clare,' he murmured, drawing back and trailing hot kisses down the length of her neck.

'R—' She bit back the name she'd been about to use. His given name of Robert. For he hadn't granted her permission to do that. And the last thing she wanted was to offend him when, so far, everything seemed to be going well. Swiftly, she substituted his title. 'Rawcliffe.' She sighed.

'Mmm…' He groaned in a way that sounded appreciative as his lips closed over one breast, through the fabric of her shift. She didn't know whether it was the hum of his voice against her, or the wetness of his tongue, or whether it was because he was paying attention to her *there*, but she became so excited she simply couldn't keep still. She ran her hands up and down the satin expanse of his back, revelling in the feel of his muscles flexing and bunching under the skin. Ran her leg up and down his, stroking the springy hairs with the sole of her foot.

Lifted herself when he began to push her chemise out of his way, so that they could be together, skin on skin, from breast to thigh.

And then it was like nothing she had ever experienced. As though she'd been lit on fire and had become one great conflagration of need. She was aching, hollowed out by needy fire. Needed him to fill that aching hollow that sprang to life between her legs, where he was stroking, and probing, and teasing with his fingers.

'Oh, please,' she sobbed, 'don't tease me any longer. I can't bear it. I need… I need…'

'I know what you need,' he growled and came over her fully, thrusting her legs apart with his own, and probing at her with something that wasn't his fingers any longer. His…his manhood. She blushed as he began nudging at her with it. She knew it was coming, of course, but the way he was opening her with his fingers so that he could thrust it inside was so…so…

'Oh!'

Painful. That was what it was. And she hadn't expected that. Not from him. He was so experienced. And she'd never heard even the faintest suggestion that he'd ever given any woman anything but pleasure.

Why was it so different for her?

He stilled, stroked her hair back from her face,

kissed her brow. 'There, that's the worst bit over with,' he said.

'Is it?' She opened one eye to squint up at him.

He ground his hips provocatively against hers.

And to her surprise, and relief, the pain turned into the achy wanting feeling again. He half-lowered his eyelids in a satisfied, knowing way, as though he knew exactly how he was affecting her.

Well, of course he did. He'd done this before. With lots of other women.

She shut her eyes again on a wave of hurt that was not the slightest bit physical and turned her head to one side in an attempt to conceal it from him.

And he kissed her neck. Fastened his lips to a point just beneath her ear as his lower half pushed slowly in and out. And then made a throaty, growling sort of noise that reverberated right through her. Right down to the tips of her toes. And somehow made her forget about all those other women. Forget everything but him, and her, together *now*.

And suddenly, almost out of nowhere, she caught fire all over again. She was all flame. Slick, burning, incandescence.

Which he stoked into a crescendo of burning, pulsing rapture. It was so consuming that for a few seconds she was aware of nothing else. But when it started to fade, it was to the discovery that Rawcliffe was panting into her ear, his own body slack over hers. As though he, too, had reached that place where she'd just gone.

It made her feel strangely close to him. Made her want to hug him, with her arms and her legs. And kiss him again. Like a besotted little fool.

Deliberately, so that he'd never guess how vulnerable she was to him, she uncurled her fingers, which were clinging into the skin of his shoulders, and began to run them down his sweat-slick back instead.

He reared back. Gave her one of his half-smiles.

'That went remarkably well, considering,' he said.

And just like that, the feeling of intimacy, of tender closeness, shattered. For his casual remark had reminded her that this hadn't been anything special, for him. She was just the latest in a long line of his conquests.

'Considering what, exactly?' Her lack of experience? Her lack of allure? She cringed to recall the way she'd writhed with pleasure when he'd sucked at her breasts—her tiny, almost non-existent breasts. In comparison with women like

Betsy Woodly, that was, whose bosom resembled a cow's udders.

'Considering your so-called virtue.'

'My *so-called...*'

'Yes,' he said, disengaging and rolling to one side. 'I had half-expected you to lie there with your eyes closed as rigid as a board. Instead of participating with such enthusiasm.'

He might as well have slapped her. It hurt so much, to hear him speak so mockingly of an experience that had been so sublime that she very nearly slapped him back.

'Oh, don't take it like that,' he said, running one forefinger over the fist she'd made in her effort to prevent her wedding night from descending into another fight. 'I am pleased with you for responding so beautifully.' He sat up and turned his back on her. Which was covered in claw marks. Which she'd made. And worse, she was able to see them clearly because it was *still light*.

'My delight in you will be reflected by the generosity of my morning gift,' he said, reaching for his shirt.

'Your...what?'

'A tradition in my family. The groom always gives his bride a gift after their first night together, to signify his approval. Or gratitude, or whatever you wish to call it,' he said with an insouciant half-shrug. 'I think your response, just now, deserves something very special.' He stood up, and went in search of his breeches. 'The traditional gift of a diamond parure seems a little inappropriate, considering your views. I shall keep the set I bought yesterday, for the birth of our first son. In the meantime…'

He got no further. From somewhere she gained the energy, and the agility, to roll across the bed and seize a water jug she hadn't been aware of until she'd started needing to have something to throw at him.

He must have caught sight of her movement because he dodged to one side, so that the jug shattered harmlessly against the wall.

'You don't want to wait until the birth of our first son for the diamonds,' he said, with raised eyebrows. 'Really, Clare, you only had to say…'

With a shriek, she seized the basin and hurled that after the jug.

He raised his hands as if in surrender. 'My presence is obviously unsettling you. I shall withdraw and leave you to calm…'

There was a candlestick and a set of brushes, and

a small porcelain soap dish on the wash stand, all of which went the same way as the jug and basin.

None of which actually hit him. Her aim grew steadily more erratic in direct proportion to her fury.

He was actually smiling, in a maddeningly superior manner by the time he shut the door firmly behind him. At the very same moment she ran out of missiles.

Clare sank to her knees on the floor beside the bed, surveying in turn the wreckage strewn across the floor and the rumpled bedding, and the blood smeared down the inside of her leg. And couldn't stand the sight of any of it. So she buried her face in her hands, but that only made it worse, somehow. Because she could still feel his hands all over her body. And the echoes of the glorious state he'd induced with them, before bringing her crashing back down to earth with those few cutting, callous remarks.

Oh, lord, how was she going to survive being married to him, if he could toss her from one extreme to the other with such ease? If he could walk away from her with a smile on his face when she was...*distraught*?

She leaned forward, pressing her forehead against

the cool silk of the counterpane. And prayed the prayer so many wives had done, she reckoned, since the beginning of time.

Lord, give me strength…

Chapter Twelve

She was sitting up in bed, taking breakfast, when Rawcliffe strolled into the room next morning wearing only, as far as she could see, an oriental-looking sort of dressing gown.

He was her husband, she reminded herself as he approached the bed, barefoot. And this was his house. Of course he thought he could go wherever he liked, dressed however he wished.

'I trust you slept well,' he said, then bent over to give her a kiss on the cheek. As though nothing untoward had occurred.

She struggled with her answer. Should she be truthful and tell him that she'd passed a wretched night? Wrestling with her conscience for hours before finally drifting off into a fitful doze. And that only after getting down on her hands and knees, and clearing up all the broken crockery, and blotting up the water with a towel so that his staff would not guess what she'd done.

Or should she take her lead from him and pretend nothing had happened?

'I cannot say it was the best night's sleep I've ever had,' she finally decided to say. Honesty had always been important to her. And she wasn't prepared to abandon all her principles the minute she ran into difficulties as a married woman. 'I was… so…'

He sat on the chair beside her bed, crossed his legs and gave her an indecipherable look.

'So…?'

Oh. So he was determined to exact his pound of flesh, was he?

'Ashamed of myself.' There, she'd admitted it.

'Indeed,' he said coolly, raising one brow. 'For what, precisely?'

'For losing my temper with you! I don't know why it should be, but you only have to raise your brow, the way you are doing now, and I want to… scream and throw things, and…'

'Is that your notion of an apology? Dear me, it seems to fall short in so very many ways.'

'I…' She took a breath. Counted to three. 'Yes,

I...' She drew on every reserve of self-control she possessed. 'That is, you are right, I *should* be apologising.'

'Your response did seem a little extreme,' he said, looking down his nose disdainfully. 'If I had known you had such a partiality for diamonds, I should not have dreamed of withholding them from you—'

'It wasn't the diamonds! And don't pretend you think it was about them. You know perfectly well you made me feel...cheap. Used. As though you had to pay me for services rendered.'

'No, no, I am sure I explained it was a family tradition—'

'I don't give a fig for your family tradition. All I wanted was for you to...' to hold her in his arms as though she mattered '...to let me know I wasn't a disappointment.'

'I believe I did exactly that.'

By saying it had gone *remarkably well, considering her so-called virtue?*

'You did it,' she said from between clenched teeth, 'in such a way that you made a mockery of my values and comparing me to all the other women you've had...'

'I did no such thing—'

'Oh, not out loud. But you did in your mind.'

'So you think you know what I'm thinking, do you?'

'Yes. You—'

But then, as if to prove she could have no idea what he was thinking, he leaned over and stopped her mouth with a kiss. It surprised her so much that she promptly forgot whatever it was she'd been about to say in the sheer delight of having his mouth on hers again when she'd been so certain, from the caustic comments he was making, that he was never going to forgive or forget the way she'd brought their wedding night to a close. She was so relieved he could still bring himself to kiss her that she put her arms round his neck and tugged him closer.

In the dim reaches of her consciousness, she was half-aware of the breakfast tray sliding to the floor, accompanied by the sound of more breaking crockery, as he threw back the covers so that he could climb in beside her. But she didn't care. He must have decided to draw a veil over her temper tantrum now he'd made her apologise, to judge from the way his hands were all over her. Not that she could keep her hands off him, either. Which was easy to do, since the dressing gown *was* all he was wearing.

* * *

Much later, when he'd taken her to the heights she'd experienced the night before, only without giving her even the slightest twinge of discomfort, he tucked her into the crook of his arm as he rolled on to his back.

'I almost forgot,' he said, reaching for his gown and drawing a square of card from a pocket. 'Your bride gift.'

She took it from him and held it up to the light filtering in through the lace curtains at the window.

'It is a voucher for Almack's,' he explained when she frowned.

'Almack's?'

'Yes. Even you must have heard of the place. Vouchers to gain admittance are highly prized by most debutantes. They will do whatever it takes to get their hands on one.'

'I am not,' she said with sinking heart, 'a debutante.'

'Nevertheless, you need to make an appearance there. You will find your future as my wife will go much more smoothly once you show that you have the approval of the patronesses. Which is why I asked them to call and look you over.'

'Oh,' she said, recalling the visit from two rather nosy women when she'd been staying with Lady Harriet. 'I thought they were interviewing Lady Harriet. They promised to send *her* vouchers for Almack's, but they never said anything to me.'

'Do you not wish to attend?'

She would rather crawl over broken crockery all the way to…to Walsingham!

'Would you have preferred,' he said, turning to his side and raising himself up on to one elbow so that he could look down into her face, 'the diamonds after all?'

She almost said something very rude about the diamonds.

'I know I ought to feel grateful that you went to so much trouble for me—'

'It was no trouble. Just had a word with one or two people…'

'And it was as much for your dear friend Lady Harriet as for me, wasn't it?' she snapped.

'You have no need to be jealous,' he said in what she could only think of as an extremely patronising tone.

'Jealous? The very idea! You seem to forget that I know that Lady Harriet dislikes you intensely.'

'Besides which, it was not for Lady Harriet that

I obtained vouchers, but for the sake of her husband. My friend, Lord Becconsall. I do not want his marriage to be a cause for regrets. Unsuitable though, in many people's eyes, she may be.'

'Unsuitable? She's the daughter of an earl!'

'Rank is not everything, my dear.'

'Well, no, it can't be, or they wouldn't have given me a voucher, would they?'

He shook his head as though in disbelief at her stupidity. 'What do you think you are, now?'

'What do you mean? I am a nobody.'

'No, you little goose, you are a marchioness. Now that you are my wife, you are Lady Rawcliffe.'

'Good grief, so I am.'

He gave her a withering look. 'You must be the only woman in England who could forget the little matter of becoming a marchioness, upon marriage to a marquess.'

'Are you saying I'm stupid?'

'No,' he said, tapping her on the tip of her nose with the end of his forefinger. 'Just very, very unworldly.'

'Hmmph,' she said. And would have crossed her arms across her chest if they weren't still linked as far round his body as she could reach.

'I know that you don't possess the clothes you

would need to attend such an exclusive club, if that is what is bothering you. But that is a matter which can easily be rectified.'

'It isn't the clothes! Well, not only the clothes.'

'What, then?'

Dear me. When he looked at her like that, as though he was really interested in hearing what she had to say, he was even more dangerous to her peace of mind than when he was kissing her.

'I'm just…not…ready. Perhaps I never will be. I'm not… I wasn't brought up to take a place in society. I'm just a vicar's daughter. And it's no use,' she carried on hastily when he took a breath as if to make an objection, 'saying that now I am your wife I have a title. I have absolutely not the first idea of how to be a marchioness. I wasn't brought up to be anything but possibly a housekeeper or companion to some elderly invalid. I have no idea how to be a grand lady.'

'First of all,' he said silkily, sliding his foot up and down her leg in a most suggestive way, 'you have already proved to be the ideal marchioness, for me, by your response to me in this bed.'

She wasn't sure whether to be flattered, or offended. After all, very many women had responded to him in his bed, she had no doubt. And he hadn't been obliged to marry any of them to prevent a scandal, either.

'And second?'

One side of his mouth hitched up in amusement. 'Second, my pedantic little bride, if you are so intent on glossing over the most basic reason any man marries any woman, you do not need to *learn* how to be a marchioness. You *are* one already, by virtue of marrying me. And you will find that there are no rules to govern the behaviour of such a high-ranking lady. You may behave however you wish and nobody will dare criticise you. Not,' he added more seriously, 'that I fear you are ever likely to do anything that might give anyone cause to criticise you, let alone bring disgrace to my family name.'

She was just starting to glow with pleasure at his praise when he ruined it all by adding, 'You are far too pious.'

How could he manage to make what ought to have felt like a compliment sound like a criticism just by injecting a certain tone to his voice?

'But—'

He stopped her next protest by the simple expedient of leaning in and kissing her again. And though she strove to hold on to her annoyance she found it impossible to do anything but melt.

'Perhaps it *is* too soon for you to face the tabbies,' he said, smoothing her hair back from her face once he'd reduced her to a pliant puddle. 'Perhaps it would be easier for you if you were more at ease with me. With your new station.'

'Oh.' Goodness, sometimes he could be so…understanding.

When he wasn't being infuriating, that was.

And since he was clearly trying very hard, by his standards, she couldn't very well do anything but meet him halfway.

'Well, yes,' she therefore admitted. 'It has all been rather sudden. One minute I was all set to start a new life as a companion to an elderly invalid and the next…'

'We shall go away for a while. Get right away from London and spend some time getting to know each other, as husband and wife. Once you have gained more confidence, I have no doubt that you will excel in your role.'

'Really? You really mean that?'

'Yes.' He frowned. 'I must warn you, however, that I will not be able to relinquish all my duties.

I have been…out of touch for some time and there are some matters which need urgent attention.'

'I would never expect you to dance attendance on me. I know you are a very important man, with a great many calls upon your time.'

'You see? You are proving to be an excellent marchioness already.'

This time, there was no sting to the compliment that she could discern. Apart from the message that she would only be a rather small part of his life. Which was all any woman he married could hope for.

She lay back and watched him through her lashes as he retrieved his dressing gown and knotted the belt loosely round his waist.

She might only be able to inhabit a very small corner of his life, but by heaven she would fill that place to the very best of her ability. He would never have cause to complain about her behaviour, or her appearance, or…she glanced guiltily at the broken breakfast dishes littering the rug…*any*thing.

Chapter Thirteen

'You look very well in that outfit,' said Lord Rawcliffe as he handed Clare into his travelling carriage. Actually, she looked utterly divine in her new carriage dress. She'd always managed to make the best of what came to hand. But now she had access to almost limitless funds he wouldn't be a bit surprised if she soon became a leader of fashion.

Clare blushed as she took her seat. Then surreptitiously smiled down at her fine leather gloves.

'You have outdone Lady Harriet already,' he added as he took the facing seat.

'Oh?' Clare looked puzzled. Suspicious. As though she expected him to say something unkind now, to rob her of her pleasure in his compliment. 'In what way?'

'Until her husband took her in hand, Lady Harriet had no idea what suited her and went about in some extremely unflattering outfits.' Which was one of the reasons he'd hired an extremely experienced dresser to oversee Clare's purchases. Lord Becconsall might not care what people said about his wife behind her back, but he was not going to leave Clare exposed to the same kind of gossip.

'Yes, I know, she told me as much,' said Clare, with a little sniff. 'I suspect,' she added sadly, 'that is why she was so keen to let me have so many of her old gowns.'

He stiffened. 'I do hope that your trunks are not full of another woman's cast-offs. Did I not give you enough time to kit yourself out, properly, for a trip to the country?' One week. Just one week had he kept her entirely to himself. He'd refused all invitations to socialise and insisted that modistes and what-have-you came to her rather than let her venture out into the streets without him. Until he'd caught her gazing wistfully out of the window and suspected she was starting to feel like a prisoner.

And so here they were, setting off for Lesser Peeving and talking about clothes as if they were all that mattered.

'They are not *full* of Lady Harriet's cast-offs,' she was saying waspishly. 'But I saw no reason to throw away any clothing that I was able to make use of.'

'That carriage dress you have on is never one of hers.'

'No. This is new.'

'I thought so.' He sat back with a feeling of satisfaction. He couldn't expect Clare to abandon her habits of thrift overnight. But at least she could treat herself to new clothing now, whenever the mood did take her. He'd done that much for her. No more dyeing coats because she couldn't afford decent mourning garments.

He'd taught her how much pleasure her body could give her, too. Although she wasn't at all comfortable with that new knowledge. Not when the pleasure came at the hands of a man she despised so heartily.

Not that she'd said as much. But then he hadn't given her the opportunity to do so. Every time she'd started to stiffen up, in his arms, and he'd seen the waves of guilt and regret wash across her expressive little face, he'd given her thoughts another direction. Had deliberately goaded her into an argument about something else, so that they wouldn't have to confront the issue which he dreaded hearing coming from her lips.

Her true feelings about him. About marrying him.

She'd never made any secret about the way she felt about him when they'd been growing up. She'd called him a libertine, a profligate care-for-nobody, a ne'er-do-well, an arrogant, unfeeling, miserly, harsh landlord...oh, there had been no end to the insults she'd flung at him.

Although to be fair, she'd only done so in retaliation to his teasing. Because teasing her had been the only way he'd been able to get her to make any sort of reply to him at all. Goading her into flying into the boughs had always been one of his greatest pleasures. She looked so funny, spitting fire and practically hopping up and down on the spot. And whenever he'd prodded her down off her high horse, forced her to lose control with him when what she most wanted to do was treat him with haughty disdain, it had felt like a victory.

Not the best way to conduct relations with one's own wife, perhaps, but then that was the way they'd always interacted and it wasn't as easy to get out of a habit, he was finding, as it had been to fall into it.

Though he could see she was trying to. He shifted guiltily in his seat as she darted him a tentative smile. Since she'd given vent to her feelings in that initial orgy of crockery-smashing, she'd been doing her utmost to keep her temper in check. He could see her wrestling with it right now, as his secretary finally clambered into the coach, his satchel of papers slung over one shoulder and his portable writing desk clutched under one arm.

'You won't mind, my dear,' he said to Clare, who clearly did to judge from the way she narrowed her eyes, 'if I spend some time attending to my correspondence? I often spend the time it takes travelling from one place to another in this manner.'

Any newly married woman would be insulted to find her husband was bringing a secretary along on her bride trip. Clare was no exception. But after sitting up very straight, she said, 'Of course not,' with a determined smile. 'I know you are a very important man and must have a great deal of work to attend to. You know, I have never travelled very far from Watling Minor before so I will be quite content watching the passing scenery out of the window.'

Dear lord, but Saint Paul had it right when he talked about heaping coals of fire upon your enemy's head. He felt downright scalded by Clare's dogged determination to enjoy the journey, so as not to be a nuisance. Especially since he'd only in-

vited Slater along to create a barrier between them.
The last thing he wanted to do was talk to her for
any length of time. Because she would probably
start to thank him for taking her out of town rather
than forcing her to go to Almack's, where she'd
have taken her place in society as his bride. And
he wasn't sure how long he would be able to let her
think he was being a caring, thoughtful husband
when the truth was he'd deliberately manipulated
her into taking this trip. First of all, he'd reduced
her to a state of boneless satiation, and then, when
her judgement was clouded, he'd scared her with
that threat of parading her before the town's tabbies at Almack's. If he'd suggested a trip to the
country to start with, she'd have been so offended
at the implication she wasn't up to snuff that he'd
have had to drag her into this carriage kicking and
screaming.

What was worse, though, was leading her to
think that they were taking this trip solely to benefit her, whereas nothing could be further from
the truth.

Slater began to pull documents from the case and
arrange them on the portable desk which he bal-
anced upon his knee. At least the man had no idea
anything was out of the ordinary. Not on this leg

of the journey, at any rate. It might well be different after they'd been to visit Clement, particularly if Clare found out that he suspected her darling brother of being involved in not only the disappearance of a large amount of jewellery, but also of the suspicious death of his friend Archie. She wouldn't be able to pretend she wasn't angry with him after that. And she would be. So angry that he wouldn't be able to manipulate her into a state of smiling compliance with his skills in the bedroom. Bedroom? She'd never let him anywhere near a bedroom ever again. In fact, if she ever *spoke* to him again it would be nothing short of a miracle.

And two miracles in one lifetime were more than any man deserved. He'd had his when he'd walked into that inn and she'd fallen into his clutches like a ripe peach.

Actually, make that two miracles. The second had occurred on his wedding night, when she'd not merely yielded to his lovemaking, but responded with an untutored enthusiasm that had stunned him. For a moment or two, he'd experienced such a strong surge of emotion that it had almost leaked from his eyes. He'd almost told her...

He pulled a face. Thank heavens, his fit of lunacy had only lasted a second or two before he'd pulled himself together sufficiently to take steps to ensure things didn't start getting...*sentimental*.

He'd managed to extricate himself from her arms, and then her room, with his own dignity intact. That he'd done it by goading her into a state where she'd found relief in throwing a selection of breakables at him also ensured she didn't notice how shaken he'd been by their encounter. And then the next morning, before she could launch into a discussion about what had happened the night before, he'd distracted her by deliberately seducing her again.

And that was the way he would continue to handle her. Handle his own weakness for her. And stop it getting out of hand.

Lord Rawcliffe was acting exactly the way a newly married man should, tenderly handing her out of the carriage at every halt, making solicitous enquiries as to her comfort and seeing to all her wants, be it delicately sliced bread to go with a cup of tea, or directions to the necessary.

The only hint that all was not as it should be was the presence of Slater and his bag of *extremely important documents*. Most newly married men would surely have consigned his secretary to one of the coaches containing all the other members of staff her husband seemed to think necessary for a trip to…wherever it was they were going. He hadn't deigned to inform her. And she was too proud to give in to her curiosity and beg him to tell her. Or to ask any of his staff, either, because that would expose the fact that he hadn't seen fit to share his plans with her.

And as the day wore on it became harder and harder to keep her feelings in check. Because none of the topics Slater and her husband discussed sounded as important as all that. Not that she supposed they would discuss state secrets with her sitting right there, she conceded. Perhaps it was just the *amount* of business her husband had to deal with that was the issue. Perhaps he just wanted to catch up with all the things that had escaped his attention while he'd been searching for the mysterious 'Jenny' Lady Harriet had mentioned before he'd made it clear she was supposed to be a secret.

He certainly hadn't liked being kept in ignorance of her father's death. And he'd been downright shaken by the news of his chaplain's horrible fate.

She let her eyes drift in his direction. And sighed. He was, in spite of all the accusations she'd flung at him over the years, a very conscientious landlord. At least he didn't regard his tenants as merely a source of income, the way so many others of his class did. Though he lived well, extremely well, actually, he never neglected repairs on the cottages of his estate workers. And he generally took such a keen interest in everything that was going on, at all his estates from what she could gather, that he had the reputation of knowing *everything*. Perhaps this was how he did it. By paying such meticulous attention to all his correspondence, no matter how trivial it appeared.

She promptly decided to give him the benefit of the doubt upon that issue. Because apart from anything else, it was a good way to argue herself out of being offended by Mr Slater's mere presence, when Rawcliffe had led her to believe this was going to be a time for them to get to know each other as husband and wife.

Though, actually, wasn't this a sort of getting to know him? She was certainly learning that he wasn't the kind of man to neglect his duties to his estates, not even when on a bride trip.

Which made his jaunt into the wilds of Norfolk in pursuit of that Jenny person all the more remarkable. He'd put himself beyond the reach of even his secretary, never mind his friends. So he must have considered it a very important matter.

Which he didn't want her to know anything about.

Even though she was his wife!

A wife who didn't feel she had the right to question him about his movements *now*, let alone before they'd married.

She sighed as they approached another coaching inn.

'Tired?'

Even though his carriage was very comfortable and she'd been regaled with all sorts of treats at every stop they'd made, she was growing rather weary of travelling.

'A little,' she admitted.

'Then you will be pleased to hear we are going to break our journey here, overnight.'

She wondered where *here* was, precisely. And wondered if now would be a good time to finally break down and ask him. Not in front of Slater, though. But later, surely he couldn't think she was being demanding, if she raised the topic…over dinner perhaps?

Yes, that was when she would ask him, over dinner. Because apart from anything else it would give them something to talk about, which wouldn't lead to an argument, the way most of their encounters did.

Unless, of course, he invited Slater to dine with them, to prevent them from descending into the kind of childish bickering that nearly always developed whenever they were alone. Except when they were in bed, of course, in which case they didn't do any talking at all. Not anymore. She just let him leave when he'd done, rather than demand more than he seemed willing to give her. It was better, she'd found, to feel a slight resentment over his behaviour than to behave badly herself.

Clare was glad to see Slater scuttle off to the nether regions of the inn while the landlord bowed and scraped her and Rawcliffe to a suite of rooms upstairs. Although it depressed her a bit to note that her husband would rather pay for two bedrooms than to have to share a bed with her all night.

'Are the rooms not to your liking?'

She lifted her gaze from an inspection of the table upon which she guessed they would be dining in due course to find Rawcliffe inspecting her sardonically.

'The rooms are lovely,' she countered.

'Then what has put that frown upon your face?'

She blushed. And decided that she wasn't going to tell him that she'd been thinking about their sleeping arrangements and wishing that after taking her to the heights of pleasure, he wouldn't always wreck it all by displaying such determination to get as far away from her as possible as swiftly as he could.

'Um…' She reached for something she might say to explain her thoughtful mien. 'Actually, it has just occurred to me that I have no idea where we are going.' Or where they were right now, come to that, not that it mattered.

It didn't matter. She blinked at the revelation. She no longer cared where she was, all that much, or where she was going. Because…she trusted him.

For so many years, she'd been the one upon whom others depended. But now, within less than a week of becoming his wife, she had a deep and abiding faith that he was going to look after her.

She went to the nearest chair and sat down upon it. He'd sown the seeds of that faith by tending to her hand after she'd punched him. Had watered it by insisting on marrying her, even though she must be the last person he'd ever have considered, had he actually been considering marriage. And it had steadily grown every time he'd greeted her outbursts of temper by walking away and giving her time to calm down. He had never responded to her with anger, or rebuked her for losing control—not even the time she'd thrown all that crockery at him—but with patience and tolerance.

'Is something amiss? Do you feel unwell?'

The look of concern on his face was almost her undoing. She lowered her head, rummaged in her reticule and pulled out a handkerchief with which to blow her nose and dab at her eyes.

Oh, dear. She'd been half in love with the handsome Robert Walmer for most of her life. Now that she was living in close proximity to him, was it any wonder that she was falling all the way?

And now he was kneeling at her feet, looking up into her face with a frown.

'I am just, I have to admit,' she gulped, dabbing at her eyes, 'rather overwhelmed by all...' she waved her damp handkerchief vaguely '...all this.'

'This inn?'

'Don't be absurd,' she said tartly. 'The inn is... just an inn. I mean, my circumstances. Us.'

His face shuttered. He got to his feet and went over to the window.

'You will feel better once you have had a cup of

tea, I should think. I have rung for some. It should be here shortly.'

Which meant, *do not become sentimental, or expect more of me than I am prepared to give.*

Well, she wasn't stupid. She could take a hint.

'Thank you,' she said meekly. And bit down on the acid retort that sprang to mind—that if he though a cup of tea was going to cure a painful case of unrequited love then he was all about in his head. Because the last thing he'd want to hear was that the bride he'd taken on sufferance was falling deeper in love with him with every day that passed.

Chapter Fourteen

And then a chambermaid bustled in with a tray of tea things, closely followed by Nancy, the maid her husband had insisted on hiring.

'I shall leave you to freshen up and calm yourself down,' he said sternly. And then headed for the door which led to his room, through which she glimpsed his own valet, Cadogan, laying out clothes into which she assumed he meant to change for the evening. Which meant he expected her to do the same. Which was why Nancy had come.

She screwed her handkerchief into a twist, the way she'd wring the neck of a chicken before plucking it and popping into the pot. How could she be falling so hard for a man who was so...*infuriating?* So oblivious to her?

Because, in so many ways, he'd been so tolerant, considerate and patient.

If he did speak to her sternly from time to time, was it any wonder? She had a terrible temper herself and knew how easily she could lose it.

Perhaps he'd thought those tears were a prelude to another crockery-throwing scene, and had withdrawn before she had the chance to behave badly.

She supposed she couldn't blame him. Besides, she did need to regain some composure. She drew in a deep breath. She could be calm. She was sure she could be calm. And, actually, having the chambermaid and her own rather toplofty maid bustling about the room did help her to control herself. She couldn't give vent to any sort of feelings when servants were about, he'd warned her. *It just isn't done, in this level of society*, he'd said, as though she'd been in the habit of discussing everything in front of servants her entire life.

Which had, of course, made her itch to slap his face right then. And, she now saw, was one reason his talking-to had been so infuriating. Because he'd initiated it in front of Nancy. After warning her she needed to watch her behaviour when servants were watching.

If she didn't know better she'd think he was deliberately provoking her. Only, why on earth would he do anything of the sort?

No, no, she was imagining things. She was tired from the journey and drained from the effort of keeping her temper in check, and unsettled by the strength of feelings she was developing for a man everyone knew had a lump of ice where his heart ought to be.

'I'll press the apricot silk for this evening, shall I, my lady?'

Clare lifted her cup of tea to her lips and took a long, soothing sip before answering her maid. Because Nancy was not actually asking her opinion. Nancy was telling her which dress was appropriate for her to wear to dine with her husband, in an inn. It was the reason her husband had hired the girl, he'd told her. So that she wouldn't make the same mistakes as Lady Harriet had. He *did not have the same level of tolerance*, he'd added, unnecessarily to her way of thinking. He *was not prepared to permit her* to go around town looking a fright. Because it would reflect badly upon his taste.

His taste.

She set the cup down on the saucer with a snap.

'Apricot silk? Do you think that is appropriate?'

'The trimmings are all black. There is no harm in wearing just a touch of colour, when dining in private, on what is, after all, your honeymoon,' replied Nancy with exaggerated patience.

'Very well,' she said through gritted teeth. 'By all means, bring me the apricot silk.'

'Shall I just help you off with your carriage dress?'

The carriage dress he'd complimented her upon. Telling her she'd outdone Lady Harriet. Which had pleased her no end, at the time he'd said it.

She supposed she ought to be grateful to Nancy. Left to herself, Clare would have purchased far cheaper, more hard-wearing clothing which he would not, she'd discovered earlier, have approved of at all. Nor would she ever have thought of changing to eat dinner in a private inn room, either, let alone into a silk gown.

'Yes, thank you, Nancy,' she said, trying to inject the gratitude into her tone of voice which she was striving to feel.

'I shall have hot water brought up directly, your ladyship,' put in the chambermaid.

Because of course she would have to wash off the grime of travelling, before donning the silk. And, yes, she did want to have a wash. It was just that afterwards she would much rather have curled up on the window seat and gazed down at the bustling inn yard. Or simply flung herself onto her bed, to rest. Neither of which she'd be able to do in the apricot gown, which was cut far lower than she was used to and therefore required the kind of underpinning that not only kept her decent, but meant there would be no flinging herself onto beds, or lounging upon comfy seats, or, if she ate too much, breathing too deeply, either.

She sighed. It was harder work being a marchioness than she would ever have imagined.

'You look very appetising in that confection,' said Lord Rawcliffe as he handed her to her chair at the table set for two. From this position, leaning over her from behind as she settled on to her seat, he had a very intriguing view down the front of it.

It made him want to slide his hands down and cup the delicate white mounds and squeeze the raspberry-pink nipples between his fingers.

Which would shock her. And be highly disrespectful, considering the waiter was still in the room, fussing over the chafing dishes on the sideboard.

And so, while the fellow's back was turned, it was exactly what he did, swiftly delving down her bodice, locating the tightly furled bud, pinching it and withdrawing his hand in the time it took her to stiffen and gasp in disbelief.

Hopefully she would now be too angry to remember whatever it was she'd been thinking of discussing with him over supper. Whatever it was that had made her look wistful, before rendering her teary-eyed. And too aware of the waiter to launch into a tirade upon his manners, either.

She was certainly angry enough to grasp the handle of the gravy boat in a very threatening manner. He had a hunch that his dignity was only spared because the waiter turned round at the very moment she lifted it from its stand. So that instead of throwing it in his face, she poured it over her plate. But she then started sawing at her food with such savagery he could easily interpret what she would rather be doing with her knife and fork.

Her ill humour was so thinly disguised that even the waiter began to grow nervous and made a strategic retreat far sooner than Lord Rawcliffe would have liked.

Still, he had not played his last card. Not by any means.

'Did you not like the food?' he enquired politely, eyeing the mangled remains of what had once been a perfectly innocent slice of steak and ale pie on her plate. 'I chose this inn particularly because the cook has a sterling reputation...'

'I have no complaints about the *food*,' she retorted.

He leaned back in his seat and put on his most patient, enquiring, innocent expression.

'Then you do have some form of complaint?'

She almost hissed with fury. 'You know very well I do.'

'And are you going to tell me what it is?'

'I shouldn't have to! The way you...' She glanced down at the front of her bodice. Went bright red.

'Ah,' he said and smiled. 'Forgive me, my dear, that I did not have time to meet your needs before supper. But with the waiter hovering...'

'Meet *my* needs?' She gripped her napkin between the fingers of her right hand as though she was hanging on to it, and her temper, for all she was worth.

'Yes,' he said, getting to his feet. 'But you have no need to be ashamed of them,' he continued provocatively, as he made his way round the table.

'Ashamed? I am not ashamed! Because—'

'Tut-tut,' he said, shaking his head. 'You are blushing so deep a shade of crimson that there is no point trying to deny it. So don't. Instead take comfort from the fact that I have been just as impatient for that waiter to take his leave as you have been,' he said, leaning down to take the hand that wasn't employed in strangling her napkin.

Her eyes narrowed. And then, as he brought her hand to the front of his breeches and pressed it very firmly against his hot, hard length, they flew wide.

'Yes,' he said mildly. 'You have the same effect upon me as I do upon you.'

'I do not… That is, I am…'

'If I were to lift your skirts now and run my hand up your thigh,' he growled provocatively, 'I would find you swollen and wet.' He noted with satisfaction the way her eyes darkened. Her breath hitched.

Yes, this was the way to play it. Keep their interactions firmly rooted in the carnal. Never let her suspect that his feelings were anything other than lustful. Never permit the more tender feelings that he seemed to be developing for her to take hold, come to that. That was how he would survive when she discovered his true motives for bringing her on this trip. By not allowing himself to feel, to hope, for anything more than what he'd get from a torrid *affaire*.

He guided her hand up the length of him and

down again. Taught her how he would like her to stroke him.

She swallowed. Kept her eyes fixed firmly on his face, though she must have been able to feel him growing under the ministrations of her hot little hand.

'That's it,' he growled, letting go of her hand. 'Keep on doing that.'

But she didn't, of course. The moment he told her to keep stroking him, she stopped, even though she hadn't whipped her hand away the moment he'd let it go.

'You are…you are…'

'Beastly?' He bent over her and fixed his mouth to the point where her neck joined her shoulder, a spot where she was particularly sensitive. And growled. She shuddered, as he'd known she would, and let her head loll to one side to give him better access.

'Shall I ravish you across the table? Sweep all the dishes to the floor, and push up your skirts, and take you, fast and hard?'

She whimpered. Reached up and grabbed hold of his shoulders.

'N-no,' she panted, kneading at his shoulders and writhing in her seat.

'No? The idea excites you, but you would deny us the pleasure of doing exactly as we please?'

'No, it… I mean, yes.' Her face flamed. She bit down on her lower lip. Her eyes filled up. 'I can't deny it. What you said…it did make me…' She glanced at the table with a sort of sick fascination. 'But we can't—'

'We can do whatever we like. Nothing is wrong between a man and a woman, if it gives them both pleasure.'

'But it wouldn't, that's just the problem.'

'Don't claim you are too shy, my little hypocrite.'

'I'm not a hypocrite! It's just that…and I won't claim it's because I'm too shy, either, when you know perfectly well that you make me too…that is, I forget about everything I ought to hold dear when you start to…work on me!'

A dark, twisted sort of satisfaction flared as she confessed he could rob her of her every principle, just by *working* on her. That she resented him for it he knew all too well. But to hear her confess how very helpless he could render her made him feel, for the first time in relation to her, as though he was starting to gain the upper hand.

'I know it ought to be that, but to my shame,

it isn't. It's…' She gave a little sob that sounded, somehow, resentful. 'It's my corsets.'

'Your corsets?' He straightened up a little, to inspect the rather rigid outline of the front of her gown.

'Yes,' she bit out. 'They are so tight, and so cumbersome, that I cannot even lounge comfortably in a chair, never mind disport myself amidst the crockery.'

And she wanted to. She'd as good as admitted she wanted to. For a moment, the knowledge brought him to a standstill.

'Then I had better get you out of them,' he said, just about regaining enough presence of mind to drop one swift kiss on the tip of her pert little nose, as though he was in full control of the situation. 'Before they do you an injury.'

She looked so relieved, and then so embarrassed, and then so guiltily excited that he changed his mind about laying her across the table like a delicacy for him to sample. Because, no matter how much she would have enjoyed it, afterwards she would have felt ashamed of herself. And though sometimes he had deliberately made her angry, he never wanted her to feel ashamed of her natural, and so far uninhibited, response to their love-making.

So he picked her up and carried her to her room. Set her on her feet and turned her round so that he could undo the lacings of her gown, and her ridiculously constructed corset, whilst pressing open-mouthed kisses to the nape of her neck. By the time he had her naked apart from her shift and stockings, she was moaning and rubbing her bottom against him in a way that was highly provocative, all the more so because he was certain she had no idea what it was doing to him. It was all instinct with her. In spite of all her much-vaunted religious beliefs, her rigid moral viewpoint, she simply couldn't help herself.

And nor could he. He was so hot for her by now, so hard, that he didn't think he was going to be able to wait much longer.

But was she ready for him? He ran his hands down her stomach, reached between her legs and delved into her moist, slick heat.

She cried out and reached behind her, running her hands down his flanks.

Oh, yes. She was ready. He'd only have to stroke into her, once or twice, and she'd explode around him. She was so passionate. So wild in his arms.

Exceeding every fantasy he'd ever had about her. And there had been many, over the years. Far too many…

So, now that he had her, what was to stop him indulging in one or two of them? Where was the harm? When he was going to make sure she enjoyed them as much as he was going to?

And so he held her trembling, responsive little body up with one arm while he brought her to a quivering, sobbing, climax with his other hand.

And then he pushed her face down on to the bed, undid his breeches, and pounded into her from behind until he reached his own release.

And then, because he wasn't sure he was going to be able to stop himself from saying something he'd regret, about how perfect she was, or how much more wonderful it felt to have her than he'd ever imagined, he pulled up his breeches and fled to the relative safety of his own room.

Chapter Fifteen

It was a good job, Clare thought as she took her breakfast in bed, that he didn't seem very keen to see her first thing this morning. She wouldn't have known how to face him, not after what they'd done last night. It was hard enough attempting any sort of conversation at the best of times, but when she thought of where he'd made her put her hand...

She went hot all over just thinking about it. And that had only been the start of what, in hindsight, she could only regard as a rapid descent into an act that had been like...like...the behaviour of two rutting animals.

Fortunately, her first sight of him was as she was climbing into the carriage to set off. And since Slater was there before her, she could hope that Rawcliffe would assume that was why she was being so stiffly polite.

Once again, the secretary was armed with an immense stack of letters and documents, and, the moment they set out, the pair of them took up where they'd left off the night before.

The coach had barely left the inn yard before growing resentment started nudging her shyness aside. He might have bid her good morning. Asked her how she'd slept. But, no. Just a curt nod was all he'd afforded her as she'd taken her seat facing him.

With a huff, she jerked her eyes away from the space he occupied and stared determinedly out of the window.

And it wasn't merely because he hadn't bid her good morning just now. It was the way he'd got up and walked out on her the night before. Leaving her sprawled face down on the bed. As soon as he'd got what he wanted.

Ooh, men were so *selfish!* She was sick, utterly sick of having to live her life on a man's terms. Her only function in the vicarage had been to make sure her brothers and her father were free to pursue their own ambitions. To smooth their way. Make life easy for them. Nobody ever asked her what she would have liked to do with her day. With her life. Not even when Father died and she could have…

could have…well, she didn't know what she could have done, there had been no time to think. But she certainly hadn't deserved to be swept to one side without even being *asked* whether she wanted to go and look after an elderly invalid.

Although she wasn't going to have to do that now, was she? Thanks to Rawcliffe. She shot him a repentant look from beneath her eyelashes, for bracketing him with her male relatives. He was holding a document between his forefinger and thumb, an expression of irritation on his face. Slater muttered something in an apologetic tone and scribbled something down in the book he had open on his portable desk. And Rawcliffe put the offending document to one side and reached for the next one in the pile that lay between them.

And just like that, she got a searing, vivid memory of him plunging that very same hand down her bodice while the waiter was busy arranging the chafing dishes on the sideboard.

Her face heating, she turned to look out of the window again. She really shouldn't have accused him of being selfish, even if she had only done so in her head. For he hadn't been totally selfish last night, had he? No, he'd made sure she'd got a great deal of pleasure from that encounter as well.

Which had, ironically, made her writhe with shame the moment he'd left. For he'd made her glory in a swift, hard, animalistic coupling, when she'd always dreamed that what a man shared with his wife would be an almost spiritual union.

Why did he always have to drag their encounters in the bedroom down to such a...well, it was almost as if he was determined to keep their encounters as basic, and brutal as he could. Even the position in which he'd taken her, on her knees, from behind, was positively *degrading*. Why, when she thought of the way he used to smile and flirt with Betsy Woodly, the charm she'd seen him exerting on a variety of females at local assemblies, she could...

Oh, she didn't know what she could do, she was so jealous of all his other conquests. Well, she always had been. Which was why she'd always vowed never to appear eager to join their ranks. And she hadn't. Except that now she was his wife, she just wished...

No. There was no point in wishing for what she didn't have. In fact, it was contrary to scripture. The bible taught that, in everything, she should give thanks. And wasn't that an attitude which had kept her going through some of her darkest moments? She'd only had to think of the things she could be grateful for and her lot had always become easier to bear.

So that was what she ought to do now.

She bowed her head, as if in prayer, and clasped her hands in her lap. And as she did so she began to rub her thumb over the ridge in her glove where she wore her wedding ring. Which was the first thing she could be thankful for. That he had married her *at all*. If he hadn't, she'd have been pitched into a household full of strangers, to care for that elderly lady about whom she knew nothing. After spending the last few years enduring that backbreaking, depressing role for her own father, whilst colluding with the curate to conceal the worst of his decline from the parishioners.

And there had been no real need for Rawcliffe to have done anything so chivalrous. It was far more than most men would have done for a woman they'd denounced, for most of their lives, as a termagant.

She supposed he felt entitled to have some reward for performing an act of such outstanding selflessness. He was a man, after all. And all men seemed to think a lot more about carnal things than women. She glanced across the coach where her eyes lit on the firm muscles of his thighs, which were lovingly outlined by the fabric of his breeches…

Which reminded her what those thighs had felt like, straining between her own, the night before.

She shut her eyes with a grimace of annoyance as her thoughts drifted back towards the things she resented about him, rather than counting her blessings.

She took a deep breath, clasped her hands tightly again and determinedly sought for something else to be thankful for today.

Once again, it was the supple material of her gloves that inspired her. And the glossy sheen of her carriage dress upon which they were now resting. It was terribly, terribly worldly of her to count shopping for clothes as something for which to give thanks to God, but truly, it had been like a sort of fantasy for her to send for dressmakers, who brought samples of the most glorious and costly fabrics, and know she could choose any of them and have them made up in whatever style she wished. Even if they did have to be predominantly black. It was such a contrast to the hours she'd had to spend mending and darning, and making over old gowns to disguise the most worn areas, that she'd gone a little mad.

To assuage her guilt over what had felt, after a day or so, like the most reckless extravagance and self-indulgence, she'd vowed to donate a tithe of her allowance to worthy causes before she went anywhere near a dressmaker in future. To charities that supported girls who couldn't afford to buy whatever they wanted, for example. Girls who were as destitute and friendless as she'd been, or at least had felt before Lord Rawcliffe had swept into that inn and transformed her life with one wave of his magical wand.

No. Not his *wand*. His wand was not magical.

Oh, dear. How very easy it was, now she was married to such an earthy, carnal sort of man, for her thoughts to turn in a carnal direction. She ground her teeth in frustration. It must have taken all of five minutes for her to descend from her ambition to apply spiritual principles to her state of mind, to recalling how it had felt to stroking and fondling his…his wand. To realise that she was the one causing it to…

Oh, dear. How she wished she had a fan in her reticule. Or had the excuse that it was unseasonably warm to explain her suddenly overheated face.

But that would make him look at her. And he'd discern somehow what she was thinking about. And he'd smile that lazy, knowing smile and half-lower his eyelids and she'd know he was now thinking about it, too. And…

Oh.

He would be thinking about it, too. Because he wanted her. Just about all the time. In the most inappropriate places. And whether there was anyone else in the room or not. It might not be the least bit romantic, let alone spiritual, but did she have any right to complain that he didn't want her in *exactly* the way she'd hoped he would? Or feel cheated because he hadn't even courted her? For here she was, married to him. As married as it was possible to be. And she was always going to be his wife.

Which was something she could be truly thankful for.

As was the prospect of one day having a baby. A baby to love. Which would grow into a child that would love her back. Even if her husband didn't.

And why would he, considering the fact she wasn't the wife he'd have chosen, if he'd actually been looking for a wife?

Perhaps she'd do better to start trying to learn how to be the kind of wife he wanted her to be, rather than complaining that he wasn't being a perfect husband. Why should he be a perfect husband when he hadn't wanted to be any kind of husband at all? In his eyes, he was probably already going the second mile.

Very well, then, from now on she would...

'Oh!' She leaned forward in her seat as she glimpsed what looked like a body of water, in the gap between two hills. A large body of water, ending at the horizon.

'Is that...?' She turned to Rawcliffe, her confused thoughts tumbling to the back of her mind in the need to ask him if that water was what she thought it was. 'Is that the sea?'

'Yes.'

She pressed her nose to the window in her eagerness to look at it. 'The sea! Oh! Are you taking me to the seaside?' She turned to look at him properly for the first time that day, no longer struggling to think grateful thoughts, so genuinely thrilled was she by this unexpected, and completely unearned, treat. 'I have never seen the sea.'

'I would never have guessed,' he replied drily.

She pressed her nose to the window again, but the carriage was rounding the foot of another hill, which obliterated her view of the sea. Almost in the same way his sarcastic attitude had blotted out her pleasure.

Why did he do that? Put her down in that odious manner? When, sometimes, he could be so kind? For instance, he'd been so gentle and tender with her when he'd bathed her injured hand with ice. But now he seemed to be deliberately going out of his way to prevent her believing there was any good in him, as if he regretted letting her see he had a streak of decency within him.

'But, yes,' he said in a voice that was no longer harsh and impatient. 'We are indeed going to the seaside.'

She turned to look at him in the vain hope he regretted speaking to her the way he had.

'We are going to spend a week in a small fishing village. Which is situated,' he said drily, 'of necessity, at the seaside.'

'It might be nothing special to you,' she said, her hurt at his attitude once again sweeping aside all her good intentions. 'But going to the seaside is the most exciting thing that has ever happened to me.' If you discounted marrying the man she'd been dreaming about ever since she'd grown old enough to know that lips were made for kissing, that was.

* * *

It felt like an age before the carriage finally drew up in front of a row of cottages, clinging to the side of a hill in a position that gave them an unobstructed view of a most picturesque little bay.

'I do hope the accommodation meets with your approval, my lord,' said Slater, pulling down the window and letting in the sounds of gulls and waves on a tide of the freshest air she'd ever breathed.

'The middle cottage is for your use exclusively,' said Slater, 'yours and her ladyship's, that is. The rest of us will take the cottages to either side.'

The rest of us were just rolling up in the three carriages that had been trundling along behind them all the way from London. Apparently a marquess could not enjoy a holiday by the sea without his French chef, who required an army of scullions, as well as his valet, a couple of housemaids, a brace of footmen, and Ponsonby to preside over them all. Not to mention Nancy, who was riding in the coach containing, to her chagrin, the other female members of staff.

Lord Rawcliffe inspected the whitewashed front of the row of cottages with faint disdain. 'I am sure,' he said witheringly, 'that you did your best, in the short space of time I gave you to procure something. Shall we inspect our lodgings?' He held out his arm to help her from the carriage and led her to the middle of the three blue-painted front doors.

It opened into a small hall, from which a staircase ran straight to the upper floor. There were chipped and dented doors to both right and left, leading to small reception rooms, one of which contained armchairs and a sofa, the other one being fitted up as a dining room. Both of them had views straight down the hill to the bay.

Upstairs there were two more rooms. But unlike the layout downstairs, where the rooms were on either side of the stairs, up here, one faced the front, and one the back. She paced to the window of the front bedroom from which she could see little boats dotted about a harbour. Men bending over fishing nets, which were spread out in all directions. Cliffs, which spread out like arms protecting the bay from harm. And beyond that, in a great, grey, sparkling silken sheet, the sea.

'I take it,' said Rawcliffe in that dry, sarcastic tone he'd been employing ever since she'd betrayed how excited she was to be coming to the seaside for the very first time, 'you would prefer to have the use of this bedroom?'

She would prefer them to share this room. To lie all night in his arms and wake up feeling… cherished.

But it was no use wanting the impossible.

So she smiled. 'Yes, please.'

He shrugged. 'As you wish, my dear.'

She watched the stiff set of his shoulders as he strolled out of the room. And wondered, which was the real Lord Rawcliffe. The one who spoke so cuttingly? Or the one who did such kind, unselfish things?

Chapter Sixteen

'Well, now that is settled, shall we go and explore and see if we can discover what passes for entertainment in this hamlet?' Rawcliffe was already out on the landing, holding out his arm, practically demanding she place her hand upon it and follow him.

But for once, she had no desire to argue with him. She *wanted* to go and explore this quaint little town, especially the parts which bordered the sea. And, since Nancy was starting to show signs of regarding her wardrobe the way a dragon did its hoard, she was going to be better off getting out of the way while the maid unpacked and arranged her room anyway.

First of all they went down the lane which led from practically their front door to the harbour. When they reached the harbour wall, Lord Rawcliffe surprised Clare by placing his hands round her waist and swinging her on to its roughened lip, which was broad enough to stand on.

'You will get a better view from up here,' he said prosaically as he climbed up beside her. And, while she wrestled to conceal the way his touch had made her pulse flutter, she noted that what he'd said was true. From this vantage point she did have a splendid view of the many boats moored beneath them, as well as a small, pebbled beach which featured a few large rocks draped with seaweed.

'I believe,' said Lord Rawcliffe, whipping out a handkerchief and pressing it to his nose, 'that fishing boats, and all that appertains to them, are more agreeable from a distance.'

Clare giggled. And reached over to squeeze his free arm. Nothing was going to dim her pleasure in this experience, certainly not her husband's fastidious manners.

He stiffened. Looked down at her with an inscrutable expression on his face. After a moment or two of studying her, appearing perplexed by her good humour in the face of his own displeasure, he leapt down from the wall and held out his hand to her. 'Come,' he said, inviting her to scramble down to the road. 'Let us walk up the hill and explore the rest of the hamlet. I believe that the air up there will be less malodorous, since there appears to be a land breeze.'

'Very well,' she said, smiling up at him. 'Though it looks as though it's a bit more than a hamlet to me.'

'It was merely a fishing village until quite recently,' he said, turning his back on the picturesque little harbour, 'when the craze for sea bathing, and exploring scenic, wild parts of the countryside, gripped the minds of those with money to spend.'

It was proving far harder to climb back up the hill in the direction of their lodgings than it had been to go down. Yet her husband was managing to carry on talking as though he was just out for an afternoon stroll. He must be incredibly strong. Well, she knew he was, since she'd had the privilege of running her hands all over his muscular body on several occasions. 'I am told,' he continued in a dry tone that showed he was completely oblivious to the direction of her thoughts, 'that the place now boasts an inn with pretensions to being a hotel, in that it has an assembly room, library, reading room and what-have-you.'

'An assembly room? Does that mean there might

be balls? Or,' she hastily added, in case he thought she was becoming flighty, 'or concerts?'

'In what they consider their high season, yes to both,' he said with a grimace of distaste. 'Fortunately for us,' he said as he turned into a street which ran parallel to the coast, rather than continuing any farther up the hill, 'that season does not commence until July.'

'Oh.' Not for another week or so. She darted him a glance. He'd got that cold, forbidding expression on his face again. And was ignoring everyone who happened to be in what appeared to be the main street. Plenty of whom, she suddenly noticed, were openly staring at them. She'd been able to understand the townsfolk's curiosity when their cavalcade had driven through this same street earlier, but it seemed rather rude of them to stare now that they were on foot.

'You'd think they'd never seen holiday makers before, from the way they are gawking at us,' she said.

He gave her a bitter smile. 'This, my dear, is what it is like to be a peer of the realm in an out-of-the-way place such as this. We are providing entertainment for the rustics who are normally starved of the sight of anyone more interesting.'

She blushed as one of the rustics, who happened to be passing, clearly heard what he was saying and scowled. Not that her husband was making any attempt to keep his voice down.

'I am sure there are plenty of interesting people who visit such a beautiful town,' she said, in an effort to counteract his insult by praising the town, 'especially in high season. Why, I'm sure it must be extremely popular.'

'Only with people from the merchant classes,' he said witheringly. 'Or so I am reliably informed. This is not, by any means, a fashionable resort.'

She grew a little indignant at his dismissal of what appeared, to her, to be a perfectly charming little place. 'So, why have you brought me here? Oh.' She flinched as one reason struck her very forcibly. She wasn't up to snuff. She wasn't fit to be seen upon his arm anywhere like Almack's, for example.

Although…no, that couldn't be right. He'd wanted her to step straight into London society and ignore whatever anyone might say or think about her. He'd only relented because she'd asked him—no, thrown a tantrum at the prospect of mingling with titled people.

Was this his idea of the kind of place where she'd

be content? Mingling with the merchant classes? Or, at least, the kind of people who relied on the merchant classes in the high season?

He glanced down at her.

'I don't know what you are thinking, but to judge from the various expressions flitting across your face, you have not as yet correctly deduced why we are here, precisely.'

'Well, no, I can't say that I have. Though it is a very lovely town,' she said, waving with her free arm at the street along which they were strolling and the bow windows of the various shops they were passing. 'It appears to have more, and better, shops than Watling Minor.'

'That is hardly difficult,' he said scathingly.

'No, but even if the harbour is a bit pungent, I am sure I shall enjoy sitting and watching the comings and goings from my window. I noticed someone had set a chair there. I expect other visitors have done the same as I plan to do.'

'Yes,' he said shortly. 'The fact is...' he said and then took a breath. His hesitation was so unchar- acteristic that she darted a look at his face and caught what appeared to be a troubled frown on his brow. 'The reason I picked this particular fish- ing village, out of all the others I might have taken you to, is that,' he said, pausing to clench his jaw, 'it is so very close to Lesser Peeving.'

'What?' Lesser Peeving? The village where Clement now lived? The place her brother had described as the back of beyond?

'Yes,' he continued in a lazy drawl. 'I thought you would be pleased. I have already made arrangements for us to visit your brother, in a day or so.'

'But, but, you…you…' He disliked Clement. And the feeling was mutual. 'Why?'

He gave a shrug with one shoulder, as though the animosity which had festered between the two men for so many years was of no account.

'He is the only one of your brothers who actually did anything for you, when you were left in such a vulnerable position, after your father's demise. For that reason, do you not think that I ought to make an attempt to…ah…go and thank him? On your behalf? And explain why it is that you have not, in fact, taken up the post he arranged for you? I am sure that there were questions arising from your apparent disappearance.'

'Oh, I thought of that and wrote to explain what had happened straight away, so that he wouldn't worry.'

'You did?' He went very still. 'When, precisely?'

'Oh, as soon as Lady Harriet could spare me and I could get my hands on some paper.'

'Has he replied to that missive?'

'Well, no, but then none of my brothers is very good at replying to any of the letters I write to them. They are all very busy men.' She paused, as a vision of her husband wading through his immense pile of correspondence flashed into her mind, along with the certainty that none of her brothers ever had to deal with a fraction of the amount of work he did. 'And besides, he may very well be…' She trailed off, biting her lip. Knowing Clement, he would be mad as fire with her for getting into such a serious scrape she had ended up having to get married. And, what was worse, to a man he heartily detested.

'You expect him to be displeased with you.'

She nodded.

'Then it is as well I have taken steps to…mend fences with him, is it not?'

'You…you have truly come all the way down here, just so that we can…' Her vision blurred as emotion moistened her eyes. 'You have deliberately exposed yourself to…the kind of attention you particularly dislike, from people you consider vulgar, for…for my sake?' She recalled the way he'd wrinkled his nose before pressing the hand-kerchief to it, the disdain in his eyes as she'd rhap-sodised about the shops, the assembly rooms, the chances of hearing a concert. 'Oh, R-Rawcliffe, that is, truly, the most…' And then words failed her. This proud, proud man had taken the first step to restoring links to her brothers which had looked precariously as though they might have been sun-dered completely, given the way they felt about him. A huge rush of emotion flattened her inhibi-tions. She couldn't help flinging her arms about him and giving him a hug.

'Oh, thank you, thank you,' she breathed into his chest. 'You cannot know what this means to me. I had quite accepted the fact that I would probably never have anything to do with any of them again, but now…'

She stopped as he gripped both her arms and set her back, quite forcibly.

'Don't,' he barked.

'I b-beg pardon,' she began, looking up into his face, expecting to see an expression of censure blazing from his eyes.

Instead, she caught a look of what appeared to be anguish. Or guilt.

No, she must be mistaken. He must be angry with her for making a scene in a public street, when everyone was already looking at them as though they were some sort of sideshow, that was what it was.

The expression only lasted for a fraction of a second, anyway. For now his face was a mask that could have been carved from ice.

'Calm yourself,' he said sternly. 'My wife should not make an exhibition of herself in a public street.'

'Not even if she has just discovered something wonderful?'

'Especially not then,' he bit out. 'Because far from doing anything the slightest bit wonderful, I have—' He shut his mouth with a snap. 'Just remember your station in life. You are not some vicar's daughter, for whom nobody cares, any longer. You are *my wife*. And as such, should make more of an effort to maintain a dignified appearance.'

She recoiled.

'Dignified,' she repeated. 'Yes, I see. You want me to try to behave in a more dignified manner.'

'Precisely.' He gave her a cold look. 'Now, do you think we might continue on our way? I should like to look in at the reading rooms and take a cup of coffee. Since you were so fired up to come out and explore, you did not give me any chance of taking any refreshment in our own lodgings.'

'I do beg your pardon,' she said stiffly, all her pleasure leeching away as though he'd just tipped a bucket of icy water all over her. 'By all means, let us go and take a cup of coffee, my lord,' she said. And then stuck her nose in the air and stalked off in the direction they'd been headed before.

Chapter Seventeen

It wasn't long before they reached a market square. The Three Tuns took up one entire side of it. A rather inexpert layer of stucco had been pasted over extensions to the original building and if she hadn't been so annoyed by the way he'd just spoken to her, she would have agreed that it did look rather pretentious.

But nothing, now, would force her to agree with his opinion, about *any*thing. There was no need for him to speak to her in that odiously condescending manner. She needed to be dignified, indeed! Why, for two pins she'd…

Hang on a minute, though. Earlier on, when she'd told him she wasn't ready to go into society because she didn't know enough about the proper etiquette, he'd told her that he wanted her to be *herself*. That she had no need to worry about what anyone else thought. So why was he now saying exactly the opposite?

She ran over the content of both conversations as they crossed the market square. During the one about Almack's he'd been trying to comfort her when she'd confessed to feelings of inadequacy. But just now, he'd acted as though she was letting him down by hugging him in the street. Which was inconsistent, to say the least.

It made her feel as if she'd tried his patience to the limit. That so far, he'd been remarkably forbearing, considering, but that hugging him in the street had been the last straw.

Although, he hadn't minded when Betsy Woodly had hung off his arm, had he? What was it—different rules for wives than mistresses?

She got a sudden, vivid image of him holding a naked Betsy in an affectionate embrace. It brought such a sharp pang to her chest that she almost gasped out loud.

'Is something amiss? Have you turned your ankle?'

She realised she'd stumbled slightly under the weight of her jealous image of how he'd been with Betsy, or how she imagined he'd been, all those years ago.

'No, I…' He was looking at her with concern. Genuine concern.

Which confused her. How could he have been so patient and kind when she'd punched him, then act so cold and cutting when she hugged him?

Was this really how marriage was going to be? Tiptoeing round her husband the way she'd had to tiptoe round her own father's increasingly erratic temper? At least she'd been able to see her father's moods brewing, and had known, for the most part, how to deflect them. But Rawcliffe's behaviour made no sense to her at all.

'It's nothing,' she said. 'The cobbles are a bit uneven, just here, that's all.'

'Hmm,' he replied, looking unconvinced.

But he didn't pursue the matter.

Well, he wouldn't. Because he would understand her need to guard her own thoughts, since he guarded his own so carefully.

She glanced up at his face as they mounted the single step and passed into the portico of the Three Tuns. It was set in the expression he normally wore. Shuttered. As though determined to keep everyone from guessing what he was thinking, or feeling.

As though determined to keep everyone at arm's

length. Instead of being open and friendly, he would put on a disdainful look and use a mocking tone of voice, and give anyone who tried to encroach upon him the most severe put-downs.

Which made many people think he was a horrible person. But he wasn't. A horrible person would not have married a woman who'd punched him, nor made any attempt to reconcile with her brother, which could only be for her sake, because Rawcliffe detested Clement and made no secret of it.

No, he was not horrible, he was just...guarded. He wrapped his dignity and consequence round him like some kind of protective shield. As though he couldn't bear to let anyone close to him these days.

And he *was* consistent in that.

When he'd heard that Mr Kellet had died, he sort of withdrew into himself, after that one, brief moment when she'd seen he'd really been devastated by the news.

From there, it was but a small step to see that it was whenever she'd started to act affectionate towards him, that he'd done something, or said something, to make her fly into the boughs, effectively re-establishing some distance between them and also enabling him to retreat with his dignity intact.

Even having Mr Slater ride with them in the carriage on what should have been their bride trip had been a way to preserve some distance from her.

And that fit in with the way he got up immediately after they'd had conjugal relations. At the very moment when she felt as if they'd really become one flesh, one person, and wanted to hug him and get closer in an emotional way.

But why? Why did he need to go to such lengths to keep her at arm's length? What did he think he had to fear from *her*? From drawing close to her?

She sighed. It was becoming increasingly obvious that she was going to have to be the sensible one in this relationship. Men were such babies when it came to their emotions. She ought to know, having had to nurse the tender sensibilities of three brothers and a father, who all threw tantrums over the most ridiculous and imagined slights on a regular basis.

Although, to be fair, so far she was the one who'd done the tantrum throwing in this relationship. Whenever he made her feel shut out, she'd practically flung herself at the barriers and tried to batter them down. She'd flung herself at him in the street just now, too, though for a different reason.

Well, she'd just have to stop doing that if it made

him uncomfortable. And accept it when he pulled away with such vehemence that it felt like a slap in the face. And then, perhaps, once he began to realise she wasn't going to demand anything he wasn't prepared or able to give, she decided as they passed through the open door into an airy hallway, he might not feel the need to be quite so nasty.

'Welcome to the Three Tuns, sir, madam,' said a man she guessed must be the landlord. He was extremely neatly dressed. In fact, he looked more like a butler than the keeper of a large inn.

Ah, yes, but hadn't Rawcliffe told her that they wanted visitors to think of the place as a hotel nowadays? That was why he'd tacked on a reading room and an assembly room, and, according to a sign hanging over a doorway to the right of the hall, a library and gift shop, too. And that was why this man was dressed the way she suspected managers of hotels dressed.

'Would you care to sign the visitors' book?' he said, indicating an immense leather-bound ledger, situated on a waist-high shelf under the stairs. 'We do like to know who is staying in Peacombe, so that we can apprise you all of the events planned during your stay and facilitate your enjoyment of all that Peacombe has to offer.'

Clare winced. If there was one thing Rawcliffe disliked it was drawing attention to his movements so that 'vulgar' persons could come and stare. At least, that was the reason he'd given her for not putting an announcement of their marriage in the papers.

So it came as a shock when he calmly followed the manager across to the stairs and added his name to the list of previous visitors, rather than giving him a sharp set-down.

The manager, too, appeared to have sustained a shock when he read her husband's name.

'My lord,' he wheezed, as though all the breath had just left his lungs in a rush. 'I am afraid we have very few notable people staying at present. Nobody suitable for introductions...'

Which immediately put her out of charity with him. For she knew very well that nobody notable *ever* stayed in Peacombe. It simply wasn't fashionable enough.

'And the season has not really begun. The first concert is not planned for several weeks, and as for dancing...'

'It is of no consequence,' said Rawcliffe dismissively. 'We have not come here to attend balls or concerts, but to enjoy the walks and the views.'

Had they? Well, that was news to her. Especially since he'd told her he'd chosen Peacombe because of its proximity to Clement. But then, he wouldn't want to share that bit of information with a virtual stranger, would he?

'The walks and the views are indeed excellent,' said the manager with evident relief. 'This part of the coastline, with its rugged cliffs and sweeping moorlands, has vistas second to none. The cliffs, angled as they are, also shelter Peacombe from the most intemperate weather. And of course,' he cleared his throat, 'the Three Tuns is open to serve refreshments whenever you desire. Please, do come and see the facilities we have to offer the discerning traveller,' he said, bowing and making a sweeping gesture with one hand. As Rawcliffe nodded in acceptance of the invitation, the man set off along a corridor that led them deeper into the bowels of his architectural abomination.

'We take the London newspapers,' said the manager over his shoulder, 'and a selection of all the best periodicals for the edification and amusement of our visitors.' With a triumphant sort of flourish, he flung open the door of what looked to Clare exactly the way she imagined the interior of a gentleman's club would look. It was all leather chairs and little tables piled with various periodicals, and a hearth containing a gently smouldering fire which made her want to remove her coat and bonnet straight away.

'Coffee, tea, chocolate?' The manager looked from one to the other as he ran through the beverages on offer.

'Ale, for myself,' said Rawcliffe, strolling over to one of the tables and flicking open the topmost newspaper as though he couldn't wait to start reading it.

'My lady?'

'He means you, my dear,' said Rawcliffe after a short interval.

'Oh, yes, um, tea would be lovely,' she said, her cheeks burning. She made for the fire which gave her the opportunity to give her prickly husband the distance he so obviously needed to preserve, pulled off her gloves and held out her hands to the fire as though warming them was the sole reason she'd gone there.

But she could feel him, watching her. Waiting, no doubt, for her to turn round and launch into a barrage of complaints about the way he'd just rebuffed her, in the street.

Well, for once, she wasn't going to do any such

thing. He wanted to keep her at a safe distance, physically as well as emotionally? Fine!

She'd give him distance.

And plenty of it.

Rawcliffe kept on mechanically turning the pages of the day-old newspaper, though he wasn't taking in a single word printed below the date. He was aware of nothing but Clare. Clare, who'd stalked across the room to the fire so that she could stand with her back to him, under the pretext of warming her hands.

Clare.

He could still feel the imprint her arms had seared into his treacherous back when she'd flung them round him. Because he'd told her a pack of lies about his reasons for coming to Peacombe.

If she knew, if she only knew…

But she didn't. Nor did she understand why he'd flung her from him with such horror. She couldn't know that, once again, she'd rewarded him when he least deserved it.

And now she was standing on the other side of the room, with her back to him, confused and hurt, and desperately trying to hang on to that fiery temper of hers, because he'd just told her he wanted her to behave in a *dignified* manner.

When what he wanted... He sucked in a deep breath as a stunning truth blazed into his awareness.

She was trying to behave the way he'd said he wanted.

And she'd flung her arms round him, with every indication of feeling some affection for him.

Even though he'd treated her worse than a whore, bedding her with all the finesse of a sailor on shore leave, then leaving her sprawled naked in her bed as he stalked off to his own. Night after night.

When all he wanted to do was roll her to his side and hold her. Tight. All night long. And wake up with her. So that she would be the first thing he saw every morning.

And then she sniffed.

He glanced over his shoulder to see her furtively brushing something away from her cheek.

Dammit, he'd made her cry.

Which was unforgivable.

'Clare,' he said. 'Don't cry.'

'I'm not crying,' she said defiantly.

'Of course not.' He abandoned any pretence of being interested in the newspaper and walked across to where she stood, her back resolutely turned in his direction.

What was he doing? Pushing her away in an effort to prevent himself from being hurt when she eventually spurned him? Which meant that *she* was the one being hurt.

And then she sniffed again and the decision was made for him. Whatever the outcome for himself, she deserved better. Much better. And, anyway, hadn't he survived the last time she'd spurned him? And he was no longer a callow youth with delusions that he could find true love. He was a man.

A man who couldn't stay away from his wife for one second longer.

Chapter Eighteen

'Clare,' he said, laying one hand tentatively on her shoulder. 'I…that is…there was no need for me to have been so brusque with you just now.'

She turned to face him and lifted her chin. 'Well, I should not have…flung myself at you in the street like that, should I? I am not surprised you lost your temper with me. I know I am not the wife you would have chosen, but I do want to be the best wife I can be and, if you do not like me to—'

He couldn't stand there letting her try to shoulder the blame when absolutely nothing that had happened was in any way her fault. But nor was he ready to explain that she was the one who'd been forced into a marriage she hadn't wanted, not him. So he took the simple expedient of stopping her mouth with a kiss.

She gasped, but then melted into his embrace.

Though she didn't respond with the kind of eagerness he'd become used to. She didn't put her arms
round him, for a start. Because his reaction to her
hugging him had made her think he didn't want
her to. And she was trying to be the best wife she
could be. Because she was that kind of girl. Giving
and brave, and loyal to those she believed deserved
her loyalty. He only had to think of how loyal she'd
been to her selfish father and spendthrift brothers.
Their father's income had nearly all gone on providing them with an education, while he knew for
a fact she didn't even have a dowry worth mentioning. And even though they now all had decent
livelihoods, not one of them had come to her aid
when she'd needed it, apart from Clement. And
all he'd done was arrange for the kind of post that
only a truly indigent female should have to endure.
Yet not one word had she ever said against them.
Even when he'd caught her travelling on the public
stage, in a coat she'd clearly dyed herself because
they hadn't given her the funds to obtain decent
mourning garments.

She wouldn't ever utter a word of complaint
against him, either, no matter what he did. It would
go against the grain.

'Clare,' he murmured ruefully, closing his eyes

and leaning his forehead against hers. 'What am I to do with you?' He'd tried to prevent her from falling in love with him. Because he hadn't wanted her to give him her heart. He didn't deserve it. And he'd only break it when she found out what he was doing with her. He hadn't wanted to live with that on his conscience.

But that hug, just now, told him that she might already be starting to think she was falling in love with him. She wasn't one to do anything in a half-hearted fashion. Many women imagined themselves in love with a man once she'd gone to bed with him. Besides which Clare had such strong religious beliefs about the sanctity of marriage, she was bound to try to convince herself it was love driving her, rather than lust. It would be the only way her conscience would be able to deal with it.

He groaned. She was the one who was trying to do her best, while he kept on hanging back, like a coward. The least he could do was match her. So he finally did what he should have done earlier. He hugged her, hard. It felt like total surrender. But he was done wrestling with his conscience. From this moment on, he was just going to live with her the way he wanted to be able to live. As though they had chosen to marry each other because it was what they both wanted, with all their hearts.

It wouldn't last, of course. But he might have one day, or possibly two before it all came crashing down round his ears. Then at least when it all went sour, when this affection she was starting to feel for him turned back to antipathy, when she routinely performed her wifely duties with the air of a martyr rather than with startled pleasure, he could look back on this short interlude and be able to treasure the taste he'd had of what marriage to her could have been like. If only...

'Wh-what do you want to do with me?' She was staring up at him, confusion pleating her brow.

'Poor love, I haven't been much of a husband to you, up to now, have I?'

'Well, you didn't wish to be one, did you?'

He sighed. It was about time he owned up to some aspects of the truth. Aspects that might stand him in good stead when she learned the rest of it.

'I have wanted to marry you since you were about sixteen.'

Her mouth dropped open. 'No.'

'Yes. Did it mean so little to you, my first proposal, that you have forgotten it entirely?'

A frown flitted across her face. 'That day at the duck pond, you mean?'

'Yes. Not the most propitious of times to ask you, I admit. I am not surprised you turned me down.'

'Turned you down? That was…you were…serious?'

He nodded.

'But you were laughing your head off. I thought you were making fun of me.'

'No…' He'd never considered that might be a factor in her total rejection of him. 'Is that what you thought? Is that why you refused to let me court you?'

'Let you court…?' She frowned in evident confusion. 'What are you talking about? You never came near me again, during that visit to Kelsham Park.'

'Because I had been told you found my proposal offensive. That you would never lower yourself to receive addresses from a man with such lax morals. That—'

She gasped. 'No. I didn't. I mean, I might have thought it, but who could have told you that without even asking me first?'

'That response did not come from your lips? From your heart?'

'No! I thought you—'

He was doomed not to discover what she thought he'd done, because the landlord chose that moment to return with a waiter bearing a tray of refreshments. And Clare, predictably, took a step away from him, disengaging herself from his arms, her cheeks flushing pink.

He let her have her space. Even though what he wanted was to haul her back into his arms and smother her face with grateful kisses.

She hadn't rejected his proposal in that offensive manner. She hadn't even known he'd proposed, not in earnest. She'd thought he'd been mocking her...

Oh, good lord, what a coil.

He ran his fingers through his hair as he watched the landlord and waiter make a production of setting out Clare's tea things and a tankard and jug for him, along with a selection of delicately cut sandwiches and tiny cakes on a low table before the fire.

'While the weather is fine, my lord, my lady,' said the landlord obsequiously, 'might I suggest taking a walk along the newly laid gravel path which extends from the town end of the harbour along the shoreline...'

And as for this time, now he came to think of

it, not one of the reasons she'd given for trying to evade marrying him had to do with him or his morals. She'd kept saying she wasn't good enough. Hadn't got a title. Or any social address...

He half-heard the landlord wittering on about admission fees for various local attractions, while his mind was turning his whole life, since the day at the duck pond, upside down.

'You can drink from the source,' he suddenly heard the landlord saying, very clearly, 'for only a ha'penny a cup. The waters are, if I do say so, as beneficial to the health as anything you could procure from any of the more fashionable resorts.'

He grimaced. What the man meant, of course, was that they tasted as foul.

Though the landlord must have noticed his lack of interest, he would not stop.

'Another very good reason for making the climb is the ice house whose entrance lies there. You can descend via man-made steps into a series of caves which stay at a constant temperature all year round. Round these parts, many such caves are used to mature cheese...'

Cheese! Good God, what did he care for cheese? He'd just discovered Clare hadn't rebuffed him. That she had never believed the proposal had been made in earnest. It explained so clearly why, after that, she behaved as though he'd been guilty of insulting her. Because she'd thought he'd been mocking her.

'...but due to a unique combination of factors, our caves keep at a very low temperature and are therefore used to store snow, which is brought down from the moorlands in winter and naturally compacts into ice.'

Just as his heart had compacted into ice once he'd sworn he didn't need Clare, nor the comfort and warmth she represented.

'It sounds like an extremely unpleasant experience,' he said when the landlord paused to draw breath. 'Grubbing about in some dark and dingy caves.'

And he should know. All his encounters with women, after Clare's rejection, had become grubby, sordid little affairs. His expectations of the entire female sex sinking to such depths he'd even treated Lady Harriet, on their first meeting, with such disdain she'd lashed out at him with her riding crop.

'Well, since it is such a splendid day you might naturally prefer to visit the beach to the far side of the cliff gardens. It contains what I am told by experts is a most fascinating selection of shells and fossils. You may descend to the beach by means of steps, provided by our town council—'

'On payment of a fee?'

'The price is included in your ticket to the gravel walk,' said the landlord, oblivious to his sarcasm. Though Clare darted him a reproachful look.

'There is no sea bathing, unfortunately, because the beach shelves so steeply. And the large pebbles would hinder the progress of bathing machines. Besides which there are strong currents close in to the shore which make swimming inadvisable—'

Rawcliffe flinched. Mentioning those currents only brought his reason for coming here to the forefront of his mind. Archie's drowning. And the need to discover what the hell he'd been doing in the water when he couldn't swim. At all.

'If we had been interested in sea bathing,' put in Clare hastily, 'we would have gone to one of the resorts where it is advertised. Isn't that so, my lord?'

She was my lording him now? When before he'd rebuked her for hugging him she'd at least ventured as far as using his title.

'Well, then, you might like to know that you can obtain a spectacular view, over both ours and the neighbouring bay, from the cliffs which you can reach by walking across a short stretch of moorland which you can easily access from a track that runs behind the cottages you are renting. It is the kind of view any artist would wish to capture on canvas.'

'Should one happen to be staying nearby,' he said curtly, hoping that the fellow would understand his total lack of interest in art from the tone of his voice and cease pestering them.

'It sounds lovely,' said Clare, shooting him a dagger glance from behind the landlord's back. 'Thank you so much for telling us. A walk up to the cliff tops sounds just the thing.'

The landlord turned and bowed to her.

'And thank you so much for the lovely plate of cakes,' she continued, waving her hand in the direction of the table upon which the waiter had deposited them. 'And the tea.' She smiled. 'Just what I was wanting.'

'Shall I pour for you, my lady?'

'Oh, no, thank you. I prefer to let it steep for a minute or two. And I am sure you must be far too busy to be kept waiting upon us.'

And with one smile, and a polite little speech, Clare obtained the result he'd been unable to produce by glowering and being rude. The landlord bowed himself out of the room and left them to pour their own drinks.

'So,' he said, as she took a seat by the table and lifted the lid of the teapot to peer inside, 'where were we?'

She glanced at him as he took the seat opposite, her cheeks turning pink again.

'You were telling me that when you saw me emerging from the duck pond, dripping with slime and holding a bag of dead puppies in my arms, you were not in fact mocking my predicament, but actually making a genuine proposal of marriage.'

Put like that, it did sound unbelievable.

'Dead puppies? Was that what you'd been doing in the pond? Trying to fish them out?'

'You surely did not think I had been wading in it for my own amusement,' she replied snippily, replacing the teapot lid with a resounding clink.

'I... I did not really think of that aspect of it at all. You just looked so...'

'Ridiculous.'

'Adorable.'

'Covered in pond slime?'

He shrugged. 'To my eyes, all I could see was a naiad come to life.'

'A naiad,' she repeated with a scornful sniff. 'Had you, perchance, just emerged from a tavern?'

'I was not foxed! You were so…'

'Wet.'

'I was going to say beautiful.'

She pulled her lips into a flat line. 'You don't have to say things like that,' she said, averting her gaze as she reached for the milk jug.

He reached out across the table and stayed her hand.

'Somebody needs to say them. And who better than your husband?'

'I don't hold with the telling of falsehoods,' she said vehemently.

'I am not telling falsehoods. You are an extremely attractive woman, Clare.'

'Fustian!'

'It is no such thing.'

'But you never… I mean, the kind of women you took up with… I mean…' She glanced down at the front of her coat. And went an even deeper shade of pink.

'You don't have the more obvious attributes that attract the notice of young men who are just beginning to notice the difference between males and females, no. But you have something of far greater merit.'

'Oh? And what's that?' She lifted her chin in what looked like a combination of defiance and hope. As though she wanted him to pay her a compliment, but was braced to receive whatever else might come from his mouth next.

'You have character. You have integrity. You have—' he shrugged with one shoulder '—passion. You never hesitated to wade in on the side of anyone you thought was enduring persecutions or tribulations, no matter what anyone else did.'

'I...what do you mean? How could you know...?'

'I have always made it my business to know everything that occurs within all the estates for which I am responsible. And your name was always coming up in connection with good works of one sort or another.'

'You cannot have wanted to marry me because of my good works,' she said with a touch of scorn.

'No, I confess, I did not think of it until that morning I saw you emerging from the pond, your gown plastered to your figure, leaving nothing to the imagination, your eyes flashing defiance, your hair escaping its proper arrangement and snaking round your shoulders like damp flames.'

'You thought of marriage, because my dress was wet? And proposed on the spot?'

'I think,' he said, feeling a creeping impatience with her flat refusal to see the romantic aspect of what had, to him, felt like the fabled *coup de foudre*, 'that we have exhausted all there is to say upon this topic.'

'Oh, no, we haven't.' She sloshed some milk into her cup and slammed the jug down on the tray. 'You said you were in earnest about that marriage proposal when I've always believed you'd been making fun of me. And what's more, that you believed I'd turned you down, which means you must have spoken to somebody about it...'

Her father. But it wouldn't do to bring up that particular conversation now. She wouldn't appreciate him speaking his mind about the old buzzard. Not so soon after his demise. He'd learned his lesson on that score in Biggleswade.

He rubbed his nose. 'That, too, is a subject perhaps best left in the past. We are married now. Let us be content with that.'

She opened her mouth to make another protest. Thought better of it. Threw a couple of lumps of sugar into her teacup instead, her brow knotted in deep thought.

Dammit, had all the men in her life done nothing but abuse her trust? Even him? Hah—especially him.

Well, it was about time somebody made it up to her. Time he made it up to her.

'I have decided to give Slater the rest of the day off,' he said, as he poured himself a measure of the local ale. 'From now on, I am entirely at your disposal.'

She darted him a suspicious glance over the rim of her teacup.

'Would you like to take that walk the landlord recommended? Or, we could just take a leisurely stroll through the streets of this town and see what the shops have to offer.'

'Which would you prefer?'

'I should prefer it if you would tell me what would please you.'

She shifted in her seat, as though struggling with the notion that she could express her own wishes and he would abide by them. As though it was an entirely novel experience to have anyone ask her what she would like to do.

'If you wouldn't mind,' she said hesitantly, 'I think I should like to climb up through the moorland above our house and see if we can find that view he was telling us about.'

'Then that is what we shall do. As soon as we have done justice to these sandwiches. I would not like you to faint away with hunger in such a remote spot.'

Her face lit up as though he'd just presented her with a rare gift. Which pierced him to the core. A walk through rugged terrain to enjoy a view, that was all he'd promised her. And she was looking at him as though he'd done something generous.

When it wasn't generous in the least. It was nothing. Less than nothing.

And when she found out what they were really doing in Dorset, she'd no doubt say the same thing.

But still, he could give her today. Small compensation for all the grief he would soon be bringing her, but today was all he had.

He downed his ale with a deep sense of foreboding.

Chapter Nineteen

'Are you quite sure,' said Rawcliffe in apparent earnest, as they trudged up the steep track which started at the end of the lane that ran past their lodgings, 'that you would not prefer to part with a penny and clamber up through the enhanced series of terraces to drink, for a further ha'penny, a cup of turgid spring water?'

'No, no,' she replied with equal seriousness, though she was almost sure he was teasing. 'I am determined to enjoy the vista from the cliff top and dream of one day being able to capture it in oils.'

'Can you paint in oils?'

'I can barely paint in watercolour. My upbringing was not of the kind where idle pursuits were encouraged. However, from the way this turf is so closely cut down, and from the number of scrapes visible, I would say that there is a large population of rabbit up here.'

'The tunnels into the gorse bushes would tend to uphold your theory. Though what has that to do with painting the scenery?'

'Not a thing. I was just going to point out that I am more the sort of girl who would be able to dress a brace of rabbit, should anyone decide to snare them for me, and turn them into a savoury dinner.'

'Pierre would be extremely upset if you were to attempt to oust him from his kitchen.'

'Oh, I didn't mean I *wanted* to cook you a rabbit stew, particularly. Just that I could, if I had to.'

'You will never have to resort to skinning rabbits again,' he said firmly. 'Besides, I am not partial to rabbit stew. All those little bones.'

'I shall bear that in mind,' she said as he held out his hand to help her clamber over a particularly rugged jumble of boulders which lay in their path. As she took it, she couldn't help thinking about that remarkable statement he'd made. Had he really wanted to marry her when she'd been a mere sixteen years old? It was extremely hard to believe. Especially as he'd said he'd reached that decision because he'd seen her wading waist deep in muddy pond water with her hair coming down in rats' tails.

But if he hadn't meant it, why had he said it?

And why had he said all that about someone telling him that she would not countenance such a proposal? If he'd really approached Father, she could imagine him claiming that a betrothal was out of the question because she was too young. And counselling the young Robert Walmer, as he'd been then, to return, if he was truly in earnest, in a year or so at which time he might, possibly, consider granting him permission to pay his addresses. Or, if he hadn't approved of the match under any circumstances, simply telling him in no uncertain terms to take himself off.

What she couldn't believe was that Father would have claimed she'd asked him to turn the proposal down on her behalf.

Yet Rawcliffe's demeanour had changed since he'd told her that was what had happened. As if, having admitted he'd been...well, smitten with her, back then, he'd been able to lower part of the defensive barrier behind which he habitually hid himself.

But all her jumbled thoughts came skidding to a halt as they crested the last of the jagged boulders.

It was as if the land ended, not ten yards farther on. From that point onward, it was just the sea, extending as far as the horizon.

'My goodness, but the sea is big,' she said, reaching up one hand to hold on to her bonnet, which was making a bid to escape. Rawcliffe's hat, which did not have the additional security of being held in place by ribbons, leapt from his head as though flicked off by some invisible, mischievous sprite and went dancing gaily off into the blue.

'I believe,' he said sardonically, watching his hat make one sally up into the air, before tumbling end over end over the edge of the cliff, 'that this is what is described in the guide books as a bracing sea breeze.'

She giggled.

'There appears to be a sort of hollow over there,' he said, indicating a natural grassy amphitheatre with his ebony cane, 'that might be sheltered from the wind. Where we could sit and admire the view. If you like,' he added as though it was an afterthought. Although he knew full well that she wanted to admire the view. Was it really so hard for him to just admit he was trying to make her day as pleasant as it could be?

'What...' She faltered to a halt. She had no wish,

really, to shatter his current affable mood and revert to their more normal habit of squabbling by asking him any one of the many questions she had teeming in her brain. 'What a lot of ships,' she finished, inanely, gesturing out to sea, at the dozens of craft of all varieties, their sails sprinkling the grey backdrop with white, mirroring the tiny white clouds scudding across the sky above.

'I believe that just offshore, there is what is known as a road. Ships sailing from places such as Portsmouth, heading out to the Atlantic Ocean, will of necessity pass by this section of the coastline.'

'And all the little boats, bobbing about nearer the shore?'

'Local fishermen, at a guess. Checking their lobster pots and so forth. I do hope they are successful, since Pierre has promised me buttered lobster for dinner.'

'No wonder you turned your nose up at my offer of rabbit stew.'

One corner of his mouth twitched up in the semblance of a smile. It was a jerky movement, as though the muscles he used for the purpose had gone rusty.

'I suppose,' she said, heartened by the way he

appeared to be relaxing in her company, 'that we ought now to turn our attention to the harbour, since that is the view the landlord of the Three Tuns recommended.'

They both turned slightly to their left. She could, indeed, see the way Peacombe curved round the bay, at one end of which the locals had constructed a harbour wall. Farther away she could also see a waterfall tumbling down a cliff and, beyond that, another curve of steeply shelving pebbled beach.

'The harbour is definitely more agreeable from this distance,' he observed drily.

She breathed in deeply. 'The air up here smells like nothing I've ever smelled before. There is a tang to it, but it's not unpleasant. Though it still reminds me a bit of what we could smell down in the harbour.'

'It is the smell of the sea, I would guess. Or perhaps seaweed.'

'Well, whatever it is, I like it,' she declared. 'I could stay here all day, just breathing it in and watching the big ships out there, and the little ones closer in, and…just be.'

'If we are to stay up here for any length of time,' he said, 'then I suggest that we make ourselves comfortable in that hollow I pointed out to you before.' Once again, he indicated the grassy amphitheatre.

She laid her hand upon the arm he held out to her and they walked the short distance to the hollow.

'If I remove my coat, we can both sit upon the ground,' he said and promptly stripped it off, spread it out, sat down upon it, and held out his hand to invite her to join him.

'Thank you.' She couldn't help smiling at him as she took his hand for help to lower herself to the ground, where she arranged her legs as decorously as she could.

For a moment or two, it felt very awkward, sitting side by side, with him in his shirtsleeves.

'You are right,' she said, feeling a need to break down the walls she could almost feel him rebuilding round himself, brick by brick, the longer the silence continued. 'It is more sheltered here. And the view is still stunning.'

He made a sort of grunt, which she took to indicate agreement, since he was gazing fixedly out to sea as though he found the ships and the waves, and the few gulls battling against the invisible currents of air, utterly fascinating.

When for her, the most fascinating thing up here was him. Oh, how she wished she could just lean her head on his shoulder and slide her arm round his waist.

'The sound of the waves,' she said in a tone that even to her own ears sounded slightly panicked, 'sighing against the shore, over and over again, is really…soothing, isn't it?'

He turned to give her one of his enigmatic looks. She bit down on her lower lip and turned away. It was so galling that he could look at her as though he could see right down into the depths of her soul, somehow, whereas she could never tell what he was thinking. Ever. Even when he'd told her he'd been in earnest about proposing to her, all those years ago, she wasn't sure if she could believe it.

And coupled with their position, on top of the cliffs, with only the sky above them, and all that expanse of sea below, she felt very small. And in-significant. Just a tiny speck of humanity perched upon the very edge of the vastness of nature.

Which made her want to snuggle up against him even more. For comfort. And reassurance.

So naturally she sat up even straighter.

'The sound of the waves *is* very soothing,' he agreed with what looked like a glint of amusement in his eyes. 'In fact, it is so soothing, I scarcely know how to keep my eyes open.' So saying, he shifted round, then startled her by spreading out his legs in one direction and settling his head on her lap. 'You won't mind if I take a nap.' He sighed, closing his eyes.

Goodness.

'You…you are missing the view.'

'I have seen it,' he murmured drowsily. 'And now I am enjoying the sensation of feeling the breeze caressing my face and the sun beating down on my body, and the softness of your thighs beneath my head…'

'Stop that! You shouldn't mention my…'

'Thighs? Why not? They are very lovely thighs,' he said, reaching round to run the back of one hand over the curve of her bottom. Sending a surge of warmth and wetness to that place between her legs that seemed to belong to him in a very special way.

She didn't know what to do. They were outside. In broad daylight. Her mind flew back to his tryst under the hedge with Betsy. *She* hadn't felt the slightest bit inhibited by either the daylight or the venue. *She'd* bared her breasts for him. Hitched up her skirts, too.

She glanced over her shoulder. From where she was sitting she could see the upper windows of their lodging house. Which meant that anyone looking out could see them, too. If they had opera glasses trained in that direction.

What was wrong with her? How could she be thinking of doing…wickedness, out in the open, just because he'd laid his head in her lap and given her bottom a casual caress?

No, she couldn't possibly…

But perhaps she could just permit herself to run her fingers through his hair. It was something she'd wanted to do for a very long time. And she'd never quite dared to do anything so bold, not even when they'd been in bed together. But perhaps he wouldn't even notice out here. Now that his hat had blown away, he might think, if she stroked it very gently, that it was the wind ruffling his hair, nothing more.

Tentatively, she lifted her hand and just touched the crown of his head. His hair was springy, yet soft. He half-opened one eye and peered up at her quizzically. She held her breath, bracing herself against a caustic comment. For he never seemed to want to indulge in any behaviour she would regard as affectionate. And stroking a man's hair, as he lay with his head in her lap, most definitely came under that category.

'That would feel much better,' he said, eventually, 'if you were to remove your gloves.'

And then he closed his eyes again, freeing her to breathe out and then to remove her gloves and put them down on the grass at her side.

Stroking his hair with her bared fingers did indeed feel much better. And, since he'd pretty much given her permission to do it, she not only ran her fingers over his hair, but plunged them through the thick, springy softness.

After a while, he reached up and caught her hand, but only to kiss her fingers, one by one. Which sent lightning bolts of excitement winging all over her body.

Making her wish she could be as bold as Betsy Woodly. Because thanks to that afternoon she'd spent stuck halfway up Farmer Westthorpe's oak tree, she knew that he enjoyed, um, *sporting* with females in the open air. And now he'd brought her down to the ground, in this sheltered little spot, with the birds mewing overhead and the waves shushing dozens of feet below, she was starting to think she could see the attraction. It would certainly be a most elemental experience to feel the sun, and wind, upon naked skin.

She snatched her hand from his and pressed it

to her mouth. Good lord, what was happening to her? Thinking such wicked thoughts?

Such tempting thoughts.

'I have changed my mind,' she said. 'I think I would like to explore the walk and the gardens, and perhaps even the caves, as well.'

Chapter Twenty

It didn't help. Not even stumbling around in the chilly, gloomy caves had been able to damp down the feelings that he'd started up on the cliff top by laying his head in her lap. By telling her that he'd truly wanted to marry her so many years ago. Because that meant that all the snide things he'd said to her since, the way he'd mocked her and taunted her, hadn't stemmed from disdain, but thwarted desire.

By the time they returned to their lodgings her insides felt as though they were melting, and her blood was fizzing through her veins like champagne. She hadn't felt as ready for him, in a sexual way, since…

She shook her head. She'd never wanted him this much. Well, she'd never allowed herself to want him. At all. Not when she'd believed the attraction was one-sided. But now, oh, how she wished she could drag him into her room and tear off her clothes, and then his, and push him to the bed. Only Nancy was bound to be waiting in her room with a basin of water and her evening clothes laid out in readiness. As though she'd been watching out for her return. It wouldn't surprise her to learn that Nancy owned opera glasses which she used for just that purpose.

The thought of Nancy in possession of opera glasses acted on her like a glass of water to the face. She actually did splash her face with water some moments later, when she reached her room to find everything exactly as she'd foreseen. For Nancy was the kind of servant who prided herself on giving superlative service.

Clare washed herself briskly and went to the dressing table where she sat down with her back to the maid.

'You should have taken a parasol out with you,' said Nancy with a little shake of her head. 'Your cheeks have become quite pink in the sun.'

It wasn't the sun that was making her cheeks pink. Clare was pretty sure she was blushing all over.

'The wind would have blown a parasol away, if

I'd taken one up to the cliffs,' she retorted, irritated by Nancy's determination to 'improve' her. 'In fact, it did blow his lordship's hat away.'

'No!' Nancy giggled. For the first time since coming to work for her. As though she was a friend, rather than a maid.

And Clare saw that, actually, Nancy wasn't that much older than her. It was just the severe way she styled her hair and the sombre hue of her clothes that made her look so strict and stuffy.

She decided there and then she was going to stop resenting Nancy, who was only doing her job, after all. And doing it to the best of her ability, for a mistress who had such a temper she'd even thrown a room full of breakables at her groom on her wedding night.

She discovered that getting ready for dinner was not such an ordeal when she was chatting with Nancy rather than glowering at her in resentful silence. That Nancy could be good company when given just a little encouragement.

She even plucked up courage to smile and tell Clare that she would *take his lordship's breath away* when Clare hesitated on the point of opening the bedroom door to go down for dinner.

Clare lifted her chin and flung open the door.

She had no need to be nervous. So why was her stomach so full of butterflies? Why was she trembling so much she had to reach out and steady herself by using the banister rail as she went down the stairs?

Ponsonby was standing sentinel outside the battered door of the sitting room, so she knew Rawcliffe must be inside. As soon as she reached the hall, Ponsonby opened the door and, since the hallway was so narrow, stepped smartly to one side so that she could get past him.

Rawcliffe was standing by the fireplace, sipping a drink. He eyed her over the rim of his glass as she entered, in such a way that he made her feel as if he was considering having her for dinner, rather than buttered lobster. Which made her turn as pink as one. Which made him smile, in a slow, knowing kind of way that made her feel as if she was standing there stark naked.

Ponsonby cleared his throat. 'Dinner is ready, should you wish to take your places at table, my lord, my lady.'

'I suppose we better,' said Rawcliffe, setting his glass down on the mantelpiece and extending his arm to her, 'or Pierre would never forgive us. He has, so I believe, been labouring under extremely trying circumstances today.'

He had been talking to his chef? Or talking about his chef? She glanced up at him out of the corner of her eye. Perhaps she ought not to be surprised. He seemed to need to know exactly what was going on, in every corner of his dominion. No matter how trivial or insignificant the matter might appear to others.

The dining room was, in keeping with the rest of the cottage, not designed to accommodate two footmen and a butler, as well as tables and chairs. But rather than permitting them to dine informally, by setting all the dishes on the table at once and letting them serve themselves, Ponsonby received each dish at the door, returning emptied ones to the footmen who hovered there.

It really was a bit ridiculous, to have so many servants scurrying up and down the passage to the kitchen, with each remove, so that she and her husband could dine in state, in what amounted to a glorified fisherman's cottage.

And yet Rawcliffe appeared to think nothing of it.

'Is the sauce not to your liking?' he enquired politely, making her realise she had been frowning at the river of cream Ponsonby had just poured over her lobster.

'I do beg your pardon, my lady,' said Ponsonby. 'I shall remove it at once.'

'No, no need. The sauce smells delicious,' she said, grabbing hold of her plate with both hands to prevent the solicitous butler from whisking it away. 'I was just thinking how very much trouble you must have all gone to, to produce such a… lavish meal, in what is only a tiny cottage, after all.'

'Chef has had to make use of all three kitchens available,' said Ponsonby gravely.

'Have you not noticed the amount of running up and down the lane behind the lodgings that has been going on all evening?' Rawcliffe arched one eyebrow at her as he signalled Ponsonby to bring the sauceboat round to his side of the table.

'Oh, dear, has there?' She hadn't noticed. She'd been far too busy fussing over her clothes and hair, and making friends with Nancy to notice what had been going on outside. 'It does seem like an awful lot of effort. For just the two of us,' she finished guiltily.

Ponsonby drew himself up to his full height and seemed to swell to twice his normal size.

'There is no excuse for lowering our standards of service to his lordship, simply because we do not have the facilities available to us in the town house. His lordship may be taking a holiday, but we,' he said repressively, 'are not.'

'Nevertheless,' said Rawcliffe, leaning back and twirling his wineglass by the stem, 'I hope that each of you will be able to take some time off while we are down here.'

'That is very good of you, my lord,' said Ponsonby, unbending a touch. 'I shall inform the staff and organise their leisure hours so that there will be no inconvenience to you, or her ladyship.'

'I don't doubt it,' said Rawcliffe tersely, 'or I would not have made the suggestion.'

Which made Clare wonder whether Rawcliffe or Ponsonby was the one being hardest on the servants. However, to show her appreciation, she made sure she sampled a little of every dish and sauce Ponsonby brought to table, declaring each one more delicious than the last. She actually had no need to pretend to marvel over the little spun-sugar baskets filled with fresh strawberries. They were works of art.

She was just beginning to wonder if her stay laces could withstand any more strain, when Ponsonby set a plate of cheeses on the table. 'Chef thought you might like to sample some local cheeses to finish with,' he announced.

Oh, thank heaven.

Rawcliffe cut a small piece from two of the truckles and placed them on his plate. She simply shook her head. Her stays had survived this far, but she wasn't prepared to test them any further. 'I couldn't eat another bite.'

Rawcliffe gave her a heated look across the cheese board. 'All the exercise, climbing up over the moors today, must have made you tired. Perhaps you would like to go up to bed?'

Oh, yes, she would like to go up to bed. It was just that she hadn't dreamed for a minute that he'd announce the fact to his butler. Who was smiling at her in a positively avuncular fashion.

'Oh...er... I...' she stammered.

'I shan't be far behind you,' said Rawcliffe, with the kind of look in his eyes that made her think of that time he had entered her from behind with animalistic fervour.

Blushing feverishly, she laid her napkin down beside her plate and allowed Ponsonby to hold her chair out for her as she got to her feet.

'I...er...goodnight!' She fled from the room and

went up the stairs in a far from dignified manner, shot into her bedroom and shut the door behind her, leaning on it for support. If he were to come in now, he could push her down on to her hands and knees, and find her ready to receive him. It was as if the whole day had been a slow, tortuous preparation for the moment when they could get to the bed.

There was a firm knock at the door which had her leaping from it with a guilty start, as though she'd been caught napping in church.

She opened the door, to find Nancy on the landing, a jug of warm water in her hands and a towel over her arm.

But just mounting the stairs, with a slow, deliberate tread, was Rawcliffe. And he was looking at her as though he felt about the same as she did. As though, if they didn't get their clothes off, and their hands on each other soon, he would explode.

'Thank you, Nancy,' he said tersely, taking the jug, basin and towel from the maid. 'I believe my wife will have no need of you tonight.'

Nancy grinned and dipped her head. As Rawcliffe stepped into the room and kicked the door shut behind him, she could swear she could hear the maid giggling.

Which was awful.

'Your servants will all know what we're about to do,' she protested. 'You might as well have issued a proclamation!'

He raised one eyebrow, then went across to the wash stand where he deposited the items he'd taken from Nancy. 'We are doing nothing we have not done every other night since our marriage,' he pointed out calmly.

'That's different. You didn't oust Nancy from the room with such…'

'Impatience?'

He stalked towards her, shucking off his jacket. 'But I am impatient. I feel as if I have been waiting for this moment all day.'

She gulped. And far from making any further protest, when he kissed her she flung her arms about his waist and kissed him back for all she was worth.

She could never hang on to a single rational thought once he started kissing her. It was as if he turned her into a creature who was all passion. She needed to feel skin on skin and to that end she began to burrow under his shirt. Just as he was burrowing under her clothes and tearing at fastenings to make their progress towards nudity as swift as was humanly possible.

She panted and moaned, and pressed herself up against him whenever he wasn't removing another layer of material. Whenever she wasn't clawing away the clothes he was wearing. She was naked well before he was. But then he had far more experience at getting females out of their clothes than she did at undressing men.

For a moment, that reflection dimmed her pleasure. But as if he sensed her withdrawal, he set his mouth to her neck and suckled on the tender spot beneath her ear that always made her knees turn to jelly.

And then he lifted her and...

Instead of carrying her to the bed, he coaxed her legs about his waist and slammed her up against the bedroom door.

Goodness. Could he possibly mean to...?

Yes, he did. He cupped her bottom and slid into her with a shocking proficiency that made her gasp. In shock, she told herself as she grabbed his head and speared her fingers though her hair. Not excitement.

Not excitement.

Not...

'Oh!'

Her fingers clenched into his hair and her legs tightened round his waist, as pleasure ripped through her like an explosion.

He groaned. Thrust into her just once more and experienced his own explosion of pleasure.

No, no, it couldn't be all over so quickly. He was going to put her down and go back to his own room. And leave her alone.

And it wasn't even fully dark outside. She could have wept.

'Clare,' he breathed into her neck. 'Don't tell me you regretted that. Admit it, you needed it as much as I did.'

'I…' She swallowed. 'Yes, I did,' she admitted. 'I am just…'

'Was I too rough? I thought you came to a spend?' He leaned back a little and looked into her face with a touch of what looked very much like concern.

'You weren't too rough. And I did…' She faltered, completely unable to use the words he could employ so easily.

'Thought so,' he said, his expression of concern turning to one of smug satisfaction.

She turned her head away. She felt so exposed,

having a conversation with him while he had her pinned to the door with her legs wrapped round his waist.

'Do you think you could put me down now?'

'Absolutely not,' he said, taking a step back and walking across to the bed, with her still wrapped round him like coat.

Where he manoeuvred them both down on to it, still locked together. 'There,' he said, flexing his hips against hers. 'Isn't this better?'

'I…' She felt a blush heating her cheeks. Because he was still quite firm. 'I thought you…'

'Oh, I did. But now I find I'm ready for more. Are you not?' He teasingly ground his hips against hers.

Well, she hadn't wanted him to leave. And if this was what it took to keep him in her bed, then…

Oh, who was she fooling? She wanted more, just as much as he did. Shutting her eyes, she ground back up against him and dug her heels into his bottom.

'I shall take that as a yes,' he growled.

And this time, he took it much more slowly.

Chapter Twenty-One

She fell asleep immediately. Which meant he didn't have to explain anything.

Which was perfect, as far as he was concerned.

He could just cradle her in his arms while she slept. Gaze down at her piquant little face and commit every plane, every curve and every freckle to memory.

She stirred in her sleep once or twice, and he let her wriggle round until she'd found a more comfortable position. And then, when she'd settled, he hooked one leg over her to prevent her sliding away from him should he happen to doze off himself.

But she didn't slide away while he slept. Instead, when he woke, it was to find she'd snuggled closer, as though unconsciously seeking his warmth, though it wasn't a cold night. He blessed the moonbeams that were streaming in through the window, since nobody had got round to drawing the curtains, for they'd woken him to a moment he would always treasure.

Her, snuggled trustingly against his chest as though…

The moment shattered. Something woke Clare, the moonlight striking their shared pillow, or some subtle movement of his, he couldn't tell.

What he did know was that she was now as tense as a plank within the circle of his arms. As though wondering what on earth he thought he was doing, holding her so tightly. And what she was going to do about it.

He held his breath as he awaited her verdict.

But when she sighed in what sounded to him like a very martyred fashion, he decided that if she wanted him to leave, tonight, then she was damned well going to have to tell him outright.

He waited for her to say something. When she didn't, he found he couldn't bear the suspense.

'Are you awake?' he murmured into her ear.

She still said nothing. Though he could almost hear her thoughts flitting through her head. Was she considering the correct way to dismiss a husband from her bed? Or…dammit! Never, in his whole life, had he wanted to know what a woman was thinking when she was in bed with him. But this was Clare. Who could tie him in knots with a sigh, a tilt to her shoulder and silence.

'You are awake,' he declared. 'So you may as well open your eyes and admit it.'

She turned her head then and by the light of the moon he could see a very determined expression settle over her features. As though she was steeling herself to face some kind of battle.

Which she wasn't, he promptly decided, going to win, not tonight. Not if it took every ounce of skill he possessed to seduce her into letting him be the husband he'd wanted to be all those years ago. Just for one night.

With what one of his conquests had termed his *I'm going to have my wicked way with you* smile, he gently tucked a stray tendril of hair behind her ear.

'I like your hair like this,' he said.

'What, in a mess?'

'Streaming across my pillow, rather than being confined in one of those braids you have insisted on adopting every night so far.'

'A braid is practical, at night.'

'It is not seductive, though. You should wear it loose, like this, in bed.'

Something nebulous flickered across her face. Something that looked...

'What thought has just crossed your mind?' he asked her. 'You got a very wicked look in your eyes. As though you were plotting mischief.'

'Perhaps,' she whispered, looping her arms round his neck, 'I was.'

'If it is the sort of mischief I am hoping it was,' he began, before pausing to kiss her, 'then I have to say...'

She turned in his arms and pressed her breasts into his chest. *She* pressed up against *him*. His heart started pounding so fast he felt dizzy with it. He swooped to her lips again and kissed her with all the finesse of a starving beggar falling upon a meat pie. He'd always known her fire would be able to warm the cold places in his soul. He'd never dreamed she'd be so hot they'd create steam.

After a few seconds, perhaps inevitably, she pulled away.

He braced himself for the recriminations.

'What,' she panted, 'were you about to say?'

'Say?' *She* wanted to know what *he* was thinking? 'Nothing of any consequence,' he replied. 'At least, it cannot have been because I have completely forgotten what it was.'

She wriggled against him, again, with a positively naughty look on her face.

No matter what else she thought of him, there was no denying she enjoyed doing this. And, it occurred to him, if he could take her to such heights that she fell asleep immediately after he finally finished with her, then he'd be able to remain in her bed without having to make any explanation at all about why he'd been so quick to leave it before tonight.

And so he paid great attention to detail. Kissing and caressing every inch of her alabaster skin. Running his tongue over the areas he'd already learned were particularly sensitive. Until she was moaning and writhing with need. At which point he honed in on the obvious target, flicking his tongue over her to tease her to the point where she was desperate for his penetration. Which he denied her. Not until she'd gasped out in surprised rapture. Not 'til he'd roused her to that same pitch all over again and she was almost sobbing with a mixture of exhaustion and frustrated need.

Only then did he slide up and into her, and give her all of himself.

His body, that was. He would never trust his heart to anyone, for them to stamp on and grind under their heels. The way she'd stamped on his when she'd…

Only she hadn't. Not intentionally.

Ah, what did it matter what had gone on between them before? When right now she was clinging to him, shuddering to her own completion in the same instant as him. Even when she slid almost immediately into oblivion, her arms and legs remained fastened round him as though she couldn't bear to let go. He buried his head in the crook of her neck, in the softness of her hair, breathing in the scent of her. Of their shared passion.

And wished it could always be like this.

Almost at once, it seemed to him, he woke to the cry of gulls. And the first rays of morning light drumming against his eyelids.

And the feel of her soft bottom pressed against his groin. And the dip of her waist, under his arm. And the fullness of her breast, cupped in his hand. It felt like heaven.

But how did she, prim little vicar's daughter, feel about waking to a man, with a man's most basic needs? When she didn't even want to let him keep a candle burning when he came to her bed at night? When she felt embarrassed and confused by the lust that flared between them in spite of all their years of antagonism for each other.

As if she was thinking along the very same lines, she stiffened in his arms.

He removed his offending hand from her breast and used it to brush her hair from her face, and tuck it behind her ear, so that he could kiss it.

'How are you this morning? I...' He faltered. It wasn't just her morals he'd violated, by forcing her into this marriage. He'd kept her body exercised practically all night long.

'I was abominably selfish last night,' he admitted. 'You must be quite...tender, after the way I used you.'

She stiffened even further, before turning in his arms to glare up at him.

'Used me? You did not use me,' she said fiercely. 'We shared a...that is—' she swallowed '—I enjoyed every moment of it.'

The reprieve was such a surprise it knocked the wind out of him. And then she surprised him even more, by putting her arms round him and hugging him. And planting a kiss on his bare chest.

'But I am grateful to you for being so considerate...in enquiring after my...that is, showing concern about me being...sore...when...honestly, I...'

She floundered to a halt on a fiery blush.

'You enjoyed *every* moment of it,' he couldn't resist teasing the top of her head, which was all he could see of her once she buried her blushing face in his chest.

She nodded.

'Even—' he ran one finger down the length of her spine until it reached the knot of nerve endings that had proved so sensitive to his explorations the night before '—even when I took you up against the door?'

There was a pause, as she squirmed with pleasure. But then she took a deep breath and nodded her head again.

'Hmmm...' Waking up with his wife wasn't proving to be as awkward as he'd anticipated, after all.

'What?'

'Well, perhaps now would be a good time to warn you that my appetite is...prodigious. And that I do like variety.'

Her head flew up. 'You mean, you want to have other women?'

'No.' His arms tightened round her. The thought of having any other woman, now he'd had Clare was almost abhorrent. 'I mean, I enjoy variety in...

the way I…' Their eyes met. And, to his amazement, he was the one who was squirming now, in response to her wide-eyed look of incomprehension.

How on earth had she managed to make him… *shy*…of speaking to her about…earthly delights? Carnal appetites. Dammit, she was now even making him censor his own *thoughts*, when before he'd married her he'd had no trouble whatsoever in describing it exactly as it was. In good old Anglo-Saxon terms.

'You mean,' she asked him, with an innocent expression in her eyes, 'that sometimes you would like to take me up against a door. And sometimes you would like to take me from behind, while I am on my hands and knees?'

God, yes! But…he swallowed. Searched her face for signs of revulsion, or rejection. Instead, he perceived a glint of humour lurking in her eyes and making the corners of her mouth twitch with suppressed laughter. The little minx! She was teasing him. Almost daring him to try to shock her.

So he decided it was about time he took back control.

'Precisely,' he said in as clinical a voice as he could muster, given his very, very aroused state.

'And right now,' he declared, rolling to his back whilst keeping hold of her, so that she ended up lying on top of him, 'I would like you to ride me.'

'R-ride you?'

Ah. That had put her off balance again. As did the way he took hold of her thighs, arranging them on either side of his legs, before pushing her into an upright position, so she could have no doubt about what he meant.

'B-but that means…' She faltered, lifting her hands to cover her breasts. He took hold of them gently, but firmly, and moved them out of the way.

'Yes, it means that I can see you. All of you. And not just your breasts. But your face, as you enjoy me.'

'I… I…' Her face went bright red. She twisted her lower lip, biting down on it in delightful confusion.

But she was also wriggling her hips experimentally as he grew harder beneath her. He thought he actually saw the moment it occurred to her that in this position, she had a good deal more power than she'd had thus far, in bed with him. And that the possibilities intrigued her.

But before she had time to feel guilty for her very natural desire to explore those possibilities, he reminded her that he had chosen this. That he was only permitting her the illusion of being in charge.

By gripping her hips and encouraging her into movement.

'Like this,' he said, showing her what he meant.

She rocked against him, tentatively, but obligingly. 'That's it,' he said, letting go of her hips to stroke his way up her flanks. 'Take your pleasure of me…'

They slept again after that. At least, she did. She sort of dived off him after and buried her blushing face in the pillows so that she didn't have to look him in the eyes.

His shy bride. He caressed the length of her spine idly as he recalled the way she'd ridden him like a stallion. With her head flung back, her wild red hair tumbling all over her shoulders. And the cry she'd made, when she'd finally reached her peak.

'Ah, Clare,' he murmured, kissing the nape of her neck. She grumbled in her sleep and made a faint movement with one hand as though she was brushing off a pesky fly. He chuckled and slid across the bed so that he could press his whole body up against the entire length of hers.

And then slid into a light doze. Feeling like the luckiest man in the world.

It was somebody knocking on the bedroom door that shattered that feeling. A feeling he might have known wouldn't last.

But even so, he couldn't keep the irritation from his voice when he bid whoever it was who was knocking to enter.

It was his voice, rather than the knocking on the door, which roused Clare. But when Nancy came in, Clare gave a little squeak and pulled the covers up over her head. As though she had something to be ashamed of.

He ground his teeth.

'Begging your pardon, my lord, my lady,' said Nancy, keeping her gaze fixed firmly on the foot-board, rather than the occupants of the bed, 'but there has been a man come to the house saying that if you still wish to take the trip in his boat you mentioned, then you won't find better conditions than what he expects today. And then he said a lot of things about wind direction and tides and so forth which none of us understood. But he was most insistent, he was, that if you wanted to take your trip, then you would need to be down by the harbour within the hour. And we did leave you as long as we could, but Slater said as how you'd gone to a lot of trouble to arrange this trip, so it must be important, and so...'

'Yes.' Yes, it was important. It was the whole reason they'd come to this benighted little hamlet rather than go somewhere with some real facilities, like Weymouth.

And it would spell the end of any more nights like last night.

But he had a duty to investigate the circumstances surrounding Archie's death. And to avenge him, if it turned out that foul play had been involved. No matter who was behind it.

'Yes, thank you, Nancy,' he said as calmly as he could, considering a part of him wanted to howl and pull the covers up the way Clare had done, and bury his face in all that soft hair and let the rest of the world, and all his responsibilities go to blazes.

But that wasn't who he was.

'We will get up now,' he told himself sternly, as well as informing the maid of his intentions. 'Bring her ladyship a can of water and get Cadogan to take some to my room. And have a light breakfast ready for us when we come down.'

Nancy bobbed a curtsy and left.

And since he wasn't the type of man to let the

world know when he was hurting, he smacked Clare playfully on the bottom, before rolling out of bed.

'You heard, sleepyhead,' he said. 'We need to be down at the harbour to catch the tide within the hour.'

'Do we,' she replied crossly, sticking her head up above the covers, 'really want to catch the tide?'

'If you want to go and visit your brother, we do.' And then, because it might be the last time she would ever be this receptive to him, he bent down and kissed her, one last time, with every atom of his being. Bidding her farewell in the only way he could, without words.

And then, since the tide waited for no man, not even a marquess, he tore his lips from hers, and strode to the door.

To face whatever the day had in store.

Chapter Twenty-Two

Clare looked at the small ketch he'd hired to ferry them along the coastline to Peeving Cove as though she suspected it of plotting to leap out of the water and bite her at any moment. He was experiencing a similar feeling. Not about the boat itself, but what was going to happen once it had brought them to their destination.

'I regret the boat is only a simple craft,' he said. 'But I have been led to believe it is the most suitable one available.' The only one available, in point of fact. No other fisherman in the area was prepared to take strangers into the lair of 'The Gentlemen', which was the way they spoke of Peeving Cove. They were afraid of reprisals.

Only the captain of this boat, who was now standing on the deck wringing his cap between his gnarled and weather-beaten hands, had been willing to take the risk. And that only after having been paid one hundred pounds.

'For that amount,' he'd said, 'I c'n buy myself a new boat, if'n the gennlemen scupper this old wreck. So long's as I'm not on it when they sink it,' he'd added gloomily. 'And as fer going fer me family, as a warning to others, well, I've only the wife and the lad left. And the lad's damn near useless and I'm sick on the owld shrew's nagging ways, anyhow.'

And so the deal had been struck.

'Won't find a better craft to take you up Peeving Cove, ma'am,' said the fisherman. Or at least, that was how Rawcliffe interpreted the assortment of strangulated vowels that emerged from the whiskers obliterating the entire lower half of the man's face.

Clare apparently thought so, too.

'Oh, I'm sure it is a very fine ship,' she said earnestly. 'It is just that I have never been on one before, and I am—' she gave a little laugh '—a bit nervous.'

'Aar,' said the captain, with a shake of his head. 'Have reason, I reckon. Warned his lordship 'ow it'd be, only he would hire 'un.'

The captain had actually warned Rawcliffe about

the inadvisability of attempting to sail any sort of craft up the inlet which led to Peeving Cove, without first gaining permission from the smugglers whose lair it was. Clare, however, not knowing the first thing about the kind of company her brother was keeping these days, naturally assumed the captain had been talking about her own reaction to going on a ship.

Which annoyed her so much, she stopped dithering on the quayside, lifted her chin and stepped onto the gangplank. It bowed under her weight, the boat bobbed lower in the water and Clare shot forward, fetching up inelegantly in the captain's arms.

Which clearly made the old fellow's day, judging from the grin that slashed a gap through his whiskers and the length of time it was taking him to let go of her.

'Ooh,' she said, as he stepped into the boat behind her and relieved the captain of his post as chief propper-up of his wife. 'It feels so peculiar! It's like…just as if I'm standing on the water itself.'

'T'will be better if you sit yourselves down,' said the captain. 'Over yonder—' he indicated, with a jerk of his head, a bench upon which Ponsonby had just finished strewing as many cushions as he'd been able to find in their lodgings '—while me and the lad cast off. That is, if you're still sure you want to sail today.'

He didn't want to sail in this old hulk today or any other day. But it was too late to draw back now.

'Indeed,' replied Rawcliffe tersely. 'Or I would not have paid you such an outrageous sum of money.'

'T'wouldn't have been worth the risk, for any less,' said the captain.

'What risk?' Clare grabbed hold of his sleeve. 'Is the boat not safe? Is it the currents that Jeavons was telling us about?'

No, the captain was not afraid of the currents and the craft itself was seaworthy. It was 'The Gentlemen' the captain feared, in spite of saying he didn't care what happened to his family.

Not that he was going to share any of that information with Clare. It would be better if she saw how Clement was living with her own eyes and made her own decisions about him. If he gave her any warning at all about his suspicions that he'd become embroiled with 'The Gentlemen', the chances were she'd think he was trying to poison her mind against her brother and she'd go into the meeting bearing him a grudge. Which Clement would then pounce upon, and work on, until he'd managed to turn her against him, somehow.

His stomach clenched.

'You have no need to be nervous,' he said as he ushered her down to sit on the cushioned bench. 'The captain is just trying to add a little touch of…the exotic to this trip, that is all. A little excitement.'

'Just being in a boat is excitement enough for me,' she said, looking about her keenly as the captain, and the lad who acted as his only crew, began looping ropes and hauling sails, and shouting completely indecipherable remarks at each other.

'Oooh,' she cried, as the boat dipped, and lurched under the auspices of a particularly playful gust of wind. She clung to his arm, her eyes wide as she watched the shore recede. She flinched when the sails made a loud cracking noise as the wind filled them completely and bore them out to the deeper waves of the Channel.

'Oooh,' she cried again, as the ketch plunged down the side of one wave, then soared up the crest of the next.

'It's…it's…' Her hand went up to the brim of her bonnet, which was making an attempt to escape from her head, dislodging a handful of hairpins in the process. 'I imagine this must be what it feels like to fly.'

'The sea is a touch rough,' he said as the ketch plunged through the crest of a wave, showering them both with salt spray, 'for you to be making your first trip.'

'I don't care,' she said, turning to beam at him. 'It's the most exhilarating experience I have ever had. Although—' her smile dimmed '—I must say, you don't look as though you are enjoying yourself. Are you not,' she said, searching his face with concern, 'a good sailor?'

How like Clare, to show concern for him when he was on the point of betraying her. Just like the way she'd tried to console him when he'd heard about Archie's death, even though he'd been in the process of exacting some petty revenge upon her.

His stomach, which had been so tense from the moment they'd awoken that he'd been unable to do justice to his breakfast, was now positively roiling.

'Look at the horizon,' said Clare, gesticulating out to sea. 'I believe that is supposed to help.'

It wouldn't. The thing that was making him sick to his stomach was the thought of losing her regard. The dread that after Clement had worked on her, she'd never look at him like this again. Never cling to his arm this way, let alone hug him in the street. He'd lose it all. And without her warmth, he'd go back to living in the cold isolation that had been his habitat since the day she'd spurned his first proposal of marriage.

Unless he explained…

Explained what? Even his two best friends had assumed he was so calculating that he'd marry his enemy's sister just to get close enough to him to find the proof they needed to bring him to justice.

Besides, he'd left it too late. If he'd only told her the truth in the first place, she might have listened. But now, if he told her that getting even with Clement hadn't even occurred to him when he'd pushed her into marriage, that it was only an additional benefit…

He groaned inwardly and shut his eyes. If it sounded that bad, even in his own head, how much worse would it sound if he said it out loud?

He should have told her how much she meant to him, that was what he should have done. The moment he'd got the ring on her finger. Or when they'd talked about his first proposal and he'd discovered she hadn't thought all those vile things that her father had told him were her reason for turning him down. She'd have listened to him then, as he told her…

Told her—his stomach constricted painfully— that he…loved her?

Did he? Was that why the prospect of losing her was making him feel so ill?

Good God. He did. His eyes flew open to stare at her. She was still clinging to his arm and looking at him with concern.

'Clare…'

His heart sped up. No. He couldn't tell her. Not now. Not just before she went to speak to Clement. Even if she believed him now, once she heard her brother's version of events, she'd look back on this moment and think he'd just been trying to *turn her up sweet*. So that she wouldn't believe what Clement had to say. They'd lived for too long in a state of mutual suspicion to easily believe anything good the other might say.

The time was not right. He passed a weary hand over his eyes. The time was never right for him and Clare. They'd both been too young when he'd made his first, impulsive and rather rash proposal. And now they were adults and free to govern their lives the way they wished, he was locked in what she'd consider a long-standing feud with her brother.

'There she is,' said the Captain suddenly. 'That be Peeving Cove. God 'elp us.'

'It's all right,' she said. 'You will be fine, soon. We are nearly there.'

He would never be fine again. Once again, Clare was going to slip through his fingers. Because he'd...he'd gone about this all wrong. He should have...

'See, the waves are less rough already,' she said, as they slipped through the gash in the cliff face that led into a narrow inlet. 'And the water in the harbour, further in, looks as flat as a mill pond.'

Even though the waves out at sea had been boisterous. It made the place a safe anchorage no matter what storms might rage elsewhere, he suspected.

'Oh, what a charming little place,' she exclaimed, straining forward now to admire the cluster of sturdy houses, built of and tiled with local stone so that they blended in with the cliffs backing the cove to the point where they looked as if they had sprouted there entirely naturally. They sat upon a sort of shelf projecting from the cliff face, down which poured a continual torrent, which was, he'd discovered by dint of studying maps of the locality, the River Peever.

She might see only a charming little village,

nestling into the shelter of protective cliffs, but he was looking at a virtually impregnable stronghold. The mouth of the river, where it emerged into the sea between two massive, sheer cliffs, which provided the only access to the village, was only just wide enough to admit their craft. And the seabed there was festooned with rocks, so that only those who knew the channel extremely well would dare attempt to sail through the gap except at high tide. Though, by some quirk of geology, the water remained deep enough for craft to sail right up to a broad quayside. So that the inhabitants could sail their own craft right up to their front doors, should they so desire, and unload whatever contraband they had on board. And, thanks to their guided tour of the caves the day before, he'd learned that all the cliffs along this part of the coast were riddled with tunnels and caves, due to extensive quarrying. Tunnels and caves in which smugglers could conceal no end of contraband.

He wondered if the smugglers had mounted guns anywhere up on those cliffs, which surrounded the village like fortress walls. He could actually see one or two ledges, which would give cover to the entire sweep of the harbour. So that they could repel any potential invaders. Such as customs men.

'I wonder which house is Clement's,' said Clare, reminding him that her motives for coming here were at such odds with his own.

'I don't like the looks of that, yer lordship,' said the captain, sidling up to him and jerking his head in the direction of the quayside, which they were steadily approaching, upon which a group of tough-looking men was gathering.

'Allow me to handle them,' he said.

'Ar, that's easy for you to say,' grumbled the captain. 'But you don't have to live in these parts.'

'Good morning,' said Lord Rawcliffe, as the captain threw a rope in the direction of a wooden post and thrust his lad up out of the sides of the ship after it.

One of the men on the quayside caught the rope before the lad could get to it and tossed it back into the boat.

'You can't land here,' he barked. 'We don't have nothing for tourists,' he finished, eyeing Rawcliffe and Clare with contempt.

'Ah, but we are not tourists,' said Rawcliffe. 'We are here to visit the Reverend Cottam.'

The men on the quayside looked at each other. Their spokesman, a tall, rough-hewn individual with shoulders a couple of yards wide, stuck his meaty hands on his hips.

'You want to speak to the Reverend, you go to church on Sunday up at Lesser Peeving and wait for him after service. He don't like being bothered during the week.'

Clare gasped. And stood up. 'That cannot be true. He would never—' she paused to swipe a tendril of hair, which had escaped from her bonnet, from her mouth '—neglect his calling by refusing to permit parishioners to come to him with their problems during the week!'

Rawcliffe sighed at her misplaced faith in her brother.

'Ar, but you ain't one of his parishioners, are you?' sneered the spokesman.

'No,' retorted Clare, lifting her chin. 'I am his sister!'

The spokesman peered at her intently. Tilted his head to one side as he noted the colour of her hair which the wind was still whipping across her face. And for once, Rawcliffe was glad that she bore such a striking resemblance to her brother.

'He never said as you was coming,' said the spokesman resentfully.

'What difference does that make? Why should I

not visit my brother whenever I wish?' Clare had become so annoyed that she did what she always did when provoked. Took to physical action. She bent to pick up the rope which the captain's lad was too intimidated to touch and threw it with remarkable accuracy at the spokesman. 'You will tie this boat to that post, if you please, and then take me straight to my brother!'

The spokesman gestured to one of the men at his side, who took the rope and looped it round the nearest bollard.

Just as he'd suspected, Clare had become the key to gaining entry to this supposedly impregnable stronghold. Not that it made him feel any better about how she'd feel when she discovered he'd been using her.

The spokesman made a signal to a sturdy boy who'd been standing on the outskirts of the group, who promptly went running off in the direction of the houses.

It took a few moments to get the gangplank in place and for him to help Clare cross it to gain solid ground.

'Oh, my word,' she said, clinging to his arm. 'It feels as if the land is pitching up and down. How peculiar.'

Just then, the boy who'd been sent away came running back and went straight to the spokesman, who bent down to hear what he had to say. Whatever it was had the spokesman straightening up sharply, whipping off his cap, and making a clumsy bow to Clare. His men followed suit.

'Beg your pardon, Miss Cottam. The reverend says as how we're to take you straight to him.'

And treat her with respect, too, by the looks of it. Interesting.

'I should jolly well think so,' she said. Not bothering, he noted with irritation, to correct their assumption that she was still a single lady.

'It's this way,' said the spokesman, indicating with a sweep of his arm that she should follow him. 'Not you,' he growled, as they set off, arm in arm.

'Not I?' Rawcliffe raised one eyebrow at the man, in his most imperious fashion.

'No. The rev said as how we was to bring his sister to him. *Only* his sister. Not nobody else, see?' To show he meant business, the man stuck his chin forward aggressively.

'How very tiresome of him,' he said mildly, though he wasn't at all surprised. Cottam would want to get Clare alone, so that he could present his own, twisted version of events, and no doubt try to convince her that whatever he'd done, he'd been acting from purely altruistic motives.

And if she believed him…

'I am so sorry,' said Clare, turning to him and placing one little hand upon his forearm. 'I cannot think what has induced Clement to be so rude. You would think—'

'It does not matter,' he assured her, though a great weight seemed to be pressing on his chest. 'You cannot think I actually wish to see him myself?' He gave a theatrical shudder. 'This entire trip is entirely for your benefit, my dear.' My darling. My love, he wanted to say, but didn't. Because this wasn't the time.

'Well, perhaps it is as well. You don't look at all the thing.' She stepped closer, stood on tiptoe and kissed him on the cheek. Sending a pang of… something, something he couldn't recognise but suspected was a noxious cocktail of regret and guilt, and despair, searing through him. 'I will try not to be long.'

However long she was away it would feel like an eternity. While he sat, powerless to defend himself against whatever lies Cottam chose to tell her.

He had never felt so helpless in his life.

'Make sure you don't, miss,' said the captain.

'We'll need to depart with the tide. You take too long and we'll never make it through the eye,' he said, waving to the narrow entrance to the inlet.

'Oh. Well, perhaps somebody could send me word before then?' She turned and smiled hopefully round the semi-circle of 'gentlemen', who either stared stonily back, or looked to their spokesman for guidance.

'But what,' said Clare with concern, 'will you do while I am gone?'

He would curse himself for being seven kinds of a fool. For not realising, until he was faced with losing her regard, how very much it meant to him. For not treating her like the treasure she was, but instead taunting her, abducting her, forcing her into marriage and then treating her like a whore, night after night. And most of all, for using her like a jemmy to prise open Cottam's fortress.

He made a languid gesture to the pile of wicker hampers stowed at the front of the boat. 'Oh, I shall make inroads into the picnic and admire the scenery,' he said with a bland smile at the group of surly men on the quayside.

'Really? Your stomach has recovered that quickly?'

'There has never been anything the matter with my stomach. I do not suffer from seasickness.'

A frown flitted across her face. 'But then, what—'

'Go,' he said, giving her a little push. 'Go and make your peace with your brother.'

'Well, if you're sure.'

No. He wasn't sure of anything. Except that somehow, Clement would use this meeting to sow discord between him and Clare. And that the worst of it was that all he'd have to do, to achieve his aim, would be to tell her some cold, hard facts.

But Clare was giving him one last tremulous, grateful smile, and turning to follow the spokesman.

The rest of the smuggling gang stood still, glowering at him. Even when he got back into the ketch, sat down on his pile of cushions and ordered his captain to open the first of the picnic hampers.

Lord, but he hoped Ponsonby had provided something decent to drink. He could do with a bottle of brandy. Or two.

Chapter Twenty-Three

Clare followed the burly giant of a man who appeared to be the head man of Clement's latest gang.

Typical. Wherever he went he managed to surround himself with the roughest, meanest boys and make himself their leader.

And would spout scripture at her whenever she, or anyone else, tried to remonstrate with him about the importance of 'being all things to all men', or 'seeking after that which was lost'. Which sounded incredibly evangelical, if you didn't happen to know that he'd never, to her knowledge, ever managed to save the soul of any single one of the miscreants with whom he enjoyed consorting.

The burly man stopped outside the largest house in the village. He knocked on the door, whipped off his cap and smoothed down his hair.

'The reverend's sister,' he said to the tough-looking, swarthy woman who opened the door.

'Indeed,' said the woman, eyeing them both, but particularly Clare's red hair. 'Yes, I can see why you might think so,' she said to the burly man. 'Very well, you may go.'

He wasted no time in doing so. 'I suppose you'd best come in,' the woman said grudgingly. 'The reverend is in his study.' She turned on her heel and Clare stepped up into the hall, then into the room to the right. A room which had a very clear view all the way round the quayside and right down the inlet. There was a telescope on the windowsill, she noted. A telescope through which Clement could easily keep an eye on everything that happened in his little kingdom.

And there, sitting behind a desk piled high with books and papers, sat her brother. Who nodded at his dragon of a housekeeper, dismissing her.

'Clement,' said Clare, stepping into the room. 'I do hope—'

He held up his hand to silence her. 'Before you go any further, Clare, let me just inform you that there is no need to beg for my forgiveness,' he said graciously. 'It would not be Christian of me to withhold it.'

'Well, thank you, Clement,' she said, lowering her head as though concentrating on tugging off her gloves while she strove to keep her temper reined in. How did Clement always manage to make it sound as if he thought she was very much in the wrong and didn't deserve his forgiveness, even as he was bestowing it? Besides which, was there anything more provoking than having someone assume he knew what you were about to say and making his answer before you'd even realised you'd been about to say exactly that?

'I know how annoyed you must have been when I didn't reach the employer you found for me,' she conceded, 'after all the trouble you went to, in order to secure my future,' she finished, quoting as far as she was able to recall, the exact words he'd used on her at Father's funeral.

'Oh, I soon found another girl, a girl who was *genuinely* grateful for the chance to better herself, by doing honest work. The cities of England are full of the unfortunate wretches.'

'Yes, I'm sure they are, but—'

'And I was not annoyed with you. I was disappointed. Very disappointed,' he added with a doleful shake of his head.

'Yes, me, too...' If only she'd been able to control her wretched temper. But no amount of scolding or preaching from either Father or any of her brothers, or forming resolutions to do better, had ever had any effect.

'I simply cannot understand how you managed to fall into that man's clutches.'

'Clutches? I am not in his clutches. And as to how I came to marry him, I explained it all. In my letter.'

'Oh, this,' he said, pulling a sheet of paper from one of the piles on his desk. 'Yes, you say he planned to get up some sort of ceremony, to persuade you that you are married, but let me tell you—'

'No. We *are* married!'

The look in his eyes was full of sympathy. 'I am sure you believe that. I know that you would never succumb to his charms, the way so many other women have, unless you truly believed he had married you. But, Clare, don't you see? He knows that, too. Which is why he wants you to believe you are his wife, since it is the only way he could ever persuade you into his bed. But—'

Everything in her recoiled at Clement's foul suggestion. 'But nothing. We are married!'

'You are living in sin.'

'Clement, you are being ridiculous. Why ever do you think that my marriage is not legal?'

'There was no notice in the papers. Which shows that this was a deliberate attempt to conceal his misdeed from the eyes of your family. If you had not written to inform me of the event, not one of us would have known of it.'

'That's... I... No, it isn't like that. Rawcliffe is the kind of man who simply doesn't care what people think.' And men of his rank rarely bothered to send notices of their marriage to the papers. They didn't think it was anyone else's business.

Clement gave a disapproving snort. 'Which we all know, to our cost.'

'Our cost? What do you mean? Honestly, Clement, I cannot think why you hold him in such dislike.'

'He may have been able to charm you into believing his smooth lies...'

Charm? The last thing Rawcliffe had been was charming, to begin with. And far from being smooth with her, at times he'd been brutally honest.

'...but I am a man of experience. I know his sort. I know that he would do anything, anything he can, to hurt and humiliate me.'

'You? What do you mean?' Why did Clement always assume everyone did things specifically to annoy him? When most of the time he never crossed her mind?

'To think that we used to be friends,' he said, with a shake of his head. 'When we were boys together. Until he found a class of people with whom he clearly felt he belonged. Young gentlemen with titles and money. He never had time for us after that.'

She was sure that couldn't be right. Oh, she knew Rawcliffe hadn't wanted much to do with her brothers from about the time he went away to school, but it wasn't anything to do with their rank or wealth. Why, Mr Kellet had been as poor as the proverbial church mouse and Captain Bretherton was merely a half-pay officer in the navy. But even though she opened her mouth to point out the flaw in Clement's logic, he just kept right on ranting.

'And he took to whoring and drinking. Not the sort of person Father wished us to associate with. His betrayal of his childhood playmates was thus twofold. He left us all behind without even a backward glance. That is the sort of man who has duped you into a semblance of a marriage. A man without conscience, without honour, or loyalty.'

'Well, first of all—' He did have a conscience, or he would never have made an honest woman of her.

And secondly, he was loyal. So loyal that he'd even given one of those friends he'd made at school a job so that he could continue with his experiments in peace, without feeling as though he was accepting charity. Everyone in Watling Minor knew it, too.

Though Clement had been furious, now she came to think of it, that Rawcliffe had made a school friend his chaplain, when he felt *he* ought to have been given the post.

Not that Clement gave her a chance to express a single one of her objections. 'No, Clare,' he said, holding up his hand to silence her the way their father had so often done when any of them had a view he hadn't wished to hear. 'You must listen to my warnings.'

Which was true. Just like their father, Clement was not going to let her get a word in edgeways until he'd said what he had to say.

She trod heavily to the chair by his desk and sat down, since she had no intention of remaining on her feet while he delivered his lecture. Father might have had the right to make her do so, but Clement was only her brother. Not even her oldest brother, come to that.

And what was more, now she was a married lady with a title, shouldn't he have got to *his* feet when she entered the room?

'I have not spoken out against Rawcliffe in the past,' Clement was saying, as Clare mentally chastised him for his bad manners, 'because I thought you had the sense to avoid such as he. A philanderer and a libertine,' he said with a curl to his lip. 'And a liar. Not only has he persuaded you that you are his lawful wife, rather than his...mistress,' he hissed the word, narrowing his eyes, 'but he has no doubt attempted to poison your mind against me.'

Far from doing any such thing, Rawcliffe had been careful never to mention him. But then she knew the two men hated each other. Why, she had no idea. It had started before Rawcliffe had appointed Mr Kellet, rather than Clement, as his chaplain, though that had certainly fanned the flames.

'No matter what he has told you, though, Clare, the fact that you have come here, to me proves that you have not yet lost complete control of your common sense. You need to hear the truth from my own lips, is that not so?'

She wouldn't mind learning why the two hated each other so much, actually. So, with a bit of a shrug, she nodded her head.

Clement's eyes gleamed with triumph.

'Good girl.'

Since she was neither particularly good, and well past the age when anyone could consider her to be a girl, she ground her teeth.

'I dare say he has told you I am embroiled in criminal activities. That I have become, in spite of my calling, some kind of kingpin in all sorts of nefarious schemes.'

Rawcliffe had never said any such thing. Why on earth did Clement assume he had?

Oh, dear...

'You don't believe it, do you? You surely cannot believe that your own brother, brought up in the sacred sphere of a family given to the service of God, could possibly stoop to the things of which he accuses me?'

Clare got a sinking feeling. It was the bag of puppies all over again. He'd used almost the exact same words to deny having anything to do with it when she'd burst into the house, dripping wet, holding that gruesome bundle in her arms. And he'd said them in the exact same tone of voice he was using on her now. He'd sounded so convincing, that day, that, had she not seen him, with her own eyes, tossing the bag off the bridge into the pond, she would have believed him.

She clenched her fists. The fact that he was denying something, so vehemently, was the clearest sign she could possibly have that it was exactly what he *was* doing.

'He is the villain of the piece, Clare, not I.'

She hadn't been looking for a villain. She'd come here to try to apologise for embarrassing him in regard to the position she was supposed to have taken with that elderly invalid. To express her hope that the lady had found another, more suitable companion—because frankly she didn't think she had been right for that kind of job at all.

But now, with all his talk of villains and philandering, and lying, she couldn't help wondering why Rawcliffe had really brought her here.

From what Clement was saying, he must believe her brother was up to no good. Which wouldn't surprise her. Not one bit.

She gazed across the desk at Clement with sadness and a sort of sick, disappointed feeling. At both of them. Clement for being up to his neck in some sort of mischief, by the sound of it. And

Rawcliffe for not warning her about his suspicions. What had he thought she'd do if he'd told her? She got a fleeting image of her shying all the breakables at his head on their wedding night. And her spirit sank still further.

'Ah,' said Clement, leaning back in his chair with a look of mock concern. 'I see that you are starting to believe me, at last. The scales are falling from your eyes.'

They certainly were. But not in the way he thought.

'Look...' She squirmed in her chair. What kind of man could sit there, lying to his own sister so brazenly? As though she was some kind of idiot, who would swallow whatever he said. Although Rawcliffe hadn't been exactly honest with her, either, had he?

'You need not be afraid,' he said with that sickly smile he wielded whenever he was trying to convince her he was full of brotherly love. The one he'd worn when he'd told her he'd taken care of her future and pressed a letter of introduction and a ticket on the stage into her hands.

'I can help you to escape his clutches. I can make you disappear so completely that he will never be able to find you. Should he bother to look, that is,' he finished on a nasty laugh.

She shook her head. 'Whatever do you mean?'

He looked down his nose at her. 'What can you possibly think I mean?'

'I don't know,' she cried. 'You are not making any sense.'

'That is because he has completely addled your brains with all his smooth talk,' he sneered. 'By now, I suppose you even think you are *in love* with him.'

'I… I…' Well, that was the first thing Clement had said that was completely true. She did love Rawcliffe. She couldn't help it. Even though he didn't trust her enough to share his suspicions about Clement with her, let alone love her back.

Something must have shown in her face, because Clement got up and came round the desk, his face creased into a careful expression of unctuous sympathy.

'You poor girl. I should reprimand you, for being so foolish, but I know how cunning he is. He caught you when you were at your lowest, did he not? When you were alone and far from home, and probably fearing the change in your circumstances. He made you think you would be safe with him, didn't he? That you would always wear fine clothes, and jewels.'

She couldn't help wincing at just how inaccurate that statement was. Far from catching her at a weak moment, she'd punched Rawcliffe. And the only time he'd threatened her with jewels of any kind, it had been by way of an insult.

And because that argument had taken place in her bedroom, when she was naked, and because it surged to the front of her memory in vivid detail, she found herself blushing and lowering her head, completely unable to look her brother in the eye.

He took her embarrassment as a sign he'd hit the nail on the head, though, apparently, because he took her hand in his and gave it a brotherly pat.

'There, there. No need to take on so. You are here now. And here you may stay.'

'What?' Her head flew up, in shock.

'You don't think I will leave you in his power, do you?'

She withdrew her hand, and got to her feet. Since she and Clement were of a similar height, she was able to look him straight in the eye.

'I am not leaving him. How can you even suggest it? He is my husband!'

Clement shook his head.

'Dear me, he really does have you completely fooled, does he not? Well,' he added with a shrug, 'at least I have done my duty. I have warned you how things stand.'

'I don't…' She pressed her hands to her temple as he stalked back to the other side of his desk. She couldn't understand why Clement kept insisting that the marriage was a fake, that she ought to leave Rawcliffe. Why was it so important to him to separate them?

'You find it hard to believe in such villainy, even when it is staring you in the face, don't you, Clare? It is something I have often observed in gently reared females. You simply cannot see what is going on, right under your noses. However,' he went on, when she took a breath to object to his latest insult, 'I am still willing to provide you with a sanctuary, when the time comes.'

'The time?'

'When he reveals his true colours. What you must do is always keep enough money about your person for you to flee him, at a moment's notice.'

She let out a wild, strangled laugh. 'Clement, you cannot be serious.'

'Oh, I am,' he said, leaning both hands on the desk and jutting his head forward, as if to demonstrate how serious he was. 'Deadly serious.'

'But—'

'And if you cannot escape him, for any reason, you may write to me and I shall arrange for you to obtain your freedom.'

'Write to you? You don't suppose that if he is such an ogre,' she pointed out, 'he will permit me to write to you, do you?'

'He hasn't done so to date, has he?,' he pointed out. 'The only letter you wrote to me was not franked by him, but by some other person.'

Ah, yes. She'd sent her hastily scrawled explanation of why she hadn't reached her employer's house from Lady Harriet's home, the day before her wedding. And Lady Harriet had handed it to her father to frank, along with all the rest of the post.

'Could you employ the same methods to communicate with me, should you find the need to do so?'

'I hardly think it will be necessary...'

'No, I can see you do not. But should it become... of dire importance to get in touch with me, without your husband knowing of it, you can always send letters to Lady Buntingford, in Lesser Peeving. So that nobody will suspect you are communicating with me, rather than a female friend of yours.'

'Lady Buntingford?' Why did that name sound familiar?

'Yes. And you need not be afraid she will read it herself. Her eyes are…not what they used to be,' he said with a strange smile. 'Which is why I deal with all her correspondence, these days. As I am her…trusted spiritual advisor.'

She must be all about in the head, then. For nobody with an ounce of sense would trust Clement, with either spiritual or any other sort of matter.

But then he'd just told her that gently reared ladies could rarely see what was under their noses, hadn't he?

He was just taking a breath to say something else she probably didn't want to hear when there was a knock at the door and his housekeeper came in.

'Message from the harbour,' she said, without waiting for permission to speak. 'Tide's turning and that boat needs to leave, else it'll be stranded here.'

Clement frowned. Glanced at her. At the door.

Through which she suddenly felt the strongest compulsion to run. To run and not stop running until she was on the boat, in Rawcliffe's arms and sailing safely away.

And yet to do anything of the sort would be to alert him to the fact she now knew he was up to no good.

She swallowed.

'I suppose,' she said, pushing herself to her feet as slowly as she could, considering the fact that something was telling her she needed to get out of there while she still could, 'I had better go.'

'There is no need,' said Clement, leaning back as though it was of no great importance to him either way. Only, he was tapping his forefinger on the arm of his chair, a sure sign he was nowhere near as calm as he looked.

'No…but…' She gave what she hoped was a resigned shrug.

'You know how I feel about you consorting with that man. But since you clearly believe you are married to him—'

'Yes,' she said, seizing on the excuse he'd handed her. 'I made vows in church and—'

'Say no more.' He flicked his hand in a contemptuous gesture of dismissal. 'Just know that when you have repented of living as his whore, I shall be here to help you. Even should you find yourself with child…' His gaze flicked to her belly.

She laid a hand over it, in an instinctively defensive manner. Help her? He didn't want to *help* her. Or any child she might have. He wanted to… destroy her marriage, by the looks of it.

She stumbled to the door and out onto the cobbled street, putting up her hand to shield her eyes from the bright sunshine. And as she did so, it struck her that though the sunlight was half-blinding her, it wasn't anywhere near strong enough to warm the coldness that was making her innards clench.

She'd only gone a few paces before she started to shiver. And her legs felt so unsteady that she wasn't sure they'd carry her as far as the harbour. Though they had to. They had to.

Because if they didn't, if she collapsed on the street and one of Clement's…*gang* picked her up… they'd carry her back to him.

And she'd never see Rawcliffe again.

She just knew it.

Chapter Twenty-Four

Clare drew on every scrap of control she could muster, stuck out her chin and made herself walk down the hill at a decorous pace. And when she reached the quayside, she allowed the captain to hand her into the boat, stepped carefully over to the cushions upon which Rawcliffe was lolling, his hat pulled over his eyes, sat down next to him and folded her hands in her lap.

He eyed her from under the rim of his hat with the cold expression he always adopted when trying to conceal what he was feeling. For once, it filled her with admiration. She'd never realised, until just now, how hard it was to prevent anyone knowing what you felt, or thought. And it was jolly hard work.

'Enjoy your visit with your brother?'

'Not really. And I am sorry, since you went to

so much trouble to arrange it, but—' she spread her hands in a gesture of exasperation '—that is Clement for you.'

'What it Clement, exactly?'

'Impossible! He—' She broke off, glancing at the captain and his lad.

'They cannot hear us,' said Rawcliffe, sitting up and setting his hat to the correct angle. 'Besides which they are too busy concentrating on steering this craft out of the cove, without running on to any of the hidden rocks which present such a danger to the unwary.'

'Really.' He had clearly spent his time, while she had been enduring that painful interview with her brother, chatting with the crew about the nature of the cove.

'Yes. Besides—'

'*Another* besides?'

'Yes,' he said firmly. 'I need to know what he said to upset you so.'

She ground her teeth. Where to begin?

'Well, to start with, he tried to have me doubt the legality of our marriage.'

Rawcliffe stiffened. But before he could say anything, she carried on. 'Which is perfectly absurd. Because if you have made me go through some

kind of bogus ceremony, then so have Lord Becconsall and Lady Harriet, who stood up before the
same officiant in the same church. And the prospect of him tricking Lady Harriet is…ridiculous.'

'But not the thought I tricked you?' He spoke
with such coldness that if she hadn't been so furious she might have tried to appease him. But her
blood was up.

'Don't be absurd. The chances of a spate of fake
marriages breaking out amongst the ranks of the
ton is so unlikely it is laughable! Why would you
all suddenly decide you want to live in sin, unless
it is so that you can get rid of your wives at some
later date, without having the bother of pushing a
bill of divorce through Parliament?'

'Why indeed?'

'Exactly! And then, for him to suggest I stay
with him, instead of returning to you, to avoid the
shame of living in sin, as he put it…'

'Now that I would not have permitted,' he
growled. 'You *are* my wife. And I would never
let you go.'

And then, to cap all the shocks she'd received
so far today, he took her by the scruff of the neck
and kissed her. Rather savagely.

When he finally let her come up for air, she

could do nothing but gulp and stare at him. And then raise her hand to her bonnet, at which the wind was whipping, because they'd emerged from the close confines of the cove and were now out at sea once more.

'Why are you looking at me like that?' he sneered. 'Did your estimable brother not warn you that I am a rake? Not safe to be alone with? Completely without morals?'

'More or less, yes,' she admitted.

'And yet you came back to me,' he said coldly.

'Well, of course I did,' she said, swatting his arm. 'Apart from the fact you are my husband, not a word of it is true.'

'You don't believe I am a rake? A libertine?'

'No. Or you wouldn't have bothered to even *pretend* to marry me. Besides, there was a huge great flaw in his argument. And I've just realised what it is.' She turned to him, her heart pounding with a sense of satisfaction in at last being able to put her finger on what it was about Clement's standpoint that hadn't added up. 'Why on earth would you *pretend* to marry me *and* try to prevent me from escaping? I mean, surely the whole point of arranging a fake ceremony is so that you can dispose of your unwanted bride when you grow bored? And also, why would you try to prevent me from writing to him, let alone fleeing to him if *I* wanted to end it? You would just wash your hands of me and think *good riddance,* wouldn't you?' She shook her head. 'Sometimes I think Clement must be touched in the upper works.'

'You are a remarkable woman.'

'What?'

He ran the tip of one finger along the curve of her jaw. 'Remarkable, I said. And I mean it. To have been able to deduce so much, while you are clearly rattled by the way Clement spoke to you, is remarkable.'

'I cannot really take much credit,' she said, blushing under the intensity of his gaze. As well as struggling with the urge to lean into his one-fingered caress like a cat. 'He went on and on about how much you hated him and what dreadful things you must have been saying about him, when you hadn't said anything of the sort. Why, in spite of disliking him, you were even prepared to offer him a sort of olive branch, weren't you, by bringing me on this visit?'

His expression closed up.

'What dreadful things did he think I had been saying?'

'Oh, a lot of nonsense about being the kingpin of some criminal gang, or something of the sort. Honestly, it was all so ludicrous I hardly remember the half of it. Though the way those fishermen on the quayside behaved, it wouldn't be surprising if everyone did think he was up to no good.'

'Hmm?'

'Yes, you know. The way they all seemed to wait for his permission to so much as breathe. And that, coupled with the way he always did make up to the worst bullies in any area, and then compel them to respect him, or even follow him like as not, well…' She finished on a shrug. 'I know he only does it to make himself feel bigger. Or more powerful, or something.' She finished on a sigh. 'Oh, there is no point in dwelling on it. He and I are… well, now that I am married to you…' She darted a glance up at his stern profile.

He did not look back at her, but kept his gaze fixed intently out to sea.

'Would you mind very much,' she said boldly, 'if I asked you a few questions?'

He sighed, as if he thought she was being tiresome. 'What sort of questions?,' he said in a tone designed to warn her that he had the greatest reluctance to answer to her or anyone.

'Well, to start with, I'd like to hear your version of how you came to fall out with Clement… and actually now I come to think of it, my other brothers, too.'

'It wasn't a falling-out,' he said, turning his face, at last, to look at her. 'It was more a realisation that they were not the sort of boys with whom I wished to spend my time.'

That was more or less what Clement had said. Only he'd made it sound as if Rawcliffe had become very high in the instep once he'd gone away to school. Which was the thing about Clement's lies. There was always just a grain of truth embedded in them somewhere, that misled you into believing the rest of what he was dishing up along with it.

'In what way, precisely?'

'Precisely?' He raised one eyebrow at her to convey his displeasure. But then, after searching her face for a moment or two, he appeared to relent. 'I discovered that I would rather keep company with boys who resisted bullies and used their intelligence to try to improve the lot of others.'

By placing a slight emphasis on the words *resist*ed and *improve*, he'd just implied that her brothers preferred being bullies and tormenting those weaker or less intelligent than themselves.

She lowered her head and stared at her linked fingers for a second or two. There was no arguing with that. All the males in her family were of a despotic disposition. Even her father used to attempt to terrorise his congregation from the pulpit with threats of hellfire.

'No wonder you didn't mind practically being forbidden to set foot on shore,' she said with a rather desperate little laugh. Because she felt, and not for the first time, acutely embarrassed at being related to Clement. 'In fact, you probably preferred waiting in the boat, if it meant you didn't have to come face-to-face with Clement.'

'I did,' he said. 'Especially since the picnic Pierre provided was of such a high standard.'

'Oh, please tell me there is some left,' she said, placing one hand on her stomach which, she suddenly discovered, felt completely hollow.

He put his foot on the hamper, preventing her from checking inside. And gave her one of those looks, with his lids half-lowered, that always put her in mind of bedroom activities.

'Will you be very angry with me if I confess to being selfish enough to have devoured it all?'

'What?' Why would he say anything of the sort? Pierre would have prepared enough to feed not only Rawcliffe and herself, but also the crew of the ketch, like as not. And why was he looking at her in that particular manner? As though he was... flirting with her.

As though she was one of the women he'd pursued because he found them so irresistible, rather than the sister of a man he detested, who'd just been pestering him with a series of questions he'd clearly found impertinent.

And why start doing so now? How typical! How vexing!

She'd always stopped him in his tracks whenever it had looked as though he'd been thinking of flirting with her, in the past. So that now she was actually of a mind to encourage him, she had no idea how to go about it.

'I... I...' She blushed and lowered her head.

'Would you like me to make a few suggestions,' he said, sliding closer and looping one arm about her waist, 'about how I could make it up to you?'

'Not while we are on this boat,' she said, going rigid within his hold. 'Not while those fishermen can overhear anything you might suggest.'

'When, then?' He nuzzled the word into her ear. 'When we land?'

That was almost as bad. Because she didn't need him to make any suggestions whatsoever. Her own imagination was supplying plenty of forfeits she would dearly love him to pay. Which made her blush all over and shake her head.

'Well, how about tonight, then?' he said, running his tongue round the outer edge of her ear. Which made her bones feel as if they were dissolving. If he hadn't still got his arm round her waist, she was sure she'd melt off the bench and all that would be left of her would be a puddle on the deck.

Thankfully, at that point, her stomach rumbled.

'Never mind what you mean to do later,' she said, lunging forward and pushing his foot off the hamper. 'As you can tell, all I can think about right now is having something to eat.' She flipped open the latch securing the lid. 'And drink. Because, do you know, Clement didn't even have the manners to offer me a cup of tea.'

'The true sign of a villain,' said Rawcliffe with a slight smile playing about his lips.

'Whereas you,' she said, finally flinging up the lid of the hamper, to find it still contained plenty of delicacies, 'are the perfect gentleman. At least, you would be perfect if you didn't try to make me believe you would actually eat an entire hamper full of food and not leave a single bite for me.'

She threw him a smile over her shoulder as she rummaged for a glass into which to pour herself a drink. And caught him looking at her bottom. In a lascivious manner.

'Perfect, eh?' He ran his gaze the length of her spine, finishing by skewering her with a look of such heat her mouth ran dry.

'Perhaps,' she said, dropping the lid of the hamper, wriggling backwards and putting herself within the circle of his arms once again, 'I was mistaken.'

'Mistaken? You? Surely not.'

'See? A *perfect* gentleman would never imply that I always think I'm right.'

'He wouldn't dare.'

'Why, you—'

She raised her fists to give him a playful punch. But she never got the chance. In one slick move, he had pinioned her arms to her sides.

And brought the conversation to an end, the way he so very often did.

By kissing her.

Chapter Twenty-Five

Thank the Lord, Cottam was such a sanctimonious little weasel. Because, by comparison, Rawcliffe appeared to Clare like a perfect gentleman.

And thank God—again—for her temper, which had propelled her away from her brother, fizzing with indignation, and right back into his arms.

He'd feared her anger would be aimed at him. Had spent the entire time she was ashore bracing himself for the confrontation which would put an end to such moments as this, filled with teasing, and hugs, and laughter.

But it sounded as if Cottam had completely mismanaged her.

Well, he wasn't about to make the same error. He was going to devote the rest of the day to keeping her off balance, to taking her mind off her brother's behaviour and directing it where he wanted it.

It wasn't going to be all that difficult. Her shy, flustered response to his gentle teasing betrayed her lack of experience in the game. Whilst also showing her eagerness to learn. So he reached for the picnic hamper and started selecting choice morsels to pop into her mouth. Kissed the juice of peaches from her lips. Showered her, for the entire remainder of the boat ride, with compliments that were so outrageous she protested with giggles and blushes.

After they disembarked they walked back to the house arm in arm. He noted with satisfaction that her eyes, which had been so stormy when she'd left Peeving Cove, now sparkled.

Ponsonby opened the door when they were still a few yards from their cottage, and bowed them into the house. Clare put her hand to her bonnet.

'I suppose I had better go and tidy myself up. I must look a perfect fright.'

'You look adorable,' he said, kissing her fingers, rather than her nose as he'd have preferred to do, out of deference to her shyness around the servants. 'You always do.'

'Even when I'm waist-deep in muddy water, with pond weed all over my face?' She laughed up at him, though there was a trace of uncertainty in her lovely golden eyes.

'Especially then.' His mind flew back to the way he'd felt at that moment and, as he handed his hat and gloves to Ponsonby, he experienced an overwhelming urge to share it with her. 'That was the moment,' he said, turning back to her and taking hold of her hands again, 'when I fell in love with you.' And then, on a wave of panic, he added, 'In a boyish fashion.'

She blushed and flicked a nervous glance at Ponsonby.

'No, really, you couldn't have…'

And there it was. Doubt in her own ability to inspire love. How glad he was that he hadn't succumbed to the temptation to tell her he loved her now. She wouldn't have believed him. He would have to convince her she was worthy of love, before he risked using the words.

However long it took.

She had shaken her head, but she'd kept her gaze fixed intently upon him and appeared to be holding her breath.

'But I did,' he assured her. 'Because that was the moment I realised you were nothing like my mother. I looked at you and knew that I would never meet any woman more diametrically opposed to everything she stood for. Appearances didn't mean more to you than doing the right thing. Your own safety or dignity wasn't more important than trying to save anyone in trouble. And you were *sober.*' He squeezed her hand hard for a moment, raised them to his lips one after the other, then let them go.

There, that should give her plenty to think about while she was getting changed for dinner. Hopefully, he'd surprised her enough that she'd want to dwell on what he'd confessed, rather than whatever poisonous notions Cottam had tried to infect her with.

'Run along and get changed, then,' he said. 'But don't take too long.'

'Why, are you hungry?'

'No,' he growled, leaning in close. 'But I don't want to spend more time away from you than is absolutely necessary.'

She lit up with pleasure, before turning and bounding up the stairs.

Ponsonby cleared his throat. 'A word, my lord, if it is convenient?'

He'd been wondering why Ponsonby hadn't melted discreetly away the moment he'd started making verbal love to his wife. So he went into the little sitting room, with Ponsonby on his heels.

'It concerns Kendall,' said the butler, after carefully closing the door.

'The footman?'

Ponsonby nodded. 'I arranged for all the staff to enjoy some extra leisure hours, in accordance with her ladyship's wishes,' he said. 'Kendall appears to have made straight for a tavern down by the harbour where, he claims, he was befriended by two locals who plied him with drinks, and then, once they were convinced he was deeply under the influence, with questions. About your lordship. And her ladyship,' he finished, looking uneasy.

'I see.' It could just have been natural curiosity, but what if the locals plying his footman with drink were Cottam's minions? 'What did Kendall tell them?'

'Nothing of any importance. He was not as intoxicated as *that*. However, once the evening air cleared his brain, he became a touch concerned about whether he ought to return to that tavern. Or any other.'

'I see…' he said again. He turned to look out of the window while he considered both what Ponsonby had said and what he'd left out. Which was that this Kendall was conscientious enough to repeat what many footmen would have attempted to conceal. And appeared to be able to keep a clear head even when everyone else thought he should be drunk enough to become indiscreet.

Which could come in handy.

'I see no reason,' he said, turning back to Ponsonby, 'to curtail his enjoyment of the local amenities. Providing, of course, that he is able to carry out his duties when needed.'

'Thank you, my lord. I was unwilling to turn him off whilst we are so far from London...'

Rawcliffe raised one eyebrow. It was unlike Ponsonby to talk about the way he governed the staff, or to bring such concerns to him. Did this sudden outburst of familiarity stem from the fact that they were in a holiday resort? Or was this Clare's influence? He'd already noted that his staff all believed they owed their increased leisure time to her, rather than to him.

Ponsonby took the hint and left the room. Leaving Rawcliffe free to go upstairs and change for dinner. Over which he renewed his sensuous assault on Clare, turning the eating of food and the drinking of wine into a protracted form of foreplay, so that by the time they went upstairs Clare was as impatient as he was to get to the main course.

He just about had the finesse to get her to the bed before ravishing her for the first time, unlike the previous night.

When they'd finished, she kept her arms and legs round him, as though she couldn't bear to let him go.

'Stay with me again tonight,' she whispered. 'I… That is…'

He stopped her mouth with a kiss. There was nothing he wanted more than to hold her in his arms all night, telling her, and showing her, how much she meant to him.

But his conscience kept him silent. Reminded him he'd just spent all day manipulating her and using her, and withholding a great deal of information from her.

Somehow it didn't feel right to say he still loved her, had never stopped loving her, while he was deliberately keeping her in the dark about…so many things. Far better to show her. Didn't they say that actions spoke louder than words? If he worshipped her body, the way he'd vowed to do in church, stayed faithful, cherished her, eventually, there would come a time when he'd be able to tell her what was in his heart, with some chance of her believing him.

So he nipped at her ear lobe. 'You know what it will entail, don't you? Inviting me to stay in your bed is inviting me to...' He ground his pelvis against hers, just in case she hadn't got the message.

She nodded. 'I know. You told me you have a big...appetite. And that is fine.'

No, it wasn't! He'd deliberately made her think he had an immense appetite for the act itself. Whereas it was his appetite for *her* that was damn near insatiable. He slid off her to lie at her side.

'I wouldn't want you to feel used,' he ground out.

She rolled to face him and looped her arms round his neck. 'If you are using me, then I am using you right back.'

'Oh?'

'Yes. Because I need someone to hold me. Someone to make me feel...after today when Clement...'

He pressed one finger to her lips. 'I don't wish to hear his name, Clare. Not while we are in bed together, at least.'

'Sorry,' she said, giving him a hug. And resting her head on his chest with a sigh.

He stroked her hair until, after only a few moments, she fell asleep. In his arms. Though his guilty conscience would not grant him the same luxury. How was he ever going to get her to trust him, with the whole situation with Cottam lying between them? He ground his teeth, wondering how the hell Damocles ever got any sleep, with that ruddy great sword hanging over his head. He probably lay looking up at what was hanging over him, rather than down at the woman in his arms, but still…

The smile she gave him on waking the next morning did not make him feel glad to be winning her trust. Instead, it cut him to the quick. So did the ones she kept on darting him over the breakfast table.

Eventually, he couldn't take anymore.

'Much as I would love to spend another day entirely in your company,' he said, screwing up his napkin and setting it aside, 'Slater will be foaming at the mouth if I do not keep up to date with business matters.'

Her face fell. But she swiftly rallied. 'Of course,' she said brightly. Like the dutiful wife she was determined to be.

'I will be going to the cottage next door,' he told her. 'Slater has fitted out one of the rooms as a functioning study for me.'

'It's a great pity you have to work so hard on such a lovely day,' she said, her gaze turned in the direction of the window and the sea beyond it.

'There is no need for you to stay indoors.' Unless Cottam, or his henchmen, had some mischief planned. 'Though you must take Kendall with you if you do go out.'

'Kendall? Not...Nancy?'

Definitely not Nancy. Nancy would be no use in a fight. Whereas Kendall was over six feet tall and built of solid muscle.

'Kendall will be better able to keep up with you than Nancy, I should think. She does not strike me as the kind of female who would enjoy hiking across the moors should you take it into your head to do so. Nor be prepared to go scrambling over seaweed-strewn rocks if the beach is your destination.'

She smiled. Again. 'You are right.'

What? She wasn't going to kick up a fuss about having a guard?

'He can carry any purchases I might make if I

go into town, or any other equipment I might decide to take with me.'

'Equipment?'

'Yes, you know, a blanket so that I can sit down without getting grass stains on my skirts, a small picnic, perhaps, if I walk a long way and get hungry.'

If she was going to have a picnic outside, he should be the man to share it with her, not his footman.

And if she intended to take a blanket with her, he could put it to far better use than merely using it to prevent grass stains.

Nevertheless, he couldn't alter the plans he'd announced, not right away. He would look weak and indecisive.

And there *would* be piles of correspondence awaiting his attention.

Ponsonby cleared his throat. 'Though the sun is shining, I have it on good authority that the wind has a sharp bite today. You might wish to take a warm shawl out with you, as well, my lady.'

'And a parasol,' she said, with a mischievous glint in her eyes. 'To protect my complexion. Yes, it is a good job you have already suggested I take Kendall with me. It is amazing how much more equipment I need to take out with me, now that I am a marchioness, than I used to need when I was merely Miss Cottam.'

If that was the extent of the fuss she was going to make, he could let it pass. He didn't want to play the heavy with her.

He wanted...

No. He'd already decided how he was going to spend his day. He got to his feet and strode to the door.

Before he weakened and changed his mind.

Chapter Twenty-Six

Clare went upstairs to fetch the requisite pelisse, bonnet, parasol, gloves and shawl with a little smile playing round her lips. It was rather lovely being married to Rawcliffe. And not, she thought as she walked past the bed, just because of *that*. It was the way he, and all his servants, treated her. Reminding her to take a shawl in case there was a cold breeze and a parasol to protect her complexion, and a footman in case she took it into her head to purchase something that weighed more than half an ounce.

As though she mattered.

She picked up her bonnet and set it on her head, then went to the mirror to make sure her hair was all tucked up out of the way. It was a troubled face that looked back at her. For thinking about her hair escaping had led her mind straight back to her encounter with Clement the day before. He hadn't even invited her to take a seat, let alone offer her a cup of tea. He hadn't asked after her health, or if she was happy, but had just launched into a tirade. To him, she was still just the pesky little sister.

She lifted her eyes to the sun shining in through the window and the sea sparkling in the distance. She wasn't going to let thoughts of Clement creep in and spoil her day. She was at the seaside, for the first time in her life—and, come to think of it, Clement could have invited her to stay with him for a short time, since he lived by the sea, while she came to terms with losing her father and her home, but, no, he'd…

She pulled herself up short. She *was* at the seaside. Thanks to Rawcliffe. And he had given her leave to go out and do whatever she wished, provided she took a footman with her. A smile tugged at her lips again as she tied the ribbons of her bonnet into a secure knot. She wouldn't be a bit surprised if Rawcliffe had really wanted her to take a footman with her, in case she got into some sort of scrape. Now that she belonged to him, he wasn't going to leave her to deal with the consequences of her impulsive behaviour on her own. Though he'd been too diplomatic to actually say he didn't trust her out of his sight. Probably with an eye to the safety of the breakfast pots.

All the while she'd been tucking up stray strands of hair under her elegant little black silk bonnet, and comparing Rawcliffe's thoughtful protectiveness with Clement's self-centred attitude, she'd been aware of a bit of a commotion downstairs. Someone had come to the door, which had resulted in lots of running feet in the lane at the back of the house which linked all three of their holiday cottages. But now she heard Nancy's distinctive tread on the stair.

Nancy barely scarcely paused to knock on the bedroom door before poking her head round it.

'You have a visitor, my lady. At least...' Her face crinkled in thought. 'At least, she came with a message for his lordship. But she don't seem like the kind of lady who is just a messenger to me. So I've put her in the sitting room and ordered tea.'

Which meant Clare was going to have to receive her, or whoever it was would take it as a snub. Clare took one last look out of window and sighed. There would be plenty of day left to enjoy the delights of the seaside after dispensing hospitality to the person Nancy had deemed worthy of the sitting room.

'I shall come down,' said Clare, removing her bonnet. 'I just need a minute to take off my coat and so on.'

Nancy whisked off to inform the visitor straight away. Clare wasn't all that far behind her.

Today it was the footman, Kendall, who was standing in the hall, waiting to open the door for her. Ponsonby must be performing that office for Rawcliffe, in the neighbouring cottage.

She gave Kendall a little smile as they went through the pantomime of sidling round each other as he opened the door, which she could far more easily have done for herself. A smile which slipped when she smelled the unmistakable whiff of alcohol on his breath.

So she entered the room with a frown on her face, as she wondered whether she was going to have to have a word with Ponsonby about the footman's drinking. Surely, it wasn't acceptable for him to be performing his duties reeking of the tavern?

Or, worse, was that why Rawcliffe had practically insisted she take the footman out with her today? Because he needed to clear his head? Or he didn't have enough to do down here and needed to be kept from the lure of the taverns?

Her eyes lit on her visitor, a tall girl who was sitting on one of the fireside chairs, twisting the strings of a very large and lumpy reticule between gloved fingers.

She leapt to her feet, as though in alarm. And only just avoided striking her forehead on one of the beams supporting the ceiling. And then as she dropped into an awkward curtsy, the tip of one flailing elbow caught a spray of roses that somebody had put into a jug on a side table. There might have been no harm done if the girl had just left it, but instead, she whirled round to try to steady the flower arrangement. And succeeded only in knocking the whole lot, jug and all, into the hearth with an almighty crashing of breaking pottery and splashing of water, and sizzle of burning roses as a few of them landed on the embers.

'Oh, no!' The girl dropped to her knees by the fire and began plucking smouldering roses from the grate, scattering them over the hearthrug in the process.

Clare got the horrid feeling that if she didn't stop her visitor, the girl would end up setting the cottage on fire in her frantic efforts to undo the minimal damage she'd already caused.

'Kendall!' Better to summon a drunken footman than attempting to deal with such a large and highly strung visitor on her own.

Kendall flung open the door, sized up the situation in a heartbeat and strode into the room.

'Excuse me, miss,' he said, taking the girl by the elbows and lifting her aside as though she weighed no more than a feather pillow.

'I'm so sorry,' said the girl, peeping round Kendall's shoulder as he began stamping out the parts of the hearthrug that had begun smouldering. 'Things of this sort are always happening to me. I'm so clumsy. I am sure you wish me at Jericho. I… It was good of you to receive me, but considering the…' she waved at the charred hearthrug and the fragments of broken pottery, causing Kendall to duck as her reticule whooshed past his head '…I had better go.'

'No, please,' said Clare, as the girl made for the door. 'The hearth rug is of no consequence. At least, I suppose we will have to pay for the damage, since it is a rented house…' She quirked an eyebrow at Kendall.

'Mr Slater will see to it, my lady. And I shall have this cleaned up in a trice.'

'There, you see?' Her heart went out to the poor girl, who was wringing her hands and looking utterly woebegone. 'And it doesn't matter that the fire has gone out, either. It is a lovely day outside and I'm sure I have no idea why anyone thought it necessary to light it in the first place. Kendall will take no time to put all to rights and then we shall have some tea.'

'Oh, no, really, I only came on behalf of my grandfather, who wanted to speak with Lord Rawcliffe. Only then curiosity got the better of me. I… I have always wanted to see inside these little cottages, you see,' she finished apologetically. 'They look so quaint.'

'Yes, they are quaint,' she said above Kendall's bent back, as he deftly rolled up the charred hearth rug round the remains of the roses and fragments of pottery. 'Though charming. But you must tell me your name, you know.'

'Oh! Oh, of course. Yes, it's Miss Hutton, my lady,' she said, blushing and dropping into another equally inelegant curtsy. And knocking Kendall, who'd been on the point of getting to his feet, back to his hands and knees again.

'Oh, I am so sorry,' she said, holding out her hand as though intending to help the hapless footman to his feet.

'Think nothing of it, miss,' said Kendall, backing hastily away, the hearth rug clutched to his chest. 'I shall…just take the worst of the…that is… I shall take this lot to the kitchen and send Maggie in with the tea tray,' he babbled, backing away to the door.

'Oh, dear,' said the lanky girl, watching his hasty departure. 'I have scared him off. I have a tendency to do that to men,' she said wistfully. 'And as for tea,' she said, turning to Clare with a sad little smile, 'you had probably better not invite me to stay. I shall probably only spill it. Or worse.'

'I am sure you will not,' said Clare, her disappointment at missing a walk vanishing when weighed against the importance of comforting the lanky, awkward and utterly miserable young giantess. 'And if you do, what does it matter? It's not as if you can ruin the rug twice, is it? And whatever you do, don't worry about the footman. I probably shouldn't tell you this,' she said, going closer, and lowering her voice, 'but I have a suspicion that he drinks. I could smell it on his breath just now. So the fact that he was a bit unsteady probably had nothing to do with you at all. Now, won't you please sit down?' Clare waved to the chair on which the girl had been perched when she first saw her.

'Thank you,' she said, subsiding morosely. 'But…actually, I cannot stay long. Grandfather will be furious with me if I keep him waiting once he's finished his business with your husband.' Her forehead pleated into two anxious furrows. 'Oh, I say, you are the Marchioness of Rawcliffe, are you not?'

'I suppose I am,' said Clare. 'Though you don't have to tell me I don't look much like anyone's idea of a marchioness.'

'Oh, no, I didn't mean…' Miss Hutton blushed.

'That's quite all right. I don't really feel like a marchioness, either. I am only a vicar's daughter, by birth, you see, not a grand lady.'

'Oh?'

'And you don't have to tell me all about the tyranny of elderly gentlemen, either. My own father was an absolute tartar.'

'I thought you said he was a vicar.'

'He was. But he was also very, very demanding. And in his last years I was the only person who could handle him.'

'Ah,' said Miss Hutton. 'Yes, it's rather like that with my grandfather. He has a tendency to lash out with his walking stick when his gout is playing him up.'

'Is his gout playing him up today?' If so, she wondered how he would deal with Rawcliffe, who would probably have resented receiving what sounded like a summons.

'No, fortunately. Or I would not have been able to escape even for half an hour. Oh,' she said, looking stricken. 'I did not mean that he…that is, that I…'

'You have no need to explain how it is. I know only too well how tempting it is to try to escape, if only for a few precious minutes, from the demands of an erratic and demanding elderly relative.'

'Yes, and then, you know, Grandfather was a colonel, as well. So he has a tendency to bark orders and expect everyone to leap to attention and salute.'

Clare had a vision of this gawky girl doing so and sweeping a whole shelf full of china ornaments to the ground in the process. And couldn't help smiling.

'You say you have always wanted to see inside these cottages? You live locally, then?'

'Well, off and on. We used to…my brother and I that is, we used to come and stay here when Papa was alive very often. But then when he died, we moved in with Grandfather permanently.' Her face fell. 'It wasn't so bad when I was little…or comparatively little, because he just treated me like a boy and I ran wild with my brother. But when I grew up—'

And up, and up, thought Clare.

'And Lady Buntingford said I ought to learn how to be a lady.' Her shoulders slumped.

'Lady Buntingford?' There was that name again. Why did everyone keep bringing her into everything lately?

'Yes, she is about the only other person, locally, Grandfather considers suitable company for us. Everyone else, he says, are yokels or mushrooms.'

Clare laughed. 'No wonder he was so keen to send for my husband and talk with him. It must feel like a rare treat to have a genuine marquess come down here for his holiday.'

'Oh, no, it isn't like that,' said Miss Hutton. 'Grandfather is the magistrate, you see. And dealt with the case of that poor young man who came down here on the pretext of visiting Lady Buntingford and drowned.'

That was it! It all came flooding back to her now. Lady Buntingford was some relative of Mr Kellet's, which was why he'd been the one to come down here and search her house for…missing jewels, wasn't it?

'He has been brooding over it ever since. And he was so pleased when he read your husband's name in the visitors' book at the Three Tuns. Because your husband was his employer. Did you… did you know him? I am sorry if you did. He was such a nice young man.'

Clare was sure she heard a kind of clattering noise as all sorts of things that had been puzzling her fell neatly into place.

Her husband's uncharacteristically meek agreement to sign that visitors' book at all, for one thing. She should have known he had an ulterior motive for doing so. And now she knew what it was. He'd wanted the local magistrate to know he was in the vicinity. He'd wanted to be able to discuss Mr Kellet's drowning without appearing to be actively investigating it. And what better way to advertise his presence than to sign the visitors' book in the establishment of the thrusting, ambitious Mr Jeavons?

That was the reason he'd chosen this resort to visit, out of all the places he could have taken her. His dislike for Clement was so intense she should have known he would not have come within a hundred miles. And as for telling her he wanted her to be able to mend fences... Her mind flew back to the way he'd settled himself in the boat, with his hat tipped over his eyes to ward off the sun. As though he hadn't a care in the world.

Because he hadn't really cared. Not about what was going to pass between Clement and her, anyway. Whatever reason he'd had for taking her to Peeving Cove, she was absolutely certain he'd never expected them to *mend fences*.

She came back to the room with a start, realising that the clattering noise was real. And that it wasn't the facts falling into place at all, but the rattle of the tea tray as Maggie set it on the table before her. And now Clare was going to have to play hostess, while her mind, and her heart, was in complete turmoil. And her hands were shaking.

She wasn't sure how she got through the rest of the half hour that Miss Hutton stayed. But the moment the girl had gone, she darted out of the house, as well. She didn't even bother going up to her room to fetch her bonnet and shawl, let alone wait for Kendall to get ready.

She had to think. And she couldn't do it in the cramped little rooms, surrounded by Rawcliffe's servants. Loyal servants. There was only one place she could think of going. Only one place where she could be free to think.

Chapter Twenty-Seven

'The Colonel is in the reading room, my lord,' said Jeavons with an unctuous smile. 'If you would care to follow me?'

'I remember the way,' said Rawcliffe curtly. 'Though I should be grateful if you would make sure we are not disturbed.'

'Of course, my lord, of course,' said Jeavons, bowing several times in a way that put Rawcliffe in mind of a jack-in-the-box with a slack spring.

There was only one person in the reading room. An elderly man with bushy white eyebrows.

'Ah,' he barked, lowering his newspaper. 'You must be Rawcliffe, eh?'

'As you say,' said Rawcliffe.

'Didn't take you long to get here,' said the Colonel in an approving manner. 'Good, good. Cannot abide time wasters.'

'No more,' said Rawcliffe, taking a chair facing the old man, and folding his hands over the top of his cane, 'can I.'

'Want me to get on with it, eh? Tell you straight out why I wanted to speak to you.'

'Precisely so.'

'Well, it's about that young feller that drowned. Employee of yours, I believe.' He crooked one eyebrow by way of query.

'That is so.'

'Nasty business,' said the Colonel with a shake of his head. 'Very nasty.'

The hairs on the back of Rawcliffe's neck stood on end. 'In what way?'

'Well, feller came down here trying to pester Lady Buntingford, or so he said. Most put out, he was, that he had to put up here—'

'Here? In the Three Tuns?'

'Yes,' snapped the Colonel, lowering his eyebrows into a scowl at the interruption. 'That's what I said—'

'But why on earth would he stay here, when Lady Buntingford is his great-godmother?'

'Makes no difference who anyone claims to be. The old girl won't let anyone in to see her these days apart from my granddaughter, to read her the

latest rubbishy novels that come into the circulat-
ing library, and the vicar, to give her communion.'

'Is that so?'

'Just said so, didn't I?' The Colonel took a deep
breath, as though wrestling with his temper. 'Anyway, back to your chaplain, or whatever he was.'

'He was my chaplain,' said Rawcliffe, defen-
sively.

'Be that as it may, he had no business throwing
himself off the cliff under my watch!'

'I beg your pardon?'

'Don't hold with suicide,' said the Colonel with
a scowl. 'Especially not over a woman. Can understand a man taking a pistol to his head if it is a
matter of honour, or—'

'He did not commit suicide,' said Rawcliffe
firmly.

'Hmmph,' grunted the Colonel. 'Well, of course,
I didn't put that down in my report. Thought it
would be too upsetting for the family. Wouldn't
have been able to give him a decent burial. Slur
on his memory and so forth. Did I do wrong? Jeavons seems to think so. And I would have thought
he'd rather the place *didn't* get a reputation for
accidental drownings, when he wants to make
his fortune turning Peacombe into a fashionable

watering hole. Not that anyone *could* bathe here anyway, couldn't get the bathing machines down that beach—'

Rawcliffe cut in. 'Would you mind telling me your reasons for suspecting it was a suicide, rather than an accident?'

'Well, what else was I to make of it? He comes down here, asking questions about his young lady, not six months after she threw *her*self off a cliff...'

'I beg your pardon? Young lady?'

'Yes. Dreadful business that. Breaking her heart the way he did. Wouldn't think he had it in him to seduce and abandon a woman to look at him, would you?'

'Definitely not.' Archie could barely string two sentences together at the best of times, unless it was something to do with science. The notion of him suddenly becoming eloquent enough to seduce a young woman, let alone behave so contrary to his gentle nature as to abandon her, was utterly preposterous.

'Wouldn't have believed it myself,' said the Colonel, 'if I hadn't got it from Cottam.'

'Cottam?' Rawcliffe's hackles rose.

'Yes. Our latest vicar. Crusading sort of chap. Thinks he can tame the local smugglers by living cheek by jowl with them and holding regular prayer meetings, or some such rot,' he said scornfully. 'From your neck of the woods, by all accounts, so I dare say you know all about him.'

'Yes,' said Rawcliffe. Though it was beginning to look as though he'd underestimated him. 'You say the Reverend Cottam informed you as to Mr Kellet's state of mind? They…spent some time together, then?'

'Oh, yes, they were thick as thieves. Terribly upset, Cottam was, after the drowning. Presented himself to me, almost as soon as we found the body, to tell me all about it.'

'I see.' Though what he saw was that he should have warned Archie to be on his guard around Cottam. That he should have listened to his instinct to prevent Archie from coming down here at all. But then, everyone had urged him to let Archie undertake the quest as an aid to his flagging self-esteem. Nobody had thought there would be any danger attached to visiting an elderly lady, to find out what she might have to do with the theft of several sets of jewels. Nobody had thought it would have ended in murder.

But…Cottam had been upset. Perhaps it was the smugglers with whom he was now involved who had so brutally disposed of Archie. 'What, precisely,' he said, hoping that he might be able to exonerate Cottam from the charge of murder, if not the rest of it, for Clare's sake, 'did Cottam tell you?'

'Well, firstly, it was on account of his work with fallen women that he knew the girl at all. He thought he'd put her back on the straight and narrow, but I could have told him how it would be. A leopard doesn't change its spots, eh? Anyway, she came running to Cottam when this young Kellet feller broke her heart. And in spite of all his counselling, she gave way to despair. Threw herself off the cliffs. I suppose Kellet did show some remorse in the end, coming looking for her the way he did. And, when he heard what happened, followed her, in a fit of despair.'

'That is the story Cottam told you, is it?'

'That's the gist of it. Thought it best to hush it up, of course.'

'Was that Cottam's idea, too? No, never mind, it really doesn't matter.' The Colonel had taken Cottam's version of events at face value. Because Cottam was a man of the cloth. And there was no point in trying to explain what sort of man Cottam really was beneath his clerical guise. Nobody would believe it. Hell, he didn't want to believe it himself.

But it was becoming increasingly clear that whatever was going on, regarding the jewel thefts, and the drownings of both Archie and the girl he was supposed to have driven to suicide, Cottam was up to his scrawny neck in it.

And then, as if to prove the old adage about speaking of the devil, the Colonel tossed his paper to one side and smiled at someone just entering the room. In spite of Jeavons promising to admit no one.

'Ah, here he is now,' said the Colonel. 'Mr Cottam, you know the Marquess of Rawcliffe, I believe?'

Rawcliffe got to his feet and turned round, slowly, desperately resisting the urge to stride across the room and knock the corrupt little clergyman down. Never had he been so glad to have his cane to grip, because if he hadn't, he would have been hard pressed not to clench his fists into the weapons he so badly wanted to use.

'Know me?' Cottam strolled forward, an unctuous smile on his face. 'Why, hasn't he told you? The Marquess is married to my little sister. I hope you don't mind, Colonel, but I would like to have a word or two in private with my brother-in-law.'

'Hmmph? Harrumph.' The Colonel made as if to move from his chair and vacate the room, with exceedingly bad grace.

'No need to get up,' said Rawcliffe. 'I believe we have finished discussing our business, Colonel, so I shall bid you good day.'

'Oh? Ah!' The Colonel looked distinctly relieved.

'Cottam, you may walk with me back to my lodgings, if you wish.'

'How very gracious of you, my lord,' said Cottam with a bow that was practically a sneer.

They left the Three Tuns, navigated the shoals of the busy high street and turned into the lane leading to the lodgings before either of them said a word.

'My sister,' said Cottam with a strange smile, 'appears to be very smitten with you, at the moment.'

They walked on in silence for a few paces.

'It would be a pity, a very great pity, if she were to discover something that might lead her to work out your true reasons for marrying her, would it not?'

Rawcliffe ground his teeth. Though the weasel

was quite right. He didn't want to upset Clare. And so they kept right on walking past the row of cottages and struck out for the track leading up to the moors.

'What reasons,' he said, once they were well out of earshot of any building, 'do you presume I had for marrying your sister?'

'Why, the very same ones that brought you down here. Your relentless need to persecute me. These… trumped-up charges you plan to bring against me, that you have sent your minions to try to pin on me…they are all figments of your imagination. And so I shall tell Clare, if you pursue your enquiries. Then we shall see where her loyalties truly lie.'

He'd already factored that into his calculations and had counted the cost.

'If they are not figments of my imagination, but are, on the contrary, facts, I will make sure the whole world knows of it.'

Clement glared at him. 'If you dare to try to humiliate me, by making accusations in a court of law, I will inform Clare exactly why you married her. That it was merely a pretext to have an excuse for pursuing me down here, and trying to…

discover what happened to your spy. Mr Kellet,' he finished on a sneer.

If the man had been innocent, there would have been no need to make threats. It was as good as an admission of guilt.

At that moment, Rawcliffe decided that Clare's brother really *was* the man behind the theft of the jewels, and the subsequent death of Archie, probably because he was getting too close to the truth. And as for the girl who drowned? Who was she and what part did she play in all this? Or had Cottam merely used her untimely death as something to pin on Archie?

'Ah, you have seen the wisdom of thinking twice,' said Clement, since Rawcliffe had made no reply to his last threat.

'If you are responsible for the death of my friend, Mr Kellet, I shall have no hesitation in having you sent to the gallows,' he breathed between clenched teeth.

'Ah, but how will you prove it?' Cottam smiled with evil glee. 'So hard to find reliable witnesses, in these parts. So hard, once a man has been buried, to prove what happened to him, one way or another.'

Rawcliffe had never felt closer to throttling someone.

'Besides, how do you think Clare would look at the man who attempted to send her favourite brother to the gallows? Do you think your marriage would succeed, under those circumstances?'

Cottam was a weasel. He'd thought it before and he thought it still. He had the uncanny knack of sending a direct hit to his victim's weakest point. And Clare's regard for him was it.

'I know you don't want her to find out what you are about, otherwise you would have been frank with her from the beginning. I have to say, as a man of the cloth, that lying to your bride is not the best foundation to a marriage.'

'Nevertheless,' said Rawcliffe, 'I cannot let you get away with it.'

'Dear, dear how very melodramatic you sound. Get away with what, exactly? Do you even have any idea?' Cottam laughed then. And never had Rawcliffe been so sure that a sound was evil.

'You never do have, do you? You look down your aristocratic nose at the rest of the world, believing yourself so superior, assuming you are in control of everyone and everything around you, but you are not. I have thwarted you once and I shall do it again.'

'Thwarted me? I very much doubt it.'

'You do not even know, do you? How I managed to foil your plans for Clare when she was still a sweet innocent.'

'What do you mean?'

Cottam turned to him, an evilly triumphant smile on his face. 'That day when she came home, dripping wet after her venture into the village pond, she told me what you had said. How you made a mocking proposal to her. She was so visibly upset that I had no trouble persuading Father *that* was at the root of her distress, rather than the fate of those stupid dogs. Because he never would listen to her once she'd reached the stage of screaming like a fishwife. He sent her to her room to calm down and put on clean, dry clothing, leaving me to relate what happened. So that by the time you came to call on Father to ask his permission to pay your addresses, he was so sure he needed to shield Clare from you, that she detested you, that nothing on earth would have persuaded him to listen to your proposal. Yes,' he breathed as Rawcliffe reeled. 'I made sure you couldn't get your hands on her then and, though I wasn't able to stop you bedding her this time round, I can make sure that any affection she might have started to feel for you will start curdling with distrust until eventually it turns into a festering mass of resentment.'

'What?' Clement had been the one who'd come between him and Clare all those years ago? And now he was going to try to do the same thing again?

No. Not while he had breath in his body.

Rawcliffe flung his cane aside before he succumbed to the urge to brain Cottam with it and grabbed him by the lapels of his jacket.

'I don't care,' he growled. Because persuading the rest of the world he didn't care about anything very much was the position he always adopted when he was hurting the most. And then, because he had to conceal his weakness from Cottam, or who knew what advantage he would try to take, he took the only course guaranteed to stop him interfering in his marriage any further.

'Do you think I care what she thinks of me? Do I look like a man who needs a woman to *love* him? All I need is for her to open her legs. The rest can—'

He heard a cry of distress. From behind a group

of rocks, just up ahead of them, he saw Clare emerge. A devastated look on her face.

He let go of Cottam so abruptly that the cleric staggered and almost fell.

'Clare,' said Rawcliffe, taking a step in her direction. 'Clare, it isn't what you think...'

She backed away, shaking her head, her mouth quivering as she strove not to weep.

'Clare!'

She turned and ran, stumbling over the rough ground.

Straight towards the cliff edge.

Chapter Twenty-Eight

Rawcliffe pounded over the close-cropped turf, steadily gaining on her. His legs were far longer and she was hampered by her skirts. Her bonnet tumbled from her head so that her hair streamed out behind her like flames from a rocket.

He caught up to her in the sheltered hollow, where they'd spent the afternoon before, in such bliss.

'Clare,' he said again, hauling her into his arms and crushing her to his chest. 'Don't, don't, don't…'

'Don't what?' She lifted her tear-stained face to look at him in confusion. 'Cry? I cannot help it. I am…' She waved her arms in agitation. 'You have…'

'I know, I know, but truly, Clare, I didn't mean what I said.'

'Didn't you?'

'No!' He looked into her eyes and then, fearing lest Cottam should still be lurking, and might over-hear what he had to say next, he simply took her face between his hands and kissed her. Kissed her until, with a half-smothered little cry, she put her arms round his waist and kissed him back.

'I know, what I said was a betrayal of what we've shared this last few days,' he breathed into her ear, since it was the only way he could be sure that only she heard his words. 'But when he admitted he was the one behind your father's decision to keep us apart, back then, and threatened to tear us apart again, I thought that if I could make him believe that I'd grown into a cynical, harsh bastard who would treat you like a whore, he might give up. I was desperate, Clare. I couldn't go back to the way I'd been for so many years. When every-thing felt like dust and ashes when I thought you meant all those horrible things you said when you turned down my proposal.'

'But I didn't say any of them.'

'Yes, yes,' he said, raining kisses on her face. 'I know that *now*. But that doesn't alter the fact that I was miserable for years. And so lonely.'

'Lonely! But you had so many other women—'

'But none of them were you. So how could any

of them heal the hurt you dealt by rebuffing me, in such terms—'

'But I didn't.'

'I didn't know that, though, did I? I thought you despised me. And it changed everything. Before that day at the duck pond, I made the most of what women wanted to share with me. It was all just… like a game. But the game turned deadly when I started to believe I could never have you. And every encounter after that just felt empty and sordid. And I raged at you for ruining it for me—'

To his shock, this time she was the one to stop his mouth with a kiss. Which was no mean feat since she was so much shorter than him.

'I raged at you, too,' she said. 'Because you flaunted your women under my nose. And made me feel small and unattractive, and unfeminine…'

'Ah, darling, I'm sorry. It was a terrible way to show you how much I loved you, wasn't it? And even now we're married, I've treated you abominably.'

'It doesn't matter.'

'Yes, I know. You believe that no wife should complain about the way her husband behaves, even if he beats her,' he reflected bitterly. 'That you must be loyal to me because of the vows you made in church.'

She reached up, grabbed him by the ears and kissed him again.

'It's because I love you, you idiot,' she said. 'Not because of the vows. Not altogether. And anyway, do you really think a woman who didn't love her husband would put up with being taken on a bride trip that was arranged purely for the purpose of investigating a crime?'

'You knew?' He felt as if someone had just punched him in the gut. 'How did you know? How long have you known?'

'I only worked it out today, really. Just now, as I was walking along the cliff tops. I started putting two and two together.'

'I will drop the investigation, Clare.'

'What? Why would you do any such thing?'

'Because he is your brother. He was right. You would not be able to live with the man who'd been responsible for sending your brother to the gallows.'

She pulled back from him and planted her hands on her hips. 'Have you thought about the other side of the coin? How *I* would feel, knowing you had let a man get away with murder, simply because he is my brother?'

'Murder? You know about that? How?'

'Two and two,' she said cryptically. 'It was Miss Hutton who helped me piece it all together.'

'Who the deuce,' said Rawcliffe, running his hands through his hair and wondering at what point he'd lost his hat, again, 'is Miss Hutton?'

'Colonel Hutton's granddaughter. The one he sent to fetch you to discuss the drowning of Mr Kellet.'

'Oh. She told you that was why he sent for me?'

'In a roundabout way, yes. And then I worked out that must have been why you were so amenable about signing that slimy Mr Jeavons's silly visitors' book. That it must have been a way of letting the local magistrate, who'd dealt with Mr Kellet's drowning, know that you were in the area, so that he would come looking for you, rather than for you to have to go and visit him, which would have told everyone exactly what you were really doing down here.'

'Clare,' he said, taking her by both arms and wishing that she wasn't quite so intelligent, 'you are correct, but—'

'No, let me finish. You've done enough to confuse and distract me to this point, but I…I can't take anymore.'

There were tears in her eyes. Because he'd hurt her so badly.

And yet she'd kissed him. Grabbed him and kissed him, even though she said she thought she'd worked out what he was up to.

'If I tell you the truth…'

'You have *got* to tell me the truth,' she said, flinging up her chin. 'It is high time you stopped… distracting me by being…kind one moment, then cruel the next. Confusing me. Keeping me off balance. Because that is what you have been doing, isn't it? I didn't realise that was the method you were employing with me until Clement did pretty much the same thing. When he cast doubt on the legality of our marriage and came up with so many contradictory theories which were so ludicrous that I got too angry to think straight. Just the way you did. Time and time again.

'Why? No, don't answer that. I know why,' she said, slapping her hands on her hips. 'Because marrying me was a brilliant excuse to come down to this neck of the woods, under the pretext of letting me visit my brother, when all the time you were really trying to find out who'd killed Mr Kellet.

Even the way we met in the inn was no coincidence, was it? Let alone the way you provoked me to throw that punch and made sure it landed on your nose, so that there was just sufficient blood to make me feel guilty enough to try to mend matters and flustered enough to let you lure me into that coffee room where you—'

'No. I won't have you thinking I engineered that meeting, or married you under any other pretext than the real one. It *was* a coincidence that I happened into the inn at the very moment you were walking along that corridor. And...' He shifted from one foot to the other. He had to tell her the truth. All of it, no matter what light it threw on his nature. 'And I didn't deliberately make sure that punch you threw landed on my nose, rather than my jaw.'

'Oh?' She searched his face keenly, as though looking into the depths of his soul. 'Really?'

'Yes, really. I was—' he took a deep breath '—I was moving in for a kiss.'

'A kiss?'

'Yes. And as for provoking you deliberately, you know that I didn't really know how hurtful my comments must have been. What I said about your father being inconsistent, it arose from seeing you looking so…threadbare. Because I would never, ever have allowed you to end up in such a state, if he'd permitted me to marry you. And all his words about my morality and exposing no child of his to my blighting influence came roaring back into my mind, when he'd neglected and used you for so long, well, that was what I meant. Though I never would have said any of it if I'd known he'd only just died.'

'Oh,' she said again. And continued to look at him expectantly. Waiting for him to make a full confession.

He took another deep breath.

'It wasn't until we reached London that I considered taking advantage of our marriage, with regard to the investigation I'd already begun. I know that sounds cold, but don't forget, at the time I thought you hated me. Had always hated me. So that there was no hope our marriage stood a chance anyway. And I knew somebody had murdered Archie. And the reason I kept you in the dark about it all was because I had no proof your brother was involved. Only suspicions. And I didn't want to put you in the position where you might be obliged to take sides.'

'Oh,' she said. And then nodded and stepped forward and slid her arms round his waist.

'He did it,' she mumbled into his chest.

'What?' He took her face between his hands and turned it up so he could look into her eyes. Eyes which were deeply troubled.

'Whatever it was you suspect him of doing. The first thing Clement said to me when I walked into his study was that he hadn't done it. Since I didn't know I was supposed to think he'd done anything, that put me on my guard. Because he always protested his innocence, even when I'd seen him do something beastly. Take...those puppies, for instance. I *saw* him throw the sack into the pond. And yet later, he shook his head over their poor little bodies and said how terrible it was that people could be so cruel, as though he was as shocked and upset as I was.

'And then,' she said, drawing a huge gulp of breath, 'when Miss Hutton spoke of how Mr Kellet had drowned, my mind shot right back to those puppies. And I couldn't help remembering how Mr Kellet always did put me in mind of a spaniel, with his big brown eyes and the eager way he used to follow you around. And I recalled how Lady Harriet had let slip that he'd come down here to search for some missing jewels. And I knew. I just knew…'

And then she went stiff and looked past him, to the jumble of rocks behind which Clement could very well be lurking.

'I thought I saw something. Someone. Just a shadow, it might have been, but…'

Of one accord, they strode over to the rocks, to see if Clement was trying to overhear what they were discussing. But he was halfway down the track to the cottages, his long clerical coat flapping out behind him like the wings of some great crow.

'How much do you think he heard?'

'I don't think he could have heard much,' he said, patting her hand. 'He was further away from us than you were when you heard my discussion with him. Besides, the wind and the roar of the surf and the crying of the gulls would have prevented much of our speech from reaching him.'

'What do you think he plans to do? Where is he going?'

He slung his arm round her waist and tugged her to his side.

'It doesn't matter. Wherever he has gone, whatever he plans to do, I will not let him hurt you. Or damage us, I swear it.'

'Yes, but you cannot let him get away scot-free. He is…he has gone bad. He was always full of mischief, was always inclined to be a bit of a bully, but…' She shook her head. 'And he would always blame everyone else. He'd sort of wind up his followers the way any other boy would wind up a top and set them off. He was always at the back of it, but nobody ever caught *him*, only those who followed him. The village boys were far less organised once he went away to university. And now he's got a gang of smugglers to do his bidding. Oh,' she said, placing one hand to her forehead. 'I'm not telling you anything you don't already know, am I? *That* is why you stopped being friends with him. Because he was a bully and taunted the other boys until they felt they had to join him.'

He hung his head for a moment. 'I stayed out of his way. I did indeed know what he was, but instead of confronting him, I just…'

'Then do it now. Stop him, before he goes any further.'

'Somebody has to stop him, yes, I agree. But it will not be me. Just think—you might say you love me, but it will always be between us. Festering.'

'No, it won't!'

'How could it be otherwise? In one form or another. You might be able to forgive me, but…there would be talk. Supposition. And I…you might not think it, but I do have a conscience. I know it would cause you grief to see your own brother brought to trial as a common criminal. And if I were the man responsible…'

She flung her arms round his waist again and hugged him hard.

He hugged her back. Rested his cheek on the crown of her head and rocked her.

After a short while, she looked up at him, her forehead creased in anguish. 'Then he has won.'

'Oh, no,' he said grimly. 'I cannot be the man to pursue him any longer, but I shall make damn sure the investigation continues. I shall pass on everything I've learned to…' No, not Lord Becconsall. Not now he had a wife. A married man couldn't risk the welfare of the one he loved. And Cottam was just the sort of adversary to defend himself by attacking the weak and vulnerable. 'Someone else.' He'd find someone. Someone tough and fearless, and clever. Someone who wouldn't be fooled by Cottam's cunning, nor vulnerable to any threat he might try to make.

'Oh, thank goodness,' she said on a sigh of relief. 'I couldn't live with myself if I thought he'd got away with whatever it is he's done, because of your scruples on my account.'

'But it will be far easier on you if another person handles his arrest.'

'Yes.'

'Then, since we have accomplished all we are likely to do, down here, I suggest we return to London—'

'Before Clement can put any plan he might be hatching against us into action...'

'That had crossed my mind. And compile all the information we have gleaned, between us,' he said, squeezing her hand.

'It isn't going to be easy, is it, to prove he's guilty of Mr Kellet's murder?'

'No. But Ulysses...that is, Lord Becconsall, is bound to be able to come up with a plan to expose him. In the meantime...how about if we let Clement think that he has won?'

'What do you mean?'

'Well, if he thinks I am so worried about losing your regard that I will do nothing against him, he might...'

'Lower his guard! That would be brilliant.'

'How much did he see, I wonder? And what might he have made of it?'

Rawcliffe swiftly went over the last few minutes, considering how they might have looked to an outsider.

'If he really couldn't hear anything we said to one another, he would have seen your devastation when you overheard me speaking crudely about our relationship...'

'Then running straight for the edge of the cliffs...'

'And me running after you, reaching you only just in time to stop you throwing yourself off...'

'As if I'd do anything so melodramatic,' she said, wrinkling her nose in disgust. 'But, yes, for the purposes of hoodwinking Clement, I am willing to go along with the fabrication.'

'Would he swallow it, do you think?'

'Oh, yes. He doesn't have a very high opinion of women.'

'Very well, then. And once I'd pulled you back from the edge, he would have seen me kissing you, desperately...promising you anything?'

'Ah,' she said, catching on. 'And then he would have seen me kissing you, for promising me that anything.'

'So. All we have to do is...'

'Oh!' She pressed her hands to her cheeks. 'He told me that if ever I needed to write to him, I should do so, care of Lady Buntingford, because he handled all her correspondence, because she doesn't see as well as she used to.'

'So *that* is how he did it. He wrote all those fake references and just got her to put her signature at the bottom.'

'References?'

'We started becoming suspicious when each family that had jewels taken, and substituted with fakes, also took into their employ a girl who had impeccable references from Lady Buntingford. That was the angle Archie was looking into. Whether she was developing some kind of mania for rubies.'

'Oh,' said Clare, a touch wide-eyed. 'Yes, that makes sense. But actually, what just occurred to me was that the reason he told me about Lady Buntingford's being a safe address to write to was so that I could write and warn him, if you were about to make a move against him. It wasn't for my benefit at all,' she said indignantly, 'but his. *That* is why he made as if he was only letting me return to you against his better judgement—so that I'd be in a position to be able to warn him if you found some solid evidence against him.

'Right! Well, I can jolly well turn his scheme against him. I can write that you are so besotted with me you would promise me anything—'

'Which would be the perfect truth,' he said, catching her round the waist and hauling her close.

She blushed.

'And in the meantime, we can also drop a hint or two along those lines to the locals.'

'How could we do that?'

'Kendall.'

She wrinkled up her nose. 'I don't think we can put much faith in a footman who drinks so heavily.'

'On the contrary. He has demonstrated a remarkable amount of trust in me by admitting what goes on when he goes to the local taverns. And it seems that certain fellows who ply him with drinks are extremely interested in our doings.'

'That doesn't mean the tale we want told will get back to Clement.'

'I think it does. The man appears to have eyes and ears everywhere. Even in London. I still can't fathom how the deuce he knew about the Tarbrook rubies.'

'People do talk to clergymen,' she said thoughtfully. 'It is a sort of relic of the confessional, from the Church of Rome. Father was very keen on utilising it. Said it made people feel better to clear their conscience.'

Clare shivered.

'Cold? You shouldn't have come out without a coat or bonnet. What were you thinking?'

'I was thinking I wanted to get out of that stuffy cottage and think,' she said, rubbing her hands up and down her arms. 'Do you really think we can make Clement believe he has won?'

'Oh, yes. He has sufficient arrogance to believe he will triumph. And I will make sure that nobody makes a move against him for some time.'

'Lulling him into a false sense of security?'

'That's right. And then, when he least expects it—' he made a crushing motion with his fist '—we will make our move on him!'

'And...and what of us?' Clare gazed up at him with wide eyes.

'We,' he said, cupping her sweet little face between his hands, 'are going to live happily ever after. I shall do my utmost to make sure of it. No woman will ever be so spoiled, so cosseted, so well loved...'

'Careful,' she said. 'If you carry on like that, people will start to think you are a romantic.'

'No, they won't. For I am not a romantic. I am just a man in love.'

She gasped.

'Clare,' he said, taking her sweet little face between his hands. 'Surely you must have guessed that, as well? You have worked out everything else I've tried to keep from you.'

'You are in love? With…me?'

'Desperately.'

'But…no…you can't be…'

'Why do you think I was so green about the gills on the way to Peeving Cove?'

She shook her head.

'Because I was sick to my stomach at the prospect of Clement would do…exactly what he threatened to do just now. Turn you against me.'

He saw her turn over that statement in her mind. And accept it.

'But—' she began.

'Now, cast your mind back to the day you punched me. Why do you think I refused to countenance any of your objections to marrying me?'

She bit down on her lower lip. But at last, he could see a spark of hope begin to gleam in her eyes.

'Yes, that's right. It was because I had finally seen a way to make you mine. After all those years of thinking my goddess was unobtainable. Why do you think I moved in for that kiss? I was attempting to compromise you. Right there in that corridor.'

'And then I ruined it for you by punching you,' she said, aghast.

'No, actually, you didn't. You made my day. You'd just given me an excuse to…lord it over you for the rest of our lives. For I would always be able to remind you that it was entirely your own fault we'd had to get married. Because you'd lost your temper and behaved disgracefully. In a public inn.'

'You are the most despicable…'

But even though she was saying the same words she'd flung at him countless times over the years, this time there was a smile hovering about the edges of her mouth.

'Ruthless…'

And now she was positively beaming at him.

'Yes,' he confessed. 'There are no depths to which I would not sink to have you in my arms. In my bed. In my life.'

'You really mean it, don't you?' She looked at him in dawning wonder. 'You love me.'

And then, because there had been quite enough talking for one day, he decided to communicate with her in the way that worked the best.

With a kiss.

* * * * *

LET'S TALK
Romance

For exclusive extracts, competitions
and special offers, find us online:

f facebook.com/millsandboon

⊙ @millsandboonuk

🐦 @millsandboon

Or get in touch on 0844 844 1351*

For all the latest titles coming soon,
visit millsandboon.co.uk/nextmonth